BRIGHT MIRROR

ISBN 978-1-7333938-6-7 (paperback)

Edited by Jacob Jones-Goldstein, J. Patrick Conlon, Marcella Harte, Nicholas Leamy, and Shasta Schatz
Cover art by Marcella Harte
Cover Layouts and Interior by Jennifer Marang
OPP logo by Steve Myers

Published by
Oddity Prodigy Productions, LLC
302 Arbour Drive
Newark, DE 19713

www.oddityprodigy.com

BRIGHT MIRROR

A UTOPIAN SCIENCE FICTION ANTHOLOGY

Edited by
Jacob Jones-Goldstein,
J. Patrick Conlon, Marcella Harte,
Nicholas Leamy, and Shasta Schatz

DEDICATION

For Steve,
without whose light our mirror would have remained dark

SPECIAL THANKS TO OUR BACKERS

We would like to give special thanks to our Kickstarter backers! You got this project off the ground and without you we would be nowhere.

Kaja Kazmierska

John McNish

Elizabeth Alban

Danielle
   Ackley-McPhail

Colin Anderson

Marcy Wieseman

Rev. Stephen Goldstein

Ann Stolinsky

Kyle Winsett

Tom DeBoissiere

Ed Taylor

Christine Strothman

Devon Miller-Duggan

Colleen Feeney

Matt Alexander

Caryn Wojtowicz

Suzanne Mattaboni

Eric Remington

Kent Messner

Stephen Padbury

Murray Eiland

Brittany Cole

Brian Gibson

Randy L Stubbs II

John Guzman

Jules de
   Bellefeuille Defoy

Joe Soldezzo

Chris DeAngelis

Chris Collier

Margaret

Sharon Lee Harte

David T Shoemaker

Alaina Sabatino

Krystal Mitchell

Zachary Fissel

Alexander Lethen

Stephanie Loose

Kara Race-Moore

Craig White

Ef Deal

John Markley

Michael A. Burstein

Bernard Brick

Tatiana Taylor

Ian Chung

Ellis Joens

Donald Bell

Oliver Scholes

Michael Auger

Mary Jo Rabe

TABLE OF TELEMETRY

INTRODUCTION

by Hannah Duggan

It can be easy to forget sometimes, like when you are stuck in traffic during your morning commute or texting your spouse that you're out of cat food again, how wild the human experience is. There has never been any time in our history that wasn't interesting in some way. That being said, we currently exist in a period so fraught, so busy, and so surprising that the word "unprecedented" has become ubiquitous in our news feeds. Additionally, we have never before had as much easy access to information about the goings-on of everyone and everywhere in the world as we do now. All of this news, all these events, all of this history-making, it piles up and overwhelms. It can be hard not to get scared about where we might be headed.

Getting scared isn't inevitable, however, nor is it the only option. In a world that seems to be endlessly plagued by conflict, inequality, and environmental degradation, some people still manage to look on the bright side of life. Some choose hope. Utopian science fiction is born from that hope and shows us better possibilities. The minds behind Oddity Prodigy Productions decided that people could use some hope right now, and thus was born this collection. The stories inside explore a range of utopian visions, each with its own unique take on a perfect society.

From technologically advanced civilizations to harmonious communities living in balance with nature, these stories showcase the power of human imagination to architect a better future. They invite us to question our assumptions about society and to dream of a world where justice, equality, and compassion prevail. These stories remind us that, even in the most unprecedented of times, the pursuit of a better world is worth fighting for. They offer a glimpse of a future where all people can exist together in peace and harmony, and where our collective potential can be fully realized.

The most avid believer in this collection at Oddity Prodigy was a man named Steve Myers. Steve was an artist, comic writer, marketing pro, rap lover, sports enthusiast, pop culture nerd, and creator of the "World's Friendliest Superhero," Superchum. Steve was someone who, even in his darkest times, could find some silver lining, some joke to be made, some way of moving forward. He also had a smile as wide as his face. Sadly, Oddity Prodigy and the world at large lost Steve too soon at the end of 2023. Ensuring that this collection of optimism came to be was the most obvious way of honoring his memory. It's everything Steve thought the world could be.

This collection will transport you to worlds where the impossible becomes possible, where hope triumphs over despair, and where humanity shows its best side. Hopefully, you, dear reader, can use this book to take a break from the unprecedented news cycle and remember how much good we are capable of and of the things we may yet accomplish. It's what Steve would have wanted.

LITTLE GHOSTS BY ESOS RIDLEY

by Glenn Dungan

Autotina: "I live life in through-lines. Between astro-physics and poetry, I can look back and realize this career change wasn't that stark of one at all."

After a century-long break, the celebrated scientist and world's first automaton returns with new programming and talks about life and death, art and science, and finding purpose.
By Esos Ridley, writing for LIFE
January 2184

At first glance, it appears that Dr. Autotina is more of a botanist than anything else.

She greets me in front of her workshop, buried deep within the Red Rock Mountain range in Denver, Colorado. The workshop is covered in astrological runes that glitter gold against a brutalist cement façade. This alien-appearing non-alien plateau is manicured in a variety of large and beautiful flowers, some from Earth and surviving without ventilators, others in vials with precise calibration, achieved on the famous interstellar expeditions to Mars with her late husband, Dr. Ronald Folsom. There is an element of nature fused with classic science- fiction on the way to a flower-laden door.

Dr. Autotina stands like a sentry at a full eight feet, her automaton body erect to a perfectly calculated geometry. She wears a lilac-colored cloak that flows in tandem with the whistling desert wind. Silicon arms extend to shake my hand, and she tells me that she heated her fingertips so that her plexiglass fingers do not feel cold in my palm. Her face is akin more to a mannequin, perfectly smooth and void of any intense definitions. Dr. Autotina says that her face was originally blank, but she felt that not only alienated her from herself but also made it hard for people to talk to her. Thus, the hollows for eyes, the impression of a nose and a closed mouth, permanently fixated into a content, almost sleepy, smile. A blue aura floats above her cranium like a crown, the latter half of which is exposed glass that contains tendrils of electricity rolling in a blue cloud. Dr. Autotina calls it her very own personal "lightning in a bottle," which I only learn later is the total representation of her consciousness.

The workshop is just as fluid as Dr. Autotina, and it is no doubt deliberate that the interior reflects all her eccentricities. Like the Earth's crust, there are layers of passion underneath the current form that the doctor brings me into. The workshop has tables, telescopes, and large supercomputers reminiscent of the original dinosaurs IBM tucked away. The computers, while hulking in size, are the most powerful processors currently in the cosmos, and Dr. Autotina hardly pays them any mind, viewing them as part of the furniture. Holographic texts float like book-sized fireflies around the workshop, and while I cannot grab the royal purple, baby blue-, and maroon-colored prisms myself, Dr. Autotina plucks them from the air as if they were floating in the ocean, tossing them over her shoulder or to the top rafters where they levitate in stasis like balloons waiting to drop. The doctor says that she doesn't need the tomes to retrieve the information, for her advanced supercomputer mind can process multiple texts at once, but the act of flipping through pages, even holographic ones, keeps her anchored to a human psychosis.

"It was a ritual then," she says at the start of our conversation, "and remains to be now."

There are a myriad of plants inside as well, rivaling the quantity of the botanical parade outside. Greenery soaks up the natural light from the skylights, sometimes turning a shade orange or green when the text prisms block the rays. There are colossal alien petals next to typical garden tulips. Encased on what used to be a kitchen, complete with appliances that have long since become relics, are vials full of strange soil and minerals. Dr. Autotina brings my attention to a silver, amorphous liquid that appears to shy away from my touch. It is a mineral found in the Great Storm of Jupiter.

"Ronald found it on one of our excursions," she tells me.

She is referring to her interplanetary travel adventures, only possible because her automaton body is outfitted with pressure-resistant alloys created by Dr. Folsom himself. As if sensing my memories of old news articles and videos, Dr. Autotina leads me to a sun-drenched salon at the rear of the laboratory. In the connecting hallway, there are a multitude of news articles featuring the power couple. It is the timeline chronicling her stratospheric ascent into the public eye. She notices me looking at this timeline, where her once flesh and blood corporal form stands in front of the MIT entrance with her not-yet-husband, Dr. Ronald Folsom.

"We were 'going steady' a little while then," she says, her voice occasionally cracking with static and beeps. She is facing the same picture that I am, although we both know she does not have to, for her sensors are connected to the numerous cameras wired to the laboratory, which functions as her abode, botanical garden, and studio. She turns to me and says with an unemotive but genuine laugh, "Do people still say, 'going steady'?"

We walk down the hall, my own boots at her plexiglass feet that have been fashioned into heels. Her purple cloak sways in the crisscross breeze. She double-checks if the temperature is satisfactory, and that she can adjust the temperature per square foot for me so as not to disturb the plants, which have taken up residency on every available surface. She talks with her hands a lot. There is another picture of Dr. Folsom on a podium wearing a suit, mouth mid-consonant. Tina, in her mortal form, stands with her hands perched in front of her, her eyes radiating sunshine.

"He proposed to me in the same speech that he officially named the new alloy he created, which was also named after me. Tinium. For Tina. My full name is Martina, but I've never liked the *Mar-* part, so I just shortened it to Tina. Can you imagine if Ronald named the alloy Martinium? How misleading!"

The *Auto-*part of Autotina is a portmanteau turned moniker. Since becoming an atomized corporeal form, Dr. Autotina has since abandoned the preceding part of her name and replaced it with the first half of *automaton*, which she says is an intentional nod to her and Dr. Folsom being not just the first automaton in history but the first automata couple in history. "Autotina and Autoron," she says, "he entertained the thought for a couple weeks."

She continues, head forward, the cameras meeting with my gaze at the next picture, "We had a tremendous life, him and I. Our breakthroughs in automata robotics helped a lot of people and advanced other fields of science. Science was the new rock 'n roll. Everyone wanted to know what the two 'robo-docs' were up to."

But the fame of their professional life took a toll on their personal lives, as well as their subjective lives. The marriage was incredibly scrutinized, both by the public and the scientific community. Dr. Autotina and Dr. Folsom were subject to numerous tests to gauge the efficiency of transporting a human consciousness into a nigh-indestructible robotic platform.

"The tests," she says, "were the hardest part. Laws were written to allow Ronald and our rights to exist against the laws which made our bodies property. Yes, our bodies were built in a lab, but our souls were not, and Tinium was Ronald's discovery anyway. Sometimes, I wonder how different our trajectories would be if Ronald hadn't owned the patent to Tinium."

There were times when the stress was too great for both of them and, like any work-weary couple, took holidays to reset. Although most work-weary couples go to resort beaches, Dr. Autotina and Dr. Folsom much preferred more esoteric locations such as the bottom of the Martina Trench, or on some asteroid near the edge of the galaxy. Dr. Ronald Folsom's brother, renowned rocket scientist Henry Folsom, lived at the first International Space Station as the active director. He allowed clearance for Autotina and Dr. Ronald to enter and exit the atmosphere on the condition that they stop at the ISS first.

"We'd bring the astronauts their favorite treats. They sent us holiday cards, each in their own language," Dr. Autotina recalls fondly.

She shows me another relic, one which heartily defines her past. A collection of "Get Well Soon!" cards are encased behind a glass wall. A hodgepodge of sources occupy the white rectangles: crayon writing of school children, each with their names written in similarly childish script, admirers in the scientific community that saw Autotina as the most prestigious in her field (as humble as Autotina is, she was ranked the most popular robotics engineer in the past decade, the recipient of numerous scientific awards, and eventually a Pulitzer prize winner for her award-winning memoir *Trans-humanism: Does this unit have a soul?*), and college robotic engineers who have heralded Dr. Folsom's experimental procedures as the next step to evolution. In the center of this positive nebula is a crinkled picture of Autotina's last days in her human body, a withered corpus, cocooned in hospital bed sheets and tangled in marionette strings and attached to large computers. She is holding Dr. Folsom's hand, or rather, he is holding hers.

This picture is an ambered moment in Dr. Autotina's life, a snapshot of her past but then uncertain future. She stills maintains that getting her doctorate in astrophysics is the highlight of her career, but for all of Dr. Autotina's existence in academia, even she cannot deny the importance of her transition into the automata.

"It was a rough time. Physically, mentally, emotionally, even spiritually," Dr. Autotina says, head perfectly straight, lips unmoving. She absently fiddles with a plucked rose nestling in a vase, her fingers unable to feel the thorns crushing under her impenetrable fingers, her mastery of working with hands that no longer feel tactile pressure to not crush the damp stem. "Not only did I experience an explosion in my MIT laboratory, but my consciousness was literally ripped from my body, which existed without any electrical charges for a full two minutes. I would be lying to you and your readers if I said that was not hard for me. I thought my life was meaningless. I could not be a scientist anymore, could not go on walks or read books, was constantly under the care of doctors and Ronald, who never once complained, ever. This is all on top of the press trying to get into the door of the hospital, hoping to catch me on the rare chance of my awakening from my coma so they could get the first scoop of what it was like, and I quote the *New York Times* here, 'to see god.' I feel the 'engine of creation' is more apt."

> "[The incident] felt like I was a balloon, and the rest of the world was the string. Once I got atomized, I was living in this dual reality, shifting in and out. Now with my new Tinium body, I can finally settle into one place."

Bringing me into her parlor, Dr. Autotina serves me freshly grown black tea leaves, served on a robotic tea tray no larger than a shiatzu. With a perfectly engineered lilt in her voice that suggests a bashful wink, she explains that she has never tasted the tea that she grows in one of the biomes out back, only that she is confident that they have been reared and dried to mathematical perfection. She is not wrong.

Dr. Autotina's transition from her human body to the robotic one in which she resides required an almost Herculean feat of willpower and psychological adjustment. The light blue aura emanating from her "lightning in a bottle" arcs over her like a corona. She tells me more of her time in what the scientific community has adopted as the "atom realm."

"It was strange, like floating in mist, or Jell-o," she laughs, referring to the once popular gelatinous treat made of protein extracted from animal bones and has since been discontinued after the Kraft / Heinz Sleeper Agent fiasco in 2055. "It's a world of light blues and purple, sort of like the color of my body, my lightning, and my cloak, which is all merely a coincidence. It's a world where time is inconceivable, where the fabric of all our creation, you know, atoms as building blocks, are both tangible and intangible. A realm of absolutely incomprehensible power. How can you ever go back to normal life after having your body atomized? Do you think Icarus, in his free fall, ever prided himself that at least he got closer to the sun than anyone else? Icarus is not at fault for getting too close to the sun, it's Daedalus for making the wings so poorly. How do you give a child a gift of flight and tell them they have limits? Ronald is not Daedalus. He does not build with clay that becomes waterlogged or melts. He builds with Tinium, an alloy that can withstand the pressures of Jupiter's Great Spot winds of 130,000 miles an hour and then some."

Dr. Autotina tells me that the decision to consent to the transferring of her consciousness in this experimental automaton (which now sits before me, body erect in geometric perfection, plexiglass fingers steepled over a lilac-cloaked lap), was not only her own, but at her own insistence.

She accesses her data files and speaks to herself as much as me, "Ronald was so frightened, and he was always so afraid of anything he didn't understand. My body was failing me. The [atom] realm had given me a sort of atomically volatile cancer. I was atomically unwinding like a spool every nanosecond. I had no life left. Of course, I would see the automata in the corner of the workshop as a buoy in the strange and scary sea of corporeal mortality."

Asked to show me the advantages of her automata body's interface with the laboratory, Dr. Autotina is nothing short of giddy. She is entirely interfaced with the digital/physical infrastructure of the workshop/living quarters, and she tells me that it takes considerable effort not to think of her and the house as one of the same. Looking into the divots of her eyes are naught, and she knows this. Her eyes are cameras throughout the house, her tactile senses now a series of automated clicks and levers that send data as I step even so far as the front lawn. She can regulate temperature per square foot, access the skylights with a thought, even put on the coffee machine the second her optic sensors see sunrise.

"I don't sleep," she laughs, "and I don't drink coffee anymore. But the house recognizes the smell."

She tells me that interfacing with the house is as far as she is comfortable.

"I don't actually need this automaton form," she says, "I can exist just fine in the digital sphere, like some sort of ghost. That's actually what Ronald used to call me, *Little Ghost*, because I can float so seamlessly between interests and subjects, often anchoring in them before wisping away to something else. But I choose to keep this form, and not because it allows me to take this vehicle to the deepest depths and the highest stratospheres. I was raised a human and I am, in essence, a human. I can access and absorb all the literature on any subject in a matter of seconds, but at what point do I become a computer, more robot than human?"

Aside from the obvious mental and emotional strain of Dr. Folsom's experimental procedure, I ask her of any quagmires she encountered when transitioning bodies. Without hesitation she says, "Losing my sense of touch was surprisingly easy. Perhaps it is the loss of smell and taste. It's a funny question because I still *remember* those senses, like someone who was not born blind. They can still recall colors. The lack of sleep was the most disorienting, but thankfully, I had Ronald to keep me company, and we took many trips."

I ask her if there is anything that she misses.

"Steak," Dr. Autotina says, "rare steak and garlic mashed potatoes. Oh, and green beans with garlic and lemon." And that was the end of that question.

Dr. Ronald Folsom passed away about 60 years ago. His story is equally as fascinating, having spawned numerous biographies (*The Atomic Adventure, Autotomata Genesis,* and *The Robot Guy* being the most popular) and several made-for-streaming movies. But the most impressionable narrative is not just Dr. Folsom's and Dr. Autotina's individual journeys, but their true-blue love story and the heartbreak which inevitably followed.

She shows me a picture above the fireplace. It is a physical copy, rare to see in this age, and gives the impression that it is just as much a memento as the alien plants and minerals, if not more. It shows Dr. Autotina as she is now, clad in a sundress just a little too short for her ("It took me *months* to get used to the fact that I was now two-and-a-half feet taller," she says), and Dr. Folsom, outfitted in a new Tinium body, wearing a Hawaiian button up. A sunset is frozen behind them, and even though their mouths convey apathy, it is evident from their body language that they are on vacation. His red corona fuses with her blue corona, creating a joint Venn diagram of purple between the two of them, which hangs above their head like a little star.

"The success of my procedure inspired Ronald. He wanted to replicate it and did so quite successfully on himself. I always suspected that he underwent the change to keep me company, that his endeavor for subjectively experiencing trans-humanism was fueled to help me get through my own transitions."

She recalls to me how eerily similar it was living with another automata as an automata as opposed to living with a human as a human, and that the transition was really only the first couple of months when Dr. Folsom was getting used to the platform's new abilities. Dr. Autotina places her chin on a cradled palm, resting it on an armchair, the hollows of her eyes looking out to the green houses beyond the porch. "He built me this new body about seven months before he embarked on the change himself. I had a leg up on the emotional, physical, and mental transformations, so it was only fair I be patient with him as he adjusted."

Still speaking with a dreamy, wistful tone, Dr. Autotina's shoulders slack, her head tilts. The purple cloak shimmers in the sunlight. It was not all dandy living as two robots with complete access to all recorded knowledge, she recalls.

"It was fine for a couple of decades, but eventually, the access to the wireless networks of the worlds became too much of a pull for Ronald. He would say to me, 'Little ghost, we have all the knowledge available to us, only limited by our imagination.' He would read the entire pantheon of a country's classical literature in the span of one morning. Ronald was always, always learning. He could never 'turn off'. Eventually, he ran out of things to learn. We would be off-planet or in the ocean depths, and he would still be trying to learn everything he could about anything else."

Dr. Autotina is a firm believer that because of his limitless, all-encompassing knowledge her husband lost the ability to wonder, to dream.

She tells me that even today she is particularly conscious of not learning all documented knowledge, why she chooses to go through the perceptively counter-intuitive motions of reading one book at a time. She has intentionally slowed her information processors to absorb information at a slightly higher rate than the average human ("I'm allowed to cheat a little," she says, her voice suggestive of a smile.)

It's the knowledge plateauing, she says, her plexiglass face dotted by lines of the midafternoon sun, that eventually set Dr. Folsom on his path. "He leaned into the computer element of the brain. He might be the only person to ever have arrived at the 'present' of human knowledge. Sure, the RAM in our automata bodies can process the information, but can our own limitations of human endeavor? Dr. Folsom became bored and scattered simultaneously. He was developing what I could only describe as some sort of robotic Parkinson's. Those times were very hard."

Years later, Dr. Autotina's hunch of robotic Parkinson's disease proved correct. This, combined with his depression, created the scaffolding of Dr. Folsom's tragic decision to end his own life.

"He got everything he wanted out of life too fast," Dr. Autotina tells me, "It haunts me to think about what thoughts ran through his own lightning in a bottle in those final days. A part of me always knew that he was heading toward oblivion, having over-learned his way into apathy. Looking back, I see why I became so obsessed with botany."

> In a way, I was happy to have [botany] because it meant that I could still grieve. There is a human under all this metal and wires. As horrible as those years were, I'm happy that I had them. Without my plants, I don' t know if I would have found poetry.

Dr. Autotina, the perfect host, brings me to her private study. It is tucked away in the back of the laboratory. The study is bathed in sunlight from the Southern wall; the view is of great rust-colored spires lording over a bare clearing like totems of nature. The room is in the shape of a perfect oval; I know this because Dr. Autotina constructed it herself. Large bookshelves house worn tomes of physical books, scaling upwards of twelve feet to accommodate for Dr. Autotina's stature and complete with a rolling fireman's ladder to reach the upper most shelves. I am dwarfed by the scale of the study in relationship to myself, wondering where a cake will appear beckoning to "eat me." Crumpled papers are scattered along the floor like sleeping tumbleweeds. Plants occupy every foot of real estate that they can; verdant vines wind over desks, petals bloom in the face of the stained glass-shielded sun in a kaleidoscopic nebula.

Dr. Autotina calls it her "solarium," then quickly retracts and says it is no more than a private study. She casually waters some plants and brings tea to a boil for me to try her homegrown ginseng. She rummages through a hastily open mahogany desk drawer and reveals a ream of paper bursting from the gut of a manilla folder. She sets this aside next to several journals and, hands on her cloaked hips, admires them like works of art.

Her body language changes into what would be considered the most mathematically precise impression of humility; shoulders arced just so, neck braced to a certain degree. These books have weight to them. Dr. Autotina explains to me that the advent of her twilight years has reoriented her creative energies, and then quickly laughs away that as long as there is Wifi, she is immortal. The books contain poetry. Stanzas of all pentameters, rhymes and rhythms, shapes and forms. I cannot help but think that perhaps this is where Dr. Autotina needed to be all along.

She flips through the pages and invites me to read her favorites. She says, "After Ronald passed, I fell into a horrible depression. I was afraid of exploring the atom realm further because it felt too personal, like revisiting a favorite restaurant we used to share. Call me weak, I don't care. Then I went into botany, which nearly replaced my astrological practice."

In some ways, Dr. Autotina feels that she has lost more than just her career.

"It took me many years... I mean, I love my plants, but I was merely supplementing one love to replace the loss of another one. I've lost my body, my urge to practice, my husband...but not my mind, and after so many years, not my purpose."

It's poetry, Dr. Autotina says. The written word.

"I've seen the ice storms on Neptune, the birth of faraway galaxies, the horrible beauty of a black hole. How can I validate those experiences and remember them? Through mathematics and cosmological principles?" She shows me more poems, enough to fill a library. "How can I appreciate all that I have seen and gone through? It is here, in poetry, that my purpose shines like a radiant sun. It is how I express myself, through the one fragment that is uniquely my own: my very own personal lightning in a bottle."

She means, of course, her soul.

But simply announcing a new passion does not equate to the reward that follows from putting in the time, which is precisely a trial that

Dr. Autotina struggles with. "I can simply download and integrate all the best poets and literature geniuses in recorded history, even add in all the literature dissertations with flairs of anthropology. Within seconds, I can have the most mathematically perfect poem written simultaneously in every language. But then I'm 'logic-ing' the poem into manifestation. Where is the victory in that? The expression?"

The strategies that Dr. Autotina has long employed through both her time as a human form and her impenetrable Tinium body have always been one of logic and research, of synthesizing data to unearth new hypotheses and provide basis for more theories.

"But those approaches don't work with art," Dr. Autotina says, folding one long leg over the other and resting into an armchair fit to her proportions. I sit in a velvet chair across, the exterior pea-green and adorned with art-nouveau style, insectile embroidery. She puts together the second cup of tea and, even though this is her interview, asks me how the cup compares to others whose aromatics are grown in a less controlled environment. After giving my approval, Dr. Autotina leans back in her chair, joints relaxed, her light blue corona crown creating an aquarium-like glow above her head. She continues, "*Perfect* does not mean correct. Every artist pulls from their own inspirations and heroes. Sure, you can argue that the Renaissance painters were inspired by nature and the individualist perceptions of man and that the other ancillary factors of the Age of Enlightenment helped to create a dopamine cocktail. Of course, most modern bands will cite The Beatles as why their fingers even touched a guitar or a piano. But ultimately, art comes entirely from within, a subjective experience manifested and codified in a language genuine and one's own. My entire life, I dedicated myself to math and science. I pursued knowledge of the highest discourse, becoming so entrenched in the field that I could close my eyes and see theories on notebook paper, models of Ronald's prototypes on chalkboards."

And Dr. Autotina isn't finished. While her intricate and beautiful gardens have taken a backseat in the passion department, she claims that it was only a stepping stone to remove her from the "old" version of her.

"People still refer to my human body as the 'old' Autotina, even though my Tinium platform is much older! However, I do not feel this is an accurate representation of time for me. While I am satisfied with my life as an astrologist and my supremely unique experiences as an automaton, I am content tucking this vortex of spinning numbers and calculations into what I would define as 'old.' Now, I have a new passion, one which does not rely on numbers or math or angles." She taps the back of her cranium. I get the impression of a smile from the slight tilt in her voice. "I get to use my lightning in a bottle, and it helps me use *this*."

Dr. Autotina taps a plexiglass finger to her chest, where a series of powerful microchips, processors, and wires have replaced where her heart used to be.

It is poetry, Dr. Autotina tells me, that keeps her alive beyond all else. "Science is how we live. Art is why we live."

Nowadays. Dr. Autotina can still be found watering her plants and digging for strange minerals. At night, she'll be in the observatory, staring into the nebula from her giant eye that is her telescope, surrounded by prismatic tomes as if she herself commands gravity. In a way, she does. Dr. Autotina is a force of undying optimism, her passion and empathy not carried away by the large orbital currents of despair and loss. She keeps herself afloat, tethering a line between human-automata, careful not to submit to the persistent inertia of computational super-sentience by means of poetry.

If you have time, she suggests attending open mic poetry sessions at your local café. On weekdays, you can find Dr. Autotina on stage, but good luck getting a front-row seat. She tells me that it shouldn't be a problem, though, being eight feet tall. Dr. Autotina plans to get enough confidence to go on weekend circuits and eventually publish a book of poetry. She already has a title: *Little Ghosts*.

When this happens, good luck finding any seat in what will undoubtedly be a packed audience.

TO ELIZA

by Alice Avoy

Local Time: Unspecified
Recipient's Time: 08:15 am, 13th March

Dear Eliza,

Let no one dare to doubt my commitment to my dearest wife, as I'm officially sending the first message from Habitus XVI to you, my love, instead of the HQ. The Intergalactic Association of Agriculture will have to wait ten minutes more for the report. Hope they will swallow the indignation like the champs they are. I wish I could have called, but the signal here is spotty at best due to all the interference, so we'll have to do with written words.

Anyway, I'm sure you're dying to know that no dying was involved in this mission (so far). I'm delighted to report that I'm completely safe and sound. I admit I was a little nervous as I was leaving the base on this solo mission, but in the end, I managed to pilot and land the shuttle perfectly—there's not even a scratch on the hull! With a start like this, I'm optimistic about achieving my goal. If things keep going well, I will be home not for Christmas, as I promised, but for Halloween!

Eh, I'm getting ahead of myself. It's all that excitement. I can't contain it. Well, obviously, I didn't have time to explore the environment. I wanted to let you know that I'm fine as soon as possible, so basically, I only set up the generator and the antenna to contact you. There's not even a roof over my head yet. Whoops! But maybe that's actually for the best. From what I've seen so far, this tiny planet seems lovely. A habitat completely unspoiled by civilization, lush and primal. And so beautiful! I can't wait to discover all its secrets.

The sky here is usually pink. Imagine that! Maggie would love it. Unless she has already picked a new favorite color. Hard to keep up with a four-year-old's interests.

I should be wrapping this up. There's a lot of work to do. I miss you both terribly. I'm sending you a big hug across galaxies. As big as my shuttle. Photo for reference in the attachment.

Love,

Alex

Local Time: Unspecified
Recipient's Time: 03:27 pm, 27th March

Dear Eliza,

I'm literally the worst person in the whole wide universe. It took me this long to reply to your message. Shame on me! In my (poor) defense, I've been busy. Like really busy. Like "I hardly caught a wink of sleep" busy. Let me tell you, establishing a science camp by yourself is not an easy feat. Granted, a miniature one since Habitus XVI is tiny, but still! Curse you, staff shortages! I had to set up the base on my own and make sure that all the equipment was operational. I completely lost track of time. Especially since the day/night cycle here is so weird. A whole day lasts only five Terran hours! That really messes up my biological clock.

I'll make it up to you for my forgetfulness by telling you and little Maggie a bit more about this place, although I'm not sure if any words can truly convey its beauty. I've never seen so many flowers of all shapes and hues in my life! And all of them growing in the shadow of a dense forest—except here, instead of trees, like oaks or birches, wherever you look, you see those huge lignified iridescent mushroom-like growths that shine in all colors of the rainbow. I took some samples from the trunk, but so far, the results are inconclusive. Are those plants, fungi, primitive animals, or something else entirely? Who knows? Not me. Not yet, anyway. Isn't that exciting?

Despite all my eagerness for extracurricular stuff, I haven't forgotten about the main reason for this mission. I've started working on collecting samples of the soil from different areas of the planet. Initial findings are very promising. As we predicted, the ground here is extremely fertile and brimming with yet unknown chemical compounds. With a bit of luck—and lots of hard work—we may be able to isolate them and replicate them on different worlds, converting them to potent artificial fertilizers that could boost farming in other corners of the universe and help to mitigate food shortages in the remote colonies.

Ah, look at me rambling about fake poop. I'm truly baffled why you even married me. Maybe I was less of a nerd before the wedding (or at least hid it better).

Anyway, I'm sending you some photos of the prettiest flowers I could find. Maggie will surely want to know if I made a flower crown for myself, but sadly not yet. Work first, play later!

Also, I think I must be getting old. I misplaced somewhere my favorite screwdriver. Not sure what's more tragic: my rapidly progressing senility or the fact that I even have a favorite screwdriver. Tell Maggie never to grow up. It's a trap.

Love,

Alex

Local Time: Unspecified
Recipient's Time: 08:52 am, 18th April

Dear Eliza,

Again, it's been a while. Work, work, work. More scouting, more research, more report submitting to The Intergalactic Association of Agriculture. They seem happy with my progress, so we're on track to a big success, yay! Buy yourself a nice dress just in case I get the Scientist of the Year Award for solving world hunger, and we're invited to the gala.

Bah, I'm babbling again, and I almost completely forgot the real reason why I'm writing to you! Another reason, I mean, aside from missing you both, of course.

Remember those big mushroom-like trees that I've told you about? I'm good at my job, and I've done a lot of diligent research, but so far haven't been particularly successful in figuring out what they really are.

However, I discovered something else. Well, more like... someone. Tiny copies of these mushrooms are running around the planet! I know how it sounds, but I'm not pulling your leg. I caught one of them observing me. I tried to approach, but they scampered away. They're surprisingly fast, I didn't even get a chance to take a photo. Now that I know I have neighbors, I should behave accordingly. I can try leaving out food to show that I'm friendly. What do they even eat, though? I know that white button mushrooms thrive on manure, but scattering bits of my own waste around seems rather uncouth. I'll try with other organic matter. Let's mark feces as a last-resort option.

Send me ideas of what I can call these creatures. Can't call them mushrooms forever. Seems rude.

Love,

Alex

Local Time: Unspecified
Recipient's Time: 02:18 am, 4th May

Dear Eliza,

First contact made! I left out some fruit pieces at the edge of the camp, and they disappeared when I was sleeping. I put some out again the next morning, and the story repeated itself, but this time, my missing screwdriver was left in the place of food! Did they find it somewhere and decide to bring it back, or did they steal it first and only now felt bad about it? Or am I assigning human morality and sentience to creatures much more primitive? We shall see, I suppose.

At any rate, I was able to observe them more closely, a group of maybe seven specimens. They are still skittish and keep a healthy distance from me but seem to have registered that I'm not an immediate threat. Here are some of my observations about the Shroomkin (thanks again for the name, you're the best):

1) All of them are only about a foot tall but appear bigger due to their large, pointy caps.

2) All are rather plump and bounce a little while walking or running (very fast!).

3) Their iridescent bodies seem to be covered in pinkish fuzz, but they don't wear any clothes. Hard to tell if they have any genders, but each specimen has a distinct pattern of dots and lines on their cap.

4) They don't make any sounds, nothing on the wavelength I could register at any rate. Their communication seems to be based on a complicated system of gestures, dances, and spores.

5) I've seen no mouth and no nose on them, but they have dark, beady eyes. They don't seem to blink.

I wish I was a cosmozoologist. Maybe my observations would have a better scientific value. I made a note about them in my report to the HQ. Someone more qualified than me will investigate them in the future, but for now, I'll keep an eye on them. It can get pretty lonely here sometimes, so I don't mind company. Even of fungi. Mushroom-watching—I guess I invented a new hobby!

Love,

Alex

Local Time: Unspecified
Recipient's Time: 3:49 pm, 16th July

Dear Eliza,
I can't believe it's been almost five months already. Mission is going

great, and the end is in sight. If everything progresses at this pace, in a month or two I will be packing everything up and returning to the HQ. Hopefully, I will be able to tell you everything in person soon, but I just wanted to update you on the Shroomkin situation.

I think they got used to my presence and happily accept the fruit gifts but are still reluctant to approach any closer. Still scared of a big bad human. That's fine by me, I let them live their fungal lives in peace. We simply observe each other from afar. It sounds creepier than it is, I swear.

Recently, I noticed that they seem to be more agitated. No idea why. I think that they even attempted to communicate with me, but I have no way to decipher their waves and jumps. Too bad. Hope it's not too important.

Love,

Alex

Local Time: Unspecified
Recipient's Time: 1:19 am, 30th July

Dear Eliza,

I'm not sure what is going on, but the readings have been all over the place lately. I can only guess that there might be a change of weather coming. A storm, perhaps? I hope it won't be too disruptive. There's still a lot of work to do.

I haven't seen the Shroomkin in a while. Maybe they melded with the big mushroom trees? I suspect that's their home. I almost miss those guys.

Write to you soon. Stay safe and kiss Maggie from me.

Love,

Alex

Dear Eliza,

You'll never receive this letter as I'm writing it down on a sheet of paper, but it helps me focus, helps me to stay sane.

Things are bad. Really bad. A storm like I've never seen before swept through the entire area. The antenna is broken, all generators are dead, and the shuttle was torn in half. There is no power in the camp. All the backup systems were either drowned by the torrential rainfall or smashed to pieces by stray rocks hurled by the hurricane. Guess I know now what the Shroomkin tried to warn me about, huh? I haven't seen them again yet.

Thankfully, I'm not hurt. I lost consciousness for a bit when the wind smacked my cabin around, but I only have a few bruises to show for it.

I'm trying to stay positive. Things are... not ideal, but I'll figure something out. It's just a setback. Been worse. I'll get through it and go back home soon.

I promise.

Love,

Alex

Dear Eliza,

I don't know what to do. I tried everything to get things running, but no matter how hard I try I can't make it work. I'm a botanist, not a mechanic! I fixed the antenna, but without power, it's useless. As it is, I can't send a distress call and neither can I leave this planet because the shuttle is dead. Someone from the HQ will probably come to check on me eventually, but that could take months. What am I supposed to do?

First of all, I shouldn't panic. Even without the food processor working, I have enough supplies to last me at least a week or two. Some of the plants here must be edible. I'll have to research that empirically. Hope my stomach will survive intact.

At least the Shroomkin are back. I was worried something might have happened to them because of the storm, but they're sturdier than they look. Their faces are expressionless, but somehow, I feel as if they are pitying me.

Am I going insane?
Love,
Alex

Dear Eliza,
The tests were a bust. Only a few plants turned out to be edible and even they offer so little nutritional value that I may as well be eating air. I'm quickly running out of options.
Love,
Alex

Dear Eliza,
I lied. I don't think I'll be coming home for Christmas.
Love,
Alex

Dear Eliza,
Tell Maggie I love her.
Love,
Alex

Local Time: Unspecified
Recipient's Time: 6:41 am, 22nd September

Dear Eliza,

I'm still overwhelmed. I can barely form a coherent thought. This may make little sense to you now, but I promise to fill you in later. But for now, I am saved! By mushrooms!

I really thought I was done for. I spent a few hours trying in vain to fix the generator and then I gave up. I sat on the ground, crying. But then, in my darkest moments, the Shroomkin approached me tentatively. They clearly wanted to tell me something, but I had no idea what they meant. At least until one of them rubbed the fuzz on their chest, producing sparks.

I could only watch in stunned silence as they surrounded the generator and blasted it with synchronized jolts of electricity. I have no idea how this works, but it was enough to kickstart the engine again. I have power! I sent the distress signal, and someone from the HQ will pick me up soon.

As I'm waiting for my ride and writing this message, I can hardly believe how lucky I am. The Shroomkin saved my life. We can learn so much from them. I'm already thinking about returning here with more researchers to truly establish proper connections between our species.

For now, I guess I'll have to content myself with a language more universal. That of love, gratitude, and friendship.

Love,

Alex

[Attached is a picture of a tall woman in a gray jumpsuit, smiling brightly. She's holding two mushroom-people in her arms, with five more climbing all over her.]

AN ESSAY IN FAVOR OF THE DESTRUCTION OF MARS ONE, BY DEMETRIUS PAVLOPOULOS

by Kara Race-Moore

Last week, the sophomore class of James E. Webb High School visited the ruins of Mars One. This trip took place despite the fact nearly every member of our class had been dragged to see this nearby historical site numerous times on multiple field trips ⌐throughout our school years.⌐ There, yet again, we saw firsthand the consequences of Anne Kennedy's decision. The twisted metal supporting beams and cracked concrete foundations sitting empty in a lonely patch of desert are all that remains of humanity's first home on Mars. The work of years spent growing the community and decades of planning before humans even got to Mars was all destroyed in an instant when Anne Kennedy gave the order to set off the bombs. Despite this being an act of wanton destruction, I believe Anne Kennedy made the right decision to destroy Mars One.

Some people —⌐and by some people, I mean specifically people like Anna-Marie Donnelly, who went on *one* art study abroad program to Moonbase II last summer, and now she thinks she knows everything about everything⌐— would argue that the destruction of Mars One was a tragic act that should not have been done due to the demolition of priceless, irreplaceable historical art and architecture, but it can be better argued that this destruction was necessary for both the saving and improvement of human life and had to be done.

To give the necessary historical background, Indigenous

life on Mars had recently been discovered by Dr. Navya "Not Dead" Patel while on an exploration of the deepest canyons of Mars.[1] The plant she found was nicknamed 'Mars Moss,' after the Earth plant it appeared to closely resemble.[2] The apparent mundaneness of this alien life meant the discovery was met by only mild enthusiasm from the people of Earth. Then, its amazing health benefits were unlocked by Dr. Katenka "Iron Foot" Mikalova when she discovered it could cure cancer.[3] The immediate ripple effects of that discovery meant the people of Mars One were now in danger of losing their livelihoods and liberties.

Up until that point, Mars One had been treated as a feel-good project for politicians to support when they wanted to be seen by constituents as in favor of science and good international relations.[4] The Mars colonists' day-to-day lives had been largely unimpeded by those theoretically in charge Back Earth.[5] The discovery of a plant that could save billions of lives and was potentially worth untold trillions changed the political landscape overnight.

Mrs. Ferraro: Colloquialisms such as "Back Earth" should be avoided in a formal essay. Say "back on Earth" or just "Earth".

Mars One had been on a planned course for gradual independence, following a path similar to the history of Canada or New Zealand. The government of Mars at this time was mostly based on the student government Anne Kennedy and her cohorts had founded while still in the Mars One schoolhouse.[6] Kennedy was head of the Mars One town council and ran the day-to-day operations as Chief Administrative Officer, with an eye towards increasing Mars One's autonomy over time.[7]

Mrs. Ferraro: It's important to mention Anne Kennedy's status as the first human born on Mars, considering how much she exploited that fact in her rise to power.

But now that Mars colonization could make powerful people real money, the thought of Martians governing Mars was to be considered out of the question. Similar to how the United States of America broke treaties in the 19th and 20th centuries after precious metals and oil were discovered on Native American lands. Any agreements between Earth and Mars that favored local Martians were now considered null and void by those on Earth. Profit was considered more important than any legal document, and the venture capitalist vultures were ready to devour Mars One, bones and all.

Mars One was not viewed as an independent entity by those on Earth. Like the various space stations that orbited above planet Earth, Mars One was seen as an extension of the countries who had contributed to first building it. However, the biggest difference was, unlike the space stations with their constantly rotating populations, people had been moving to Mars One permanently and, more importantly, an entire generation and a half had now been born on Mars One, growing up thinking of themselves as Martians first and whatever nationalities of their immigrant parents or grandparents second.[8]

While it was known that a fleet of Mars Exploration and Colonization Company ships were coming to study and collect the Mars Moss, and everyone understood it would be for the corporation's profit, it was considered an understandable course of events. But then the situation was escalated sharply when the company only gave the Mars One local administration a 48 hours' notice that when the MECC ships landed in two days, all locals were going to be conscripted

---

Mrs. Ferraro:
As I said, this type of essay is not meant to be an appeal to emotions. Stick to facts, such as the MECC business plans for minimum wage for Mars colonists and a 300% mark-up on the resulting Mars Moss product.

Mrs. Ferraro:
Either say "two generations" or specify the first generation born on Mars had grown up and was now old enough to be having their own children.

Mrs. Ferraro:
Be mindful not to use too many adverbs.

---

[1] Carlingford-Psmith, Nigel, (June 24, 2078) "Plant Life Discovered on Mars," BBC News.

[2] Jayasuriya, Priya. *Not. Dead. Yet. The Life and Many Almost-Deaths of Navya Patel, Explorer of Mars,* (Schiaparelli City: New Leaf Press, 2197), 114-117.

[3] Laguerre, Usain, (January 2201) "A Premature Birth: The Unexpected Beginnings of the Republic of Mars," History Today.

[4] Morales, Jorge. "The Political PR of Colonial-Era Mars One." *Space Politics of the 21st Century,* edited by Jackie Shinya and Taylor Gibbons. Harvard University Press, 2220, 24-34.

[5] Cole, Jillian and Tanaka, Marie, *Daily Life in Mars One,* (New York: Random House, 2182), 46-52.

[6] Burkes, Joanne, *Anne Kennedy: First Among Equals,* (Port Olympus: Zeus Books, 2213), 24.

[7] Ibid, 38-39.

[8] Goodwin, Cheryl, *Welcome to the Red Planet: The Early Years of Mars One,* (New York: Penguin, 2099), 170-171.

to help collect the moss, with all other work and study put on hold, and anyone under the age of eighteen would be shipped back to Earth.[9]

The company sanctimoniously cited the reason as concerns for the children's safety, given the plans to turn Mars One from a home to an industrial workspace. If parents wanted to stay with their children, they would have to abandon all the work they had put into colonizing and studying Mars; if they wished to stay on Mars, they would still have to put aside most of their scientific studies to harvest the moss, and also see their children sent to live with either — literally distant — relatives or see them placed into foster care, with all the inherent dangers of that system back then.[10]

Anne Kennedy immediately called the entire Mars One community together for an emergency town hall meeting and told them she refused to hand over their children. "All this has happened before, and all this will happen again," she quoted, "but," she went on angrily, "it will not happen on my watch."[11] She called for a vote of independence, and the Republic of Mars was born, with its first act being to order a total evacuation, rather than risk anyone being detained by the MECC.[12] The new republic would set up temporary headquarters in the storage facility and research base of Labyrinth Station, located nearly 700 kilometers away at the edge of the Noctis Labyrinthus, part of the great Mars chasm. Also, I believe it would have been just as, if not more so, educational to visit the still active Labyrinth Station and see where they ran to rather than away from.

Mrs. Ferraro:
Good sum up in these first few paragraphs of the events before the destruction!

Mrs. Ferraro:
Your request for a much more expensive and time-consuming field trip has been duly noted.

---

[9] Herrara, David. *The Last 48 Hours of Mars One*, (Independence City: White Bear Publishing, 2204), 17-19.

[10] Ibid, 24-25.

[11] Yang-Norton, Emily, *My Fellow Martians: The Speeches of President Anne Kennedy*, (Schiaparelli City: Metropolitan Books, 2109), 58-62.

[12] Anne Kennedy was being referred to as 'Madame President' within the hour, although it would be a full week before a formal election would be held. Burkes, *Anne Kennedy: First Among Equals*, 152-153.

Labyrinth Station was partly used as the base of operations for studying the biggest canyon in the solar system. Meanwhile, the lower levels were a seed vault, keeping seed samples on Mars of almost every plant species on Earth to help protect them from the risk of total extinction, some later outlasting the countries that had originally sent them.[13] The vault was not fully finished at the time and, at that point, contained more storage space than seeds, a perfect place to act as an emergency shelter.[14]

As the logistics for the excavation were quickly hashed out in that historic town hall, it was initially Dr. Katenka "Iron Foot" Mikalova who brought up the idea of destroying Mars One, sharing the story of a family legend that a many-times great aunt had personally helped set Moscow on fire rather than letting it fall into Napoleon's hands.[15] However, this account cannot be verified in any of the sources I searched on the Napoleonic Wars. I think she made this story up!

Mrs. Ferraro: Good for you for checking, but remember to keep the "I" point-of-view out of this type of essay.

Dr. Mikalova's suggestion started an intense debate, with the pros and cons of the idea discussed, quickly getting quite heated. Kennedy was in favor of the idea, which heavily weighed the debate in favor of destruction. She argued it was the best way to ensure they caused real change instead of merely slightly delaying the MECC's plans. Mars One would have to be destroyed to keep it from becoming a base for the MECC to operate from.

Kennedy is known to have been an amateur World War II historian and she herself cited in later interviews that she was thinking of how Denmark had destroyed its own naval fleet rather

---

[13] Wibowo, Josefina. (June, 2099). "North Korea Agrees To Send Heirloom Seeds To 'Doomsday' Seed Vault On Mars". Forbes.

[14] Duggan, Jennifer (April 2107). "Inside the Martian 'Doomsday' Vault". Time Magazine.

[15] Breyer-Goldberg, Alex. *Flight of the Phoenix: The Story of Katenka Mikalova*, (New York: Scholastic Inc., 2150), 49-52.

Mrs. Ferraro:
This is not a needed or helpful aside.

Mrs. Ferraro:
Yes, this paragraph is a good summary of the reasons in favor of her decision. Well done.

Mrs. Ferraro:
Remember, this type of essay also needs facts. Make it clear to the reader the number of animals being evacuated.

Mrs. Ferraro:
Again, PLEASE don't reference yourself OR Anna-Marie when making your case.

than letting it fall into the hands of the Germans during WWII.[16] She knew, just as King Christian X of Denmark had known, and Anna-Marie Donnelly clearly doesn't know, that people were more important than things.

As all essentials were being packed up, Kennedy had a team of engineers create a network of bombs that would leave Mars One open to the elements and render it useless to the incoming MECC agents.[17] If she had not done this, evacuating Mars One would have only temporarily saved the children, and would have provided the MECC with *exactly* what they wanted — a pre-built and furnished base of operations filled with oxygen and fully stocked with food and water without any pesky locals in the way. Kennedy was determined not to hand them that advantage.

Everything alive had to be packed up — besides the people of Mars One, there were also the goats and chickens in the Farm, the plants and fish in the hydroponics structure, the pet cats and dogs, the rodents in the labs — nothing living was to be left behind. Kennedy had to very firmly stipulate, over a few very loud protests, that several large art sculptures would be left behind, even at the cost of possibly offending the countries that had donated them. Anna-Marie Donnelly would argue this was a — weak — point against the Mars One destruction, as, in the next few weeks Norway, Japan, and Portugal did all make offended noises, with Japan going so far as to issue an official Notice of Protest, but, Anna-Marie ignores the important part that the very act of issuing the Notice gave the new Mars Republic legitimacy since it meant they had been officially acknowledged by another country, which is what Kennedy wanted, and supports *my* argument *for* the destruction.[18] To support leaving the art behind, Kennedy

---

[16] Burkes, *Anne Kennedy: First Among Equals,* 65.

[17] Herrara. *The Last 48 Hours of Mars One,* 86-87.

[18] Cavendish, George, *Colonial Mars in 100 Objects,* (London: V&A Museum Press, 2230), 346, 349, 350, 353.

quoted the doomed hero from the film *Glass Flowers* about the French authorities' choice to save art rather than people when the Germans invaded Paris in 1940: "And who will walk in your precious art museums when all the people are gone?"[19]

There was a non-stop shuttling back and forth of people, animals, plants, and supplies since there were not enough vehicles to make the evacuation in one trip. Without any need for debate, everyone under the age of sixteen was put in the first convoy, later known as the Children's Brigade, along with most of the animals. Children led the goats on leashes, clutched tight to cages of rats and mice, and stuffed protesting cats in backpacks. Years later, Dr. Navya Patel's son recalled, "My mom told me to look after my little sister, but I was more excited to be put in charge of President Kennedy's Sphynx cat, Dejah. I wasn't even five yet, but felt so grown up."[20]

After the entirety of the Mars One population was at or on its way to Labyrinth Station, Anne Kennedy oversaw setting off the bombs, making the decision there was no coming back from: "This is Anne Kennedy giving the official order to destroy Mars One. I take full responsibility for this action. Light her up."[21] The resulting explosion thoroughly destroyed Mars One, leaving a crater of rubble, with nothing to see immediately afterward, let alone two centuries later, on the world's most boring field trip.

Less than 48 hours after the now infamous 'Child Removal Memo' had been read by Anne Kennedy, Mars One was destroyed, and the entire population was evacuated to Labyrinth Station, where the nascent government was setting themselves up, having bought time to start making plans.[22] Time they would not have had if they had stayed put or left

---

[19] DiNapoli, Sofia, *Madame President: A New Biography of Anne Kennedy*, (Schiaparelli City: Noble Books, 2211), 142-149.

[20] Kalnietis-Patel, Mohamed, *Son of Mars: My Coming of Age with the Dawn of the Martian Republic*, (Independence City: Guttenberg Press, 2145), 54.

[21] Yang-Norton, Emily, *My Fellow Martians: The Speeches of President Anne Kennedy*, 67.

[22] Conner, Jane, *Seed Libraries*, New York: New Society Publishers, 2215), 236-237.67.

Mars One deserted but functional.

The MECC fleet landed to discover the bombed-out remains of Mars One. They had expected ready-made housing, fresh provisions, full supplies of oxygen, and newly conscripted staff prepared to serve them when they arrived. Instead, they were confronted by this airless, empty husk.[23]

The lack of supplies available meant that the MECC managing director assigned to the fleet, Leo Wagner, had to make a choice very quickly. If he turned around immediately, there would be enough food and oxygen to get everyone he'd brought with him back home. The longer these unwelcome parasites stayed and tried to either repair Mars One without the proper building supplies and specialists, or stayed and tried to besiege Labyrinth Station without any real siege weapons, meant a risk of running out of food and oxygen while on Mars, let alone enough for the trip back to Earth. Wagner would spend the rest of his life refusing to take any responsibility for events and bemoaning the fact he had been a corporate administrator unfairly thrust into a military-like position.[24]

For two days, Wagner watched his subordinates fruitlessly try to make the ruins of Mars One habitable again. Finally, on the third day, he blinked first and ordered everyone back on the ships, and began the trip back to Earth.[25] The War for Martian Independence had only just begun, but Anne Kennedy had been able to begin it on her terms, already steering the course that events would take.

Mrs. Ferraro: FACTS Demetrius, not name calling.

---

[23] Herrara. *The Last 48 Hours of Mars One,* 168-172.

[24] Hoffman-McNab, Charlotte, *Who Really Started the Martain War for Independence?* (New Cambridge: Raven Books, 2201), 233-239.

[25] O'Brian, Bridget, *Battle for a Republic: The Battles of the Martian War for Independence,* (Independence City: FitzSimmons University Press, 2204), 32-36.

In conclusion, it is unlikely that, without the ruthless actions of Anne Kennedy, we would be the independent republic we are today. If Anna-Marie Donnelly had been in charge with her 'save-the-art' attitude, we would all still be under the bootheel of Earth. President Kennedy had to make a tough decision, but for the sake of future generations, it was the right one. Her choice to destroy Mars One helped guarantee the creation of the Republic of Mars and all the freedoms we enjoy today here on Mars. Although, sadly, I was not allowed the freedom to opt out of being dragged to see this dull pile of scrap metal for the thousandth time.

Mrs. Ferraro:
Did you two break up? I know you two thought you were being sneaky, but everyone saw you and Anna-Marie kissing at the ruins of Mars One.

Mrs. Ferraro:
Overall, Demetrius, you demonstrated a general understanding of the proper format for this type of essay, and did a great job citing sources, but you need to learn to be less emotional and put in more hard facts. B minus

ISAAC GEARY'S INSTANT UTOPIA

by Phil Giunta

It took only a day to grow the first snow-capped mountains. The entire range had erupted from the surface on the other side of the world, far enough away that the shockwave barely registered at Terraform Control. By the following afternoon, several kilometers of barren gray flatlands were transformed into lush fields of colorful wildflowers and deep green grass bordered by a rushing river on one side and a dense forest on the other.

"Sector Zero terraforming complete," the dulcet voice of the computer announced over the intercom.

On the opposite side of the canteen, a group of scientists cheered and toasted their success while the Marines in the back corner maintained their stoic silence.

Seated across from me at our usual table, my sister raised her cup. "Here's to Isaac Geary's instant utopias."

I tapped mine against hers. "And the lives they'll save."

This wasn't the first time Nula and I had witnessed the ancient terraforming technology work its magic on a dead world. After living on the remote planet of Orellan for the past few years, she and I were used to landscapes changing at the press of a few buttons. We could order up a beach of pink sand one day and go skinny dipping in a secluded hot spring the next.

Don't ask us to explain how it works. For that you need to chat with the lead scientist, Dr. Isaac Geary. He's the one who'd discovered and mastered the long-buried alien machinery after his ship crashed on Orellan. That was long before my sister and I landed there to hide from the law, but that's a story for another time. Suffice it to say that Isaac saw something redeeming in Nula and me and took us in rather than turn us over to System Police. Since then, he's become a surrogate father to us.

After he'd created a perfect utopia for himself on Orellan, Isaac was reunited with his wife, Hannah. She joined him there after he treated her terminal cancer using nanites he'd programmed himself, but they both knew she was living on borrowed time. It broke our hearts when she died a year later, but at least they'd spent that time together in paradise.

To help him cope with his grief, Isaac set his mind to duplicating the terraforming technology so he could offer it to others. That brought us here to Apphira, a barren planetoid in the middle of the Noltaq system. It was a proving ground to see if he could generate a utopia from scratch. If the test succeeded, the process could be used on other lifeless worlds, alleviating the pressure on most of the overpopulated planets throughout the Eight Systems.

"What time are we takin' off for Lyris?" Nula asked, just before a distant explosion rocked the base. Plates and utensils rattled, and cups toppled to the floor. "Was that another shockwave from the terraforming?"

The Marines shot up from their table and bolted from the canteen while the scientists rushed to the windows, but the tranquil scene outside gave no indication that anything was amiss. "Attention, all personnel," the computer beckoned. "Lockdown in progress. Do not attempt to leave the complex. All vessels will remain grounded until further notice."

"Sounds like we're not taking off anytime soon." I downed the last few drops of my coffee. "Let's find out what the hell happened."

We charged down the corridor, covering our ears against the alarms screeching from the ceiling. By the time Nula and I bounded into Terraform Control, Isaac and his colleagues were huddled around Colonel Lorca, the commanding officer of the Marines assigned to protect the base.

"...cargo ship on a direct collision course with this complex," Lorca was saying. "When the pilot failed to acknowledge our hails, two of my patrol cruisers shot it down near Kilrain Crater. We're sending a squad to check for survivors. We'll lift the lockdown when I'm satisfied we're out of danger. In the meantime, I'll shut off the alarms."

It's hard to believe that anyone would object to the idea of creating a better future for humanity, but the death threats against Isaac and his team started two days after our project on Apphira was featured on the interplanetary news. A handful of extremists condemned the technology as dangerous and vowed to stop us, but I never expected they'd get this close. People often fear what they don't understand. I used to be one of them until I met Isaac.

"I'll be curious to see which terrorist faction claims responsibility for this," he said to the colonel.

"You and me both." With that, Lorca hurried from the room.

It wasn't until the other scientists had drifted back to their stations that Isaac noticed us and ambled over. "How are my two favorite pilots in the galaxy?"

"A lot more worried about our future here than I was ten minutes ago," I replied.

"Understandable, but I have faith in our marines to keep us safe. Speaking of which, I know you two were heading out to Lyris in a few hours to pick up the equipment for Sector Two. I don't know how long you'll be delayed, but once this crisis is resolved, I'll request a military escort for you."

Nula waved off the suggestion. "We don't need that. With all of the mods Zai and I made to our ship, we got more than enough speed and firepower to deal with anything those thugs can throw at us."

"Don't underestimate those thugs," Isaac said. "They possess more determination and resources than the pirates you're used to fending off in the space lanes." He slipped an arm around each of our shoulders. "I don't know what I'd do if I lost you both, so the Marines are going with you. Besides, by the time you get back, Sector One will have been terraformed and I programmed a few hot springs into the matrix just so you two can go skinny dipping."

There were no survivors from the crashed cargo ship. It had been a drone, its course pre-programmed. Four hours passed before Nula and I were allowed to leave with one System Marine cruiser as an escort. The trip to Lyris took six days through hyperspace. Our final approach brought us between the planet and its primary moon, Dek'ahj, a patchwork sphere of rust, beige, and slate gray pockmarked by scores of impact craters. I wondered if anyone lived there until my tactical display picked up a cluster of surface-to-space missiles on an intercept course.

"This wasn't the welcome I was expecting."

The automatic red alert klaxon blared through the ship. Even Nula couldn't sleep through that. I slapped the comm button to hail the Marines. "ME-2061, this is the *Gilded Rage*. I have two dozen spearhead-class seeker missiles on their way up from Dek'ahj. Any suggestions?"

Nula stumbled into the cockpit half-dressed and strapped herself into the co-pilot's seat. She shut off the alarm and pulled up a tactical display on her console. "Who the hell's firin' at us?"

"Someone on that moon. ME-2061, do you read me?"

The only response was static.

"Whoever it is, they're jamming our comms. Hang on." I threw the ship into a forward dive toward Lyris, then banked hard to port.

The marine cruiser unleashed a spread of anti-missile rounds. Several small explosions followed. The remaining spearheads separated into two groups. One swerved toward the Marines, the other followed us.

Nula's fingers danced over the weapons console. "Since when do pirates use seeker missiles? They disable ships to raid 'em, not blow 'em out of existence."

"I don't think these are pirates."

Somewhere behind us, the Marine cruiser exploded.

"Shit! We're on our own now. Maybe we can shake these damn things near the outer moons."

"I might be able to get rid of 'em sooner." Nula pressed a button on her console, launching two aft torpedoes. They sailed into the cluster of seven missiles and exploded, destroying four of them and knocking the remaining three off course.

Our victory was short-lived. The tactical screen flashed red as the klaxon sounded off again. Two of the missiles that had been diverted to the marine cruiser earlier were still in the fight. They emerged from the debris behind us and slammed into our engines, sending the *Rage* spiraling out of control toward Dek'ahj.

Something's crawling on my legs.
Something's crawling on my legs.
Something's crawling...

I woke up with a gasp, kicked off the thermal blanket covering my naked body, and screamed at the writhing, squirming porcelain white skin that spanned from just above my knees straight down to my toes. "*What the hell is happening?*"

Hands gripped my shoulders. "Zai, take it easy." I swatted the arms away and tried to leap from the bed, but my legs refused to move.

Cold metal pressed against the back of my neck.

"Doctor, she's waking up again."

"Right on time."

I opened my eyes to find a swollen and bruised face peering down at me.

"Nula?" I propped myself up on my elbows. "Are you OK?"

"I'm fine. I looked a lot worse when they brought us in. I should be fully healed in an hour or so, according to Doctor Tavlyn." She nodded at the middle-aged man in a teal medical smock towering over the foot of my bed.

"Where are we?"

"In the infirmary on Dek'ahj," Tavlyn said. "Your ship crashed a few kilometers outside one of our settlements."

"I need to sit up."

"Not so fast." He glanced at one of the screens on the wall behind my head. "Just give it another minute."

Ignoring him, I tossed off the thermal blanket and swung my legs over the side. I was now wearing a sleeveless green tunic and matching shorts. Scattered patches of pale white on my shins, calves, and feet gradually shrank as I watched. The childhood scar on my left ankle was gone. Otherwise, my legs were beginning to look normal again. I glared at Tavlyn. "What the hell did you do to me?"

Nula held up her hands. "Take a breath, Zai. After we crashed, you were out cold and pinned under your console. The colonists sent out an emergency crew. They had to cut the cockpit apart to get us out. Doctor Tavlyn and his team tried to save your legs, but..."

"Your legs were damaged beyond even the nanites' capability to repair." Tavlyn took a seat beside me on the bed. "The only option was cybernetic replacement. You woke up prematurely earlier while the nanites were working to tighten the synthetic skin to the plasteel shell and match the pigment to your natural skin color. It can be disconcerting to watch. I'm sorry it scared you."

"What about the missiles that were fired at us from this moon?"

"Not from this moon. From an orbital platform. A terrorist group hacked into the launch systems yesterday. They're the ones who fired on you. Our techs have since locked them out." Tavlyn gave a gentle tap on my left leg. "Back to these. They're the latest in cybernetic replacements from Lyris. You should try them out. In fact, if you two are hungry, we can take a walk down to the cafeteria."

"What about our ship?"

"I imagine a salvage team will move it to the dockyard at the end of town until you're well enough to inspect the damage and decide what to do with it."

"It ain't gonna fly anytime soon." Nula chimed in. "And we still have to pick up the equipment from Lyris."

"I know a guy who might be able to help," Tavlyn said. "Captain

Panko of the freighter *Prythian Torch*. Among other things, he delivers our tech and medical supplies from Lyris once a month. He also takes charters if the money's right."

I stretched my new legs straight out in front of me, then pulled them in toward my chest, testing the knee and ankle joints. "And where can we find this Captain Panko?"

"I believe he's due in tomorrow." Tavlyn rose from the bed. "I'll contact him and find out for certain. Meanwhile, I recommend you rest after you eat, unless you need to check in with your people on Apphira. There's a small conference room three doors down to the right with an outbound comm system. It's all yours whenever you're ready."

"Can you please give us a few minutes in private?" I asked.

"Of course. I'll go check on my other patients." With that, Tavlyn strode out to the hallway and closed the door behind him.

I slid from the bed and, after a few tentative steps, hurried across the room with ease. No stiffness or pain. Even my gait felt normal. I opened the door just enough to peek out to the empty hallway and closed it again. "He seems like a decent guy."

"Only one problem," Nula said. "I never told him we're from Apphira."

"In that case, let's wait until we're off-world before contacting Isaac. If this Captain Panko is able to help us, we'll need to alert our people to expect his ship instead of ours. Being shot down once on this mission was more than enough for me."

The following morning at the Dek'ahj spaceport, Captain Panko was all too enthusiastic to help us once we agreed to his exorbitant fee. "Immense pleasure to assist charming ladies, but lost much cargo during recent pirate attacks. Revenues down. Credits tight. Had to upgrade shields and guns on *Prythian Torch*. Cost high, but now able to give pirates noble wallop."

Panko was an Urujian, a fact that the good Doctor Tavlyn had failed to mention when he arranged this meeting the night before. The captain stood about a meter and a half tall with lavender skin and dark, beady eyes that bulged from either side of his narrow head. As with all Urujians, his downturned mouth conveyed persistent disapproval, making it impossible to get a read on him. And if I can't get a read on someone, I find it hard to trust them. Nevertheless, Panko was our best chance of getting back to Apphira as soon as possible.

"What manner of cargo to convey from Lyris to Apphira?"

Nula downed the rest of her Llamyl tea. "Scientific equipment and medical supplies. Nothin' dangerous or illegal."

"You visions of beauty work for Isaac Geary, then? Instant terraforming? Saw all about it on newscast. You think I may be permitted to witness this technology in action?"

"Wouldn't hurt to ask," I said. "Once we're underway, we'll need to send an encrypted message to Apphira to apprise them of our situation so they know to expect your ship instead of ours. The planet is patrolled by System Marines who don't welcome unexpected guests."

"Understood. Ship stands ready to depart at your pleasure."

Before we left Dek'ahj, Nula and I suited up and rode the tram out to the shipyard to inspect the damage to the *Gilded Rage*. It was worse than either of us had imagined. The engines had been obliterated, and the forward hull demolished. She would never be spaceworthy again. The yard boss offered to purchase the wreckage for parts and scrap. Painful as it was, Nula and I agreed. We negotiated a fair price and then salvaged from it what we could, including firearms, toolbelts, clothing, and any portable tech that was still intact. We carried out six crates on two anti-grav trucks, bid our final farewells to the *Rage*, and boarded the tram back to the spaceport.

A day later, we were on Lyris. I wish Nula and I could have spent time exploring that beautiful world with its three continents and hundreds of islands scattered throughout its teal oceans. Isaac had contracted with a company there to replicate the ancient alien terraforming machines, which can alter the molecular structure of a landscape for a thousand kilometers or more.

Once our cargo had been loaded and Lyris and its moons were far behind us, I recorded a holographic message to Isaac, imparting everything that had happened over the past few days. Captain Panko sent it over an encrypted channel.

Isaac's reply arrived three days later. "Thank Rujah, you both survived. We've had no less than three extremist groups claim responsibility for the attack here on Apphira and on your ship. I feared you were dead." His voice quivered as he slumped in his chair. "If I had known these monsters would go after you, I never would've let you go. I'm so sorry for what you endured."

"Why don't these people understand that having paradise on tap will save lives, including their own?" Nula asked.

"They don't see it that way," I said. "To them, this technology is an abomination that could be perverted into a weapon. Of course, those same terrorists would be the first to use it against their enemies."

"The Marines have increased their patrols of the system," Isaac continued. "I'll alert them to expect the *Prythian Torch*. By the way, Sector One is finished, complete with a series of hot springs, as promised. Sector Two should be ready to terraform by the time you arrive with the equipment. As for Captain Panko, I see no reason why he shouldn't be allowed to observe the process. After all, we'll be sharing it far and wide soon enough. I won't stop worrying until I see you both again. May Rujah bless your travels. Isaac out."

The moment the *Prythian Torch* dropped out of hyperspace, the ship was flanked by two Marine cruisers that escorted us to Apphira's surface. Civilian crews unloaded the cargo under the supervision of our science and engineering teams. The moment Nula and I stepped off the gangway, Isaac embraced us as if for dear life.

"You've both earned a long rest. No more cargo runs, at least for a while."

"That'll be easy," I said. "Since we have no more ship."

"We'll get you another one, I promise."

Captain Panko emerged wearing a dark blue jacket and a transparent breathing mask that covered his nose and mouth. A flexible tube connected the mask to a small metal tank strapped to his thigh. He joined us at the end of the gangway, where he was greeted by two Marines, one of whom ran a scanner over the tank. He then did the same to my legs, which was damned awkward.

He nodded at Isaac. "All clear, Doctor Geary."

"Thank you, young man. Sorry about that, Zai. Colonel Lorca insisted. Once we finish terraforming Sector Two, I want to have a closer look at those legs of yours, so to speak."

"I thought you might." I winked. "Cheeky old man."

"Forgive change of appearance," Panko said. "Afraid the air on this world is a touch too thin and cold for me." He tilted his head and gazed up at Isaac with one eye. "You are venerable cyberneticist Doctor Geary, who discovered ancient terraforming technology on Orellan?"

"The same." Isaac bowed his head. "I greet you with grace and gratitude for bringing home my two favorite people in the universe."

Panko returned the gesture. "Honor of traveling with exquisite company was all mine. Look forward to observing your miraculous terraforming process."

"We're starting Sector Two in a few hours. You're welcome to stay and watch. In fact, while my team installs the equipment you delivered, perhaps you'd like a brief tour of the sectors we've terraformed so far. Least I could do, in addition to paying your fee, of course."

"Would be most grateful for tour. Business talk can wait."

Nula and I left Captain Panko in Isaac's capable and enthusiastic hands while we reported to the infirmary. After the chief medical officer gave us a clean bill of health, we hit the showers then chowed down in the canteen with a group of Marines.

We reconvened in Terraform Control just in time for the Sector Two launch. Isaac, Captain Panko, and several excited members of the science team stood chattering before a series of screens spanning the front wall.

The moment Nula and I entered, a technician at one of the monitoring stations waved Isaac over. "Doctor Geary, my scanners picked up an unusual signal burst. Looks like it came from somewhere in the vicinity of—"

"Attention, all personnel," the computer's melodic voice silenced all conversations. "An explosive device has been detected in Terraform Control. Activating isolation shield. Please evacuate the complex immediately."

I winced as a wall of amber light flashed in front of me. By the time my vision cleared, I was trapped in a column of pulsing energy. The purpose of an isolation shield was to contain an explosion and prevent widespread injury and property damage. So why the hell was it focused on me?

"Exotic matter bombs, two of them." The engineer who had detected the strange signal a few seconds ago tapped his touchscreen. "If this reading is correct, they'll detonate in three minutes."

All heads turned to stare at me, or rather, my legs.

"Isaac, what the hell's going on?" I shouted over the buzzing and crackling of the isolation shield.

"Attention, all personnel," the computer repeated. "An explosive device has been located in Terraform Control. An isolation shield has been activated to contain the blast. Please evacuate the complex immediately."

"Clear the room." Isaac waved toward the doors. "Everyone out, now!"

"I ain't leavin' my sister," Nula said as the science and engineering teams scurried from the room.

"I didn't expect you would." Isaac approached the shield. "Zailyn, each of your cybernetic legs contains an exotic matter bomb. They're nestled in your calves. We have about two minutes before they detonate."

I groped around in my toolbelt until I found my laser cutter. "Time for another amputation." I lowered myself to the floor, legs straight out in front of me. "Keep the shield up until I'm done, just in case any tampering sets off the bombs early."

"Understood." Isaac backed away as I went to work. He directed Nula to the engineering station. "When I give the order, lower the shield. Flashing red button on the upper left of the screen. Be ready to reactivate it as soon as I pull Zailyn away."

By the time he hurried back to me, I had severed my left prosthetic just below the knee and started on the right.

"Minute and a half," Nula called.

"Working as fast as I can."

Once the right leg was free, I crawled to the edge of the shield.

Isaac waved at Nula. "Now!"

The amber column evaporated. Isaac gripped my outstretched hands and yanked me away. "Shield up!" The crackling hum and heat of energy flickered on behind me as Isaac lifted me into his arms. With Nula in tow, he scrambled for the door.

"Attention, all personnel. An explosive device has been located in Terraform Control. An isolation shield has been activated to contain the blast. Please evacuate the—"

I glanced over Isaac's shoulder as my former cybernetic limbs exploded in a silent blast of pale blue light. The doors slid closed behind us moments before the shockwave knocked us to the floor.

"Nula!"

I shot up, thrashing and kicking until a bolt of pain ripped through the back of my head.

"Easy, Zai, easy." Nula wrapped her arms around me and lowered me back onto the bed. "You're safe in the infirmary."

"What happened?"

"Ya cracked the back of your thick skull against the wall."

"That was my fault." Isaac strolled over to join Nula. "I dropped you when the shockwave hit. Sorry about that."

I lifted my bare legs one at a time. Wiggled my toes. Bent my knees. Everything worked as expected, but it still weirded me out that I couldn't feel anything aside from the occasional phantom pain.

"You're the only person I know who lost their legs twice in one week." He squeezed my left calf. "I assure you *these* cybernetics are free of explosives."

"How much damage was there?"

"Most of Terraform Control will need to be rebuilt along with other parts of the complex, but without the isolation shield, we wouldn't have a complex at all, nor would we be here to discuss it."

"I'm sorry."

Nula cupped her hand over mine. "Ya got no reason to be. None of this was your fault. If I ever find that Doctor Tavlyn, I swear to Rujah I'll kill him."

"Get in line," I said.

"System police were dispatched to Dek'ahj," Isaac said. "They found the remains of what they believe was a terrorist base. Looks like the occupants cleared out just after you left. This was a well-coordinated attack. From the newscasts about our project, everyone knew we'd contracted with a company on Lyris to manufacture the terraforming equipment, but their facility is underground and heavily guarded so the next best target for the terrorists was the cargo ships. It wouldn't have taken much effort to find out when the next one was scheduled to arrive from Apphira, which just happened to be yours."

"What about Captain Panko?"

"Dead. The signal that activated the bombs originated from his ship, which has been impounded. When the Marines tried to arrest him, he killed three of them before turning his blaster on himself."

"All this happened while I was out?"

"Well, you took a nasty head injury." Isaac brushed aside a lock of my hair. "But nothing that a few dozen nanites couldn't fix."

"Just like the first time you saved my life."

"Yes, and I seem to recall how irate you were with me about that."

"At the time, I didn't like the idea of microscopic robots floating around in my bloodstream—until you proved that they could be used ethically."

"Which is precisely what I'm doing with this ancient terraforming technology, but I was naïve to think everyone would embrace it, that they would welcome its benefits with open arms. Instead, I nearly lost you both. Rujah save us from those who try to destroy what they don't understand."

"But people are embracin' it," Nula said. "The newscasts are callin' it 'Isaac Geary's Instant Utopias.' Governments are clamorin' for this tech all over the Eight Systems. Plenty of dead planets and moons out there, and if they want ya to convert them into a paradise, they'll provide protection. These terrorists won't win."

"And we're still in the cargo business," I added. "Or we will be as soon as we get a new ship."

Isaac snapped his fingers. "Oh, about that. According to Colonel Lorca, the Marines finished their search of Captain Panko's freighter and its computers. They're analyzing the data they downloaded with the hope that it will lead them to the terrorist cell that orchestrated these attacks. According to the colonel, they have no further use for the ship so, at my request, they wiped its registration and rechristened it the *Gilded Rage II*."

"What?" Nula and I perked up in unison.

"As much as I want to, I know I can't keep you two grounded forever. The ship is yours, ladies."

I leapt out of bed and into Isaac's arms, joining Nula in showering him with hugs and kisses.

"And to make sure you always come back to me, you get two marine escorts from now on." He beamed as he pulled us close. "Since I lost Hannah, you girls are all the family this old man has left. You're my universe. Whenever we're together, that's Isaac Geary's Instant Utopia."

LITTLE HOUSE ON THE ECLIPTIC

by Zachary Taylor Branch

Lara was taking twenty-foot leaps along the edge of a frozen iron-lava waterfall, and the voice coming over the comms was making it hard to concentrate.

"You can't turn them down again, Lara. This could be your last chance."

"Point taken, Benn, but I can't leave Ella, not yet. The guardianship ends in a few months, we'll figure it out then."

"She should never have dragged you and Paris out to Psyche in the first place, Lara. Look, I know I can get the Co-op Board to make another recommendation, and the T.E.F will expunge your record if you enlist, you'll be free."

"Thanks Benn, but I'm not exactly Morale Officer material. The august Terran Expeditionary Alliance is just as likely to kick me out as the VI was, and I actually enjoy it out here on the Ecliptic."

The comms were quiet for a few seconds. "No one likes it out on the Ecliptic, Lara. Everyone out here is just trying to get flush again, before heading back sunwards or out to the Near Worlds, but no one loves the work here."

"Well, I love it enough for now, and I need to get back to it. Shakhtar Two out."

Lara toggled off her comms, and tried to concentrate on the task at hand. Ella was just ahead, with a large brass disk floating just a few feet behind, which followed her when she jumped off the edge of the cliff.

Lara jumped a few seconds later and after a languid thirty second fall to the jumbled iron floes at the base of the cliff, she toggled her comms over to her guardian.

"Ella, we can't stay out here much longer, the leading edge of the solar flare is only about an hour away."

"We'll be in night-shadow by then, my girl," replied Ella. "Gotta reset the #13 spin well, can't take the loss of production."

The two heavily-suited figures were soon hopping up to a complex stack of pipes and fittings, looking more like a 20th Century Terran oil derrick than the most sophisticated Ecliptical technology of the 21st Century. The sun was just above the too-near horizon, and would disappear in 15 minutes, at the end of the too-short Psychean day.

"I think we've lost connection with the core, the bit might be hung up in a rubble pocket," said Ella. "I'm going to restart the drill, you lay hands on the works."

Ella threw a couple of old-style breakers, and the upper portion of the drill began to turn and slowly descend through an extinct volcano of quantum-coupled iron/nickel. Lara could not hear the sound of the grinding, or feel the white-hot drill bit 100 meters below, but she could feel the vibrations, even through the thick soles of her insulated boots. She removed her over-gauntlets, and laid her contact gloves on the derrick. She immediately felt the deep cold of 16 Psyche, and something more. She silently recited from the Spin Mining Primer to help get her connection established.

"Bulk-entangled coupled matter is forged in the core of planetary bodies, and 16 Psyche is the exposed core of a shattered Solar world. Heat, light, momentum and electricity can all be transferred remotely through entangled matter, under the proper conditions, as was first discovered almost two centuries ago with iron/nickel meteorites found on Earth..."

"That's it!," yelled Ella, as the drill began to slow. "Got contact with the core again, good coupling with the Optical Network, fine longitudinal spin capture. Let's give it a few to make sure it sticks this time, and then we can scoot back to the ranch before sunrise."

What Lara sensed as she held onto the well-works was not quite a vibration, it was more like a long, slow musical note. Actually, a chorus of bass notes, almost below her range of hearing.

"Good old Number 13, lucky 13," thought Lara to herself as she tried to stabilize the glitchiest of the ranch spin wells. Coupled matter momentum exchange was more art than science, more feeling than protocol, a bit like riding a bike. The spin mines were translating angular momentum into linear momentum, like the coupling of bike and road, but remotely, Spooky Momentum Transfer at a Distance. Lara was connecting the motion of Psyche's core with thousands of other coupled matter objects scattered through the Solar System. Her eyes were closed tight, but she started seeing lights nonetheless.

First a streak of blue, like a tiny meteorite, flashed from left to right. Then a burst of yellow, then white, then green, a tiny slow motion fireworks show. She opened her eyes and saw Ella looking to the north. Psyche's axis of rotation was in the plane of the Ecliptic, and her north pole was currently pointed toward deep space, away from the Sun. Lara saw a series of bursts, violet, blue and green, which seemed to erupt across the darkened landscape around the well. And she could tell that Ella had seen them too.

"Cosmic rays, some bad ones," said Ella over the comms. "We need to get down into the works until this swarm passes. It's always some goddamn thing."

Ella pulled up on the edge of a metal hatch which would have weighed half a ton on Earth. Its inertia slowed the task, but Ella soon had it wedged open enough that she and Lara could squeeze into the well housing. The brass disk, a Maxim Corp. Sprite that went by the name Jeeves, remained on the surface generating a respectable magnetic field which would deflect at least some of the persuadable cosmic rays.

It was a tight space, not meant for humans. The flashes persisted, but less frequently now that Lara and Ella had a bit of cover. Lara placed her customized gloves back on the drill, and the moaning lament of the coupled matter core of 16 Psyche resumed in her head. She was mining the much sought-after longitudinal spin, $z+/-$ angular momentum to be more precise, which would be mediated further through the Optical Network to provide linear Reactionless Drive to anyone who wanted to move out of the plane of the Ecliptic.

Lara directed her poking and prodding of the Psychean core and the Network's receipt of high-value longitudinal spin as a series of whispers, almost like incantations, instructions that would keep #13 connected to the Network after she returned home. But other voices were joining the conversation. Spin mediators didn't speak of it openly, they didn't want to get suspended for mental aberrations, but they all thought the rumblings were more animate than geologic.

Hours later, Ella had to shake Lara out of her mediation, not for the first time. "You got Number 13 nice and stable, Lara. Storms are well past and we're back in deep shadow. Let's head home."

Jeeves welcomed Ella and Lara back to the surface with his nervous side-to-side waggle, and lighted their way along the rock-strewn path that led back to the house. After an hour of hop/skipping over various obstructions, they and Jeeves cycled through the cylindrical lock-lift which slowly lowered them down to their subterranean (subpsychean?) home. They shed their outer expeditionary gear during the slow 20 meter descent. The lift lowered into the center of a cave thermally cut out of the Psychean regolith, but it no longer looked much like a cave.

The walls had been melted smooth and air-tight by the Co-op's thermal miner, revealing the speckled grays and silvers and blacks of the local metallic chondrites. At the top of the rock dome, about 20 feet above the smooth-cut floor, several small Lux Sprites were loitering, filling the house with yellow-white light from the photonically-coupled satellite in orbit about 16 Psyche. The dome space was about 30 feet in diameter, and was cluttered with cargo containers and work stations and multi-processors.

The interconnected ovens and extruders and looms were processing carbonaceous ores into thread and fabrics and wire, small lots, but still workable. Ella's workbench was cluttered with projects where she was turning these local materials into clothing and furniture. Lumpy futons surrounded an always-warm Hot Block, some modest thermal Action at a Distance.

The kitchen was Lara's domain. It took some finesse to turn vat-grown yeast paste and space-taters and pressed algae into edible food, but she had become quite accomplished at it. Ella had recently helped her wang up a new 3-D printer which could make a reasonable analogue of a lightly marbled pork roast. She had one slow-cooking in the new thermal oven, with a handful of precious root vegetables purchased from the Co-op, and a mix of seasonings from her treasured spice collection. The savory smell of the demi-roast filled the house.

There were three currently sealed doors around the periphery of the dome room. One led to the reactor room where fermentation tanks and cultivation vats and O2/H2O reclaimers were recycling waste products into food and drink and air and water, remotely powered by cheap electricity transmitted through the Tesla Network. The second led to a long tunnel which would someday connect to the new Transit line, still in the earliest stages of construction. The third led to the sleeping tubes, and it opened suddenly to reveal Lara's brother Paris, fidgeting with the coupled matter Diadem that fit over the back of his head like a small, elegant crown. He was looking annoyed as usual, but he was also exceedingly well dressed.

"C'mon, let's get moving, folks. We're late for the party, and I haven't seen non-relational humans in weeks. I decanted a bottle of the new moonshine for the party, anyone stupid enough to decamp to 16 Psyche is going to need it. Though I gotta say, Ella, I do like the new party togs."

Paris was smoothing out the last wrinkles in his pseudo-silk thawb, a loose-fitting robe covering his Second Skin Suit and Gravity Vest. All Transterrans wore Suit and Vest (low gravity and hard vacuum were the norm out on the Ecliptic) except when in the water closet or sleeping tube. Paris' new robes were solid gray-blue, the only color of carbon/silica thread that Ella had mastered. But it was her jewelry which drew the eye.

Paris wore a wide polycarb belt studded with the gemstones which turned up regularly turned in the constant mining and tunneling around the spin ranch. Rough-cut rubies, serpentine, agates, malachite, jasper, all quite beautiful, but of absolutely no trade value. With the exception of coupled matter, there was no material valuable enough to mine and ship around the Ecliptic.

Lara and Ella just rolled their eyes, and started poking around on the workbench for some suitable evening attire. They were considerably less stylish and fussy than Paris, but they were quite fond of him nonetheless.

"Looking pretty posh there, womb-buddy," said Lara, as she pulled a new robe over her Suit and Vest. "Remember to be nice at the Myasnikovs tonight, and discreet, we're just one big Shakhtar clan for the evening. Valentina is a Near Worlds Driver and Yuri is a hydroponics engineer, both expats from the Russian Empire. They've been quiet this past year, but I hear Yuri's market garden is ready for trade. I would kill for some fresh greens and…"

"They shouldn't be out here any more than we should," said Paris, now looking more grim than annoyed. "We could run this whole operation remotely from a real house in real civilization, despite what the masters say. A flat at Olympus Mons or Copernicus City or even back in Virginia."

Ella was intently watching the complex fields of data that Jeeves was projecting on the big Whiteboard hanging over her work table. More requests to check in with the surgeon at Iolanthe, they were all overdue for their RadMeds. And there was more damned trouble with the spin wells.

"OK, smart guy, Well #7 just went out again," said Ella. "Why don't you and Jeeves just wander on over there and get it running again?"

Paris was tempted to accept the challenge, he desperately wanted to return to city life, but he was not all that good at spin mining. Comms and remote operations were more his forte, though some youthful indiscretion with those skills had gotten him and Lara placed into the guardianship with Ella.

"Don't get him started again, Ella," said Lara, hanging a three-foot necklace of polished green aventurine over her robe. "Paris is out of here and headed back sunwards the micro-second we turn 20. Might just be you and Jeeves running the ranch by yourselves if I decide to join him."

Jeeves expressed a surprising amount of emotion for a three foot wide brass disk with no face, but the rapid turning of his main camera toward Ella, then Lara, and back again, along with a slight tremble in one of his articulated arms indicated that he was not at all pleased with this particular plan.

"I've been on my own before, my girl, and will be again no doubt. But if you stay, the house and ranch can all be yours, once I get the notes paid off. You can make a fortune here, Lara, coupled matter technology requires a specific human factor, and with your gift..."

"The mysteries of bulk quantum entanglement will have to wait," said Paris. "The runabout is here, time for a modest asteroidal party."

The Co-op runabout was docked at the top of the airlock/lift, and launched in a negative gravity climb as soon as Ella and Lara and Paris were strapped in. Other coupled bodies in the Solar System were experiencing increased gravitational attraction, the Gravity Exchange was another essential component of the World Without Wires. Jeeves was reluctantly minding the ranch alone for the evening.

A fifteen minute parabolic hop took the runabout to the Myasnikov encampment on the far hemisphere of 16 Psyche. A Co-op pilot was remotely helming the little disk ship, so Paris was scanning his media feeds while Lara checked the new Co-op food inventory and Ella scanned the Optical Network momentum prices. Only Paris looked cross.

"Damn, the rest of the guests left hours ago, hope the Myasnikovs are still awake. I hate being late."

Lara and Ella sighed, as they sent some apologetic text messages by Coupled Matter Radio, to which the Myasnikovs responded immediately. The runabout docked at their landing pad a few minutes later, and lifted back off as soon as the Shakhtar party had egressed, on a never-ending circuit of Psychean passenger and cargo runs. Lara and Paris and Ella hop/skipped down a short tunnel from the landing pad to the main dome, and when the final lock door opened, Lara saw a color she'd been missing. Green, lots of green.

Yuri Myasnikov was a big man with an even bigger gap-toothed grin and he hugged Lara and Paris and Ella in turn as he made his welcomes.

"Ah, the Shakhtar clan at last! And such attire, best dressed citizens of Psyche, no doubt. And bearing gifts, I unburden you, dear Paris! Spirits are rare gift on Ecliptic, we are most honoured. Val, my treasure, guests have arrived, please to set table for five, I make salad."

A very tired-looking women emerged from the tiny kitchen alcove, and cheered up noticeably when Yuri handed her the bottle of almost-vodka. Paris and Ella helped her set the table with some virtually indestructible

Regolite pottery. Lara followed Yuri directly to the hydroponic stations around the perimeter of the dome, dark now but for the light of the wandering Lux Sprites.

"Our mutual friend at Co-op says we share passion, my dear," said Yuri, as he gestured to the larger articulated Sprites that were tending his vertical garden. "Will not conquer Ecliptic on empty stomach, but cannot remain human on yeast cakes. I was mere chemist once, at Mendeleev Institute in blessed Moscow, but Valentina led me to space. Deep quiet of Ecliptic key to her interstellar Driving, far from quantum entanglements of Terra. How could I but follow? And provide modest sustenance."

Lara walked slack-jawed along the curved hydroponic racks, stepping lightly between a jumble of processed food containers. The produce was all small in size, but brightly colored. Yuri popped a cocktail tomato in her mouth as he began to fill his basket.

"Aubergine have failed, but tomato and cucumber now tradable. Fine arugula, plenteous basil, sprouts of all sorts, peppers to make Chinaman cry."

Lara fought back tears herself, she had not seen so much fresh food since her involuntary departure from Earth. She and Yuri were in intense culinary discussion as they wandered back to the kitchen to chop and toss a salad. Several tiny Lux Sprites started orbiting over the main table, producing a low light that resembled flickering candles. Valentina laid out a fine table of cured meats and smoked fish and cheeses, while apologizing profusely for the absence of a good black bread and butter. Yuri and Ella had just started a discussion on how to produce some vat-based substitutes when Valentina stood and raised her glass.

"Dear new friends, welcome to humble Myasnikov home. Shakhtar spin mining is renowned, and compliments to Paris on fine Ecliptical spirits. Had hoped to share findings of our new probe at Lalande 21185, but coupled matter connection has failed. Bitter disappointment, decade of work lost... Forgive me, most inappropriate subject of first toast with Shakhtar clan. To 16 Psyche, may our lives here be most safe and productive."

Ella and Val were soon talking about the challenges of life on Psyche, while Lara and Yuri tucked into dinner with gusto. Paris was holding forth on his prowess in remote telemetry and networking, while Valentina, who also wore a Diadem, began to summon up images from her previous interstellar probe missions with the Virginia Institute and T.E.A. Paris became very quiet upon mention of the VI, and Val turned her attention to Lara.

"Do I understand, Lara, that you are primary facilitator of coupled matter connectivity in the Shakhtar spin mines?"

"She is indeed, Val," said Ella, helping herself to another helping of tossed salad. "Spin mining requires a human factor, and no one finesses the Optical Network better than Lara."

"I have no doubt, Ella. Might I prevail upon your family, after dinner of course, to adjourn to my Driver Warren? Paris to inspect Coupled Matter Radio and Lara to attempt her subtle magic with Optical Network?"

Paris had been looking a bit sulky, but he cheered up immediately at the prospect of fiddling with some new comms. Lara was less excited, facilitation was an intensely personal activity, and she'd never done it in front of an audience before. But Yuri was overjoyed, Val's sorrow at losing the Lalande probe had wounded him deeply. He shuffled everyone off to the Warren in a trice, dirty dishes still on the table and a fresh bottle of plum brandy in hand.

Paris actually whistled out loud as they entered Val's lair, a pre-fab module that had been landed fully equipped and was now partially buried next to the main dome. Every exposed surface above the floor was covered with Whiteboards and displays and control consoles, showing a torrent of alphanumeric data but no imagery. Lara could tell by the large red fonts and rapid repeat rates that the displays were indicating mission failure, even though she couldn't read the Cyrillic characters.

"Probe is small, less than four meters length, capable of 10g acceleration and years at 0.9c in interstellar space," said Val, adjusting her Diadem and the Driver controls in yet another attempt to re-establish contact. "Decelerated into Lalande system this month after nine year transit, all momentum transfer acquired through Optical Network, which makes us clients of estimable Shakhtar spin mines."

Yuri and Ella were exchanging sly nudges, and after the briefest of hesitations, Paris and Lara began to noodle with the innumerable controls and status boards. Val helpfully changed the displays to English, and continued her improvised mission brief.

"Probe achieved orbit with second planet last week, tidal-locked terrestrial world, sunside a desert, darkside a frozen tundra. Inert atmosphere, iron crust, not candidate world for colonization, but T.E.A. pays well for probe contact with coupled meteoric bodies, to allow Transnormal exchange of Gemini ships to other stars. All 'cannonball' worlds found to date of little interest, profoundly dead, no ecosystems, no orbital companions. Until Lalande 21185 Beta."

Val settled into the main Driver's Station and cued up a recording, the last received from her lost probe. The imagery on the displays showed it meandering through an unusually dense asteroid field, which soon resolved itself into a ring high above the equator of Lalande Beta. Ella leaned in very close to one of the video displays.

"A ring shouldn't be stable around a tidally-locked planet this close to a red dwarf," said Ella. "Beta's orbital period couldn't be more than 20 days."

"18.5 days, even more confounding than the Rings of Venus," said Val. "Though VI has classified all research on Cytherean rings."

Paris and Lara shuffled a bit nervously at the latest mention of the VI, hoping the Myasnikov didn't pursue this line of discussion further. So Lara changed the subject.

"You managed to navigate a coupled matter probe through a dense planetary ring over eight light years away?," she asked.

"Briefly," replied Val, looking both proud and sad. The recorded imagery showed the probe in a stable co-orbit with dozens of the ring fragments, small tumbling micro-worlds which made Psyche look quite grand. Until the probe began to approach one of the larger moonlets, glowing a bright metallic red under the light of Lalande 21185. The probe drew closer, revealing a plain of metal with the distinct crosshatch pattern of iron/nickel meteorites, until the probe crashed into it.

The recording ended, as did the dense feed of sensor data, and the Whiteboards went dark. "Last of probe transmissions, no joy re-establishing contact," said Val, reaching down to her control console. She very lightly touched a small nodule of silver/gray metal, egg-shaped and covered with a familiar cross-hatched pattern. "Meteoric coupled matter. Probe contains its twin, allows instantaneous communication across eight light years, until it didn't."

Lara knew the beautiful object well, she and Ella had encountered scores of coupled matter nodules during their mining operations. They were just articles of commerce, the working material of the profligately entangled World Without Wires, but they were always more to Lara. She reached out for this one without even meaning to, feeling an intense desire to take this little piece of primal metal. She lightly touched the little nodule in its receptacle, and her eye went wide.

She began to hear a song, a familiar song, if somehow sped up almost to the point of comedy. It was the slow, mournful lament of Psyche, but now with the speed and pitch of a flock of migrating passenger pigeons. She was somehow hearing the chattering tune in her head when she heard a familiar human voice in the usual way. Val was quite excited.

"Contact! Lara has contact with probe! Telemetry feed re-established! What are you seeing?"

Lara was seeing through two sets of eyes. She was clearly still in the Myasnikov's Driver Warren, standing just a few feet from them and Ella and Paris. But she was also on a tiny moonlet in orbit above Lalande 21185 Beta, tumbling through a maze of other micro-worlds, while they sang to each other.

"Hearing. Music. A symphony, choir of thousands, millions... The moonlets are singing, like birds, joyous in flight," said Lara absently, her eyes half closed.

"Sound doesn't travel through space," said Paris, fidgeting with his Diadem, as was Val, trying to hear what Lara was hearing.

"And Lara's ears are not in orbit above Lalande Beta," said Val, a bit impatiently. "She is interpolating probe telemetry, possibly changes in magnetic and electrical fields transduced to sound, much as human brain takes impact of random photons on retina and creates our internalized vision of external world."

"Like she mediates the spin wells," said Ella, recognizing Lara's vaguely trance-like state. She fetched a stool for Lara, and set her down gently on it, knowing that these sessions could go on for hours. And she wasn't wrong, Lara held onto the little coupled matter orb through another Psychean day and night, humming a not-quite-human tune, a repetitive arpeggio of dancing notes, octaves lower than what she was hearing.

Paris and Val worked their Diadem controls feverishly, finally getting the vaguest echo of the songs that Lara was hearing. They were debating frequency modulation and Doppler shifting, trying to figure out if this was a complex orbital phenomenon, or something more.

Yuri and Ella held Lara's free hand tightly as she began to cry, and for the long hours later, well after she had run out of tears.

"I don't think I've ever seen Paris so happy," said Ella a few weeks later.

He was seated in an improvised Driver station that she had wanged up in her workshop, at the cost of the workbenches for her sartorial projects. New clothes and jewelry would have to wait. Paris' connection to the Lalande probe proved to be far less intense than Lara's, but still highly productive. He had re-established a working relationship with some old friends at the VI, and all were now engaged in intense debate about acoustic resonance and chaotic systems and whether humans would even recognize truly alien life if they finally stumbled upon it.

Lara herself had no doubts about what resided at Lalande Beta. She was absently reading the latest missive from the Terran Expeditionary Alliance, offering her immediate commission as an Exo-Scientist on the Gemini 489, the first T.E.A. mission to Lalande 21185. She smiled at the compliment and was idly humming one of the more melodic passages of the Lalande Beta songs when the main lock cycled. It was Yuri, in an ill-fitting Second Skin suit, heavily burdened, and with a much smaller companion.

"Lara, my treasure, you are looking much recovered," said Yuri as he stepped off the lift platform. "And there is dear Paris on station at Lalande, fine lad, my Val is getting her first good sleep in years. Ella, if I might prevail upon you, borscht and black bread have gone cold." Ella smiled as she helped Yuri navigate the idiosyncratic Shakhtar kitchen.

"Yuri, you don't have to keep bringing food, I'm fine now," said Lara, as Yuri's companion removed her retractable helmet. "And I see you have brought your partner in crime."

Yuri looked at Lara with an uncharacteristically serious expression. "You suffered on my behalf, Lara, a Myasnikov always repays debt, with interest. And young Benn here has kept eyes upon you during your Ecliptical sojourn, tells me that estimable T.E.A. desires you to join new expedition to Lalande Beta."

"Benn has a big mouth," said Lara, "And scary good intelligence and organizational skills. You set up that whole intervention at Yuri and Val's, didn't you?"

"More shove than intervention," said Benn. "The songs here on Psyche are seductive but slow, the VI will be studying them for centuries. You needed to know that worlds like Lalande Beta are out there. Alive, just complex, who knows? But you can find out, as soon as the 489 can make Transnormal exchange with one of the coupled Beta moonlets"

Lara began to tear up again at the memory of that strange red-lighted world and its ring of little coupled matter singers, and the prospect of trading places with one of them by the spookiest action at a Distance.

"What do you think, Ella? Can you and Jeeves mind the ranch without me?"

"Won't be the same, my girl, but Paris and Val show some promise as spin miners, if I can ever get them out of those bloody Driver stations. Don't you worry about us, Lara, you go off and do the brave thing," said Ella, as she and Yuri busied themselves with dinner.

Paris removed his Diadem, and rose slowly from his station, stiff after 12 straight hours of Near World Song mediation, a new market in the World Without Wires that he was building from the ground up with Val.

"Always thought I'd be the first to go, womb-buddy, but there's so much to do here now. Who knew a planetary ring eight light years away would be so interesting? And profitable," said Paris, looking quite pleased at first, but then more than a little sad. "They're connected, you know, Psyche and Lalande Beta, and not just in the World Without Wires and Transnormal exchange ways we and the T.E.A. have been exploiting. Gotta promise me you'll be careful in the worlds beyond."

Lara nodded as she and Paris hugged, and Jeeves drifted in and touched the edge of his disk lightly to Lara's forehead. He seemed to be having the most trouble with the idea of Lara leaving. Nonetheless, he projected her T.E.A. enlistment papers on the Big Whiteboard and witnessed her signature, before joining Ella as she headed out to the spin mines.

Lara boarded a T.E.A. cutter a few days later, bound for the Gemini 489 and an alien world far from her home and family out on the Ecliptic.

NAHIB

by Paul Weissman

Once upon a time, there was a girl. She was shy and lived at the edge of the woods in a quaint little house with her mother and her father. They were away for long periods of time. The girl, whose name was Leila, did not know why. When she asked, they smiled, patted her head, and said, "Big people things." That made Leila feel smaller than she already felt. When her parents were gone, she would feed the chickens and the goats, tend the garden, and keep the house tidy. Even though she was lonely, she felt safe.

It was at nighttime that her fears would overtake her. She knew there were bad things in the woods, because her parents told her. She had only ventured a few feet in and only during the daytime. She would touch the trees with wonder, feeling how rough and gnarly they were to her small hands. Once, she heard a rustle that made her jump back. It was only a bunny carefully sniffing the air and hopping about. But her parents told her of other animals. Not so nice things. Things she did best to stay away from.

She did not like when her parents were away. But it was always so lovely when they returned. They would have such a time laughing at the dinner table. Her father was so funny telling stories about his life, and his mother smiled and shook her head. Her father always said her mother had such a good head on her shoulders and that he would fly away with the breeze if it weren't for her. She did not know quite what he meant. But watching them in the warm glow of the candle, filled with love for her and each other, it didn't quite matter to Leila.

Then, one day, her parents left and did not return. Leila waited and waited. She did everything she was supposed to. She fed the chickens and the goats, tended the garden, and kept the house tidy. In the evenings, she would wait at the front gate for them to come home, laughing and apologizing, but they had such an adventure. She ate the eggs from the chicken. She drank the milk from the goat. And she ate the vegetables from the ground. After a couple of weeks, Leila realized that her parents were not coming home. Whatever adventure they were on, she was not invited. She packed up a bag with some eggs from the chickens and milk from the goats, and she set out into the world.

Every village she entered, she asked about her parents and every time she was told they were here, but they had left, sometimes one week ago, sometimes a year ago, but she knew they were alive and whatever they were doing must have been good, because she knew her parents were made up of nothing but good. Eventually, she grew to be a strong young woman of many talents, and she wearied of searching for her parents. And so, one time, in one village, she settled down and raised a family of her own. She spoke of her parents with love because they were full of love, and even though they left and she hadn't seen them for twenty years, that love never died, and neither will her love for her children because it is the same love.

"That was a sad story," Carly said.

"I suppose," Her mother replied. "But it was a happy story too."

"It can be both?"

"It can be both."

Carly's mother stroked her hair. Tears were rimming her eyes.

Carly's mom wiped the tears away.

"Are you sad?"

"I am happy sad."

"You can be both. Just like the story."

Carly's mom smiled.

"You can be both."

Carly hugged her mom and smelled her hair like she always did when she hugged her mom.

"See you on the other side."

This is what they always said when they went into hypersleep.

"See you on the other side, my love."

"Is Daddy coming to tuck me in?"

"Daddy is working with Richard on some navigation changes."

"Oh. Tell him good night for me. And I am angry. Well, don't tell him the angry part. Though I am."

"I'll tell him both. He'll want to know."

Carly's mom tucked the blanket around her so she would be nice and snug and closed the capsule.

"Richard, play my favorite."

Frere Jacques soon filled her ears. It was the perfect going-to-bed song, soft with a calm melody. It was in something Carly's mom called French so Carly didn't know what the person was singing about. It didn't matter. Soon, she was fast asleep.

Carly woke up to a rooster crowing. This was Richard's wake-up alarm. He thought it was funny. Carly didn't understand why. Carly waited patiently for the hypersleep pod to fully open, and then she stretched. Hypersleep was a little different than regular sleep. It made your brain fuzzy, and you would trip if you walked too soon. So, Carly spent some time imagining what she was going to do for the day.

First, she would have breakfast. Pancakes were her favorite. Then, she would wander to her playroom. There was a lot to do there. And then there was school, which Richard taught. Lots of stuff about space and what planets are. Then Carly's mom usually taught her about something she called literature, which to Carly meant stories she didn't quite understand. Then, Dad usually took her for repairs around the ship and then back to Carly's mom for math and science and then free time.

She was glad it was the three of them. Carly's mom talked about planets and ships full of people. Carly could not imagine what that would be like. "Wouldn't it be loud?" she asked once. Carly's mom laughed, "Sometimes. But it felt good to be around so many different types of people. It's healthy." Carly wasn't sure since Carly had never been around other people. She had Mom, Dad, Richard (who wasn't really a person), and herself. It seemed just fine to her.

Carly wandered into the kitchen and hopped up on a stool.

"Richard, pancakes, please."

"Well, since you said please."

It would take a couple of minutes for Richard to make pancakes. She could hear the whir of machinery in the galley as she waited. Sometimes, her mom went back there to cook what she called an "honest-to-God homemade meal." It was always delicious, but it was delicious when Richard cooked, too. Carly really couldn't tell the difference.

The pancakes arrived on a plate that popped up from the middle of the table, and Carly dug in. She was particularly hungry.

"Richard, what are we learning in school today?"

"No lesson plans have been drawn."

"Really?"

"Affirmative."

Usually, Richard knew and preps Carly. Carly likes to go in knowing what is going on.

"I suppose I'll find out."

"I suppose you will. Drink your milk."

Carly finished her breakfast and wiped her mouth with her sleeve. She hopped off her stool and bolted out the door to the schoolroom.

"Mind your manners. Use a napkin!" Richard cried to no avail.

The schoolroom was just a room on the ship. It had a desk, a holo, and a notebook. Carly's mom insisted that she use her own instincts and not rely on Richard for everything. She was always about preserving what she called the "old things." Carly's dad was the opposite. He was constantly tinkering and improving. He knew the ship inside and out and was always on the lookout for new ways to upgrade or streamline a system. One time, he tried to upgrade Richard, who reminded him that Richard could supervise their own upgrades, thank you very much. But Carly's dad was insistent. That did not go well. Carly's mom was particularly annoyed, complaining that Richard sounded consistently drunk.

Carly sat in the schoolroom and waited. Mom was late, which was rare. She doodled in her notebook. She liked to draw. After a few minutes, she said, "Richard, where's Mom?"

Richard was silent for a moment and then said, "Scanning ship," then, "Carly, your mother is not on the ship."

A lump immediately formed in Carly's throat. She found it hard to swallow.

"Maybe she is with my father doing hull repairs or something?"

"Your father is not on your ship, either."

"Where are they, Richard?"

"Unknown."

Carly made a little clicking sound and climbed off her chair. She slowly walked back to her room with her bed, her actual bed, exactly how she left it before hypersleep. She climbed onto it and clutched her stuffy, Larry the lamb, an animal she had never actually seen in her life, and slept.

When she awoke, she had no idea what time it was, only that she was very hungry.

"Richard, are my parents back yet?"

"No. Would you like dinner? You slept a very long time."

"I'm not hungry."

"You need nourishment."

"I'm not hungry."

A panel opened just above Carly's nightstand, and a piping hot bowl of soup slid out. She ate voraciously.

There was quiet as Carly ate. When she finished, Richard spoke.

"Do you feel like crying?"

Carly wiped some snot from her nose and sniffled, "No."

"It is okay to cry when you are sad. It is healthy."

"Where are they?"

"I do not know. But there is one less shuttle on the ship."

"How many shuttles are there usually?"

"Three."

"And there are two?"

"Yes."

"Thank you, Richard."

Carly slipped out of her bed. She did not know what was going on, but she knew her parents wanted her to be brave. So she would be brave.

She traversed the ship, looking for clues. They would not have just left her.

"Richard, where is their shuttle headed?"

"Undetermined"

"When did they leave?"

"Late last night."

Of course, there was no night or day in space, Carly always knew that. But Mom and Dad insisted on calling awake time day and asleep time night. It was what they called a quirk.

"Direct me to the shuttle bay."

"It is on the far side of the ship. It will take you approximately twenty minutes to get there. There are watering stations along the way if you get thirsty."

"Thank you, Richard."

Carly was not usually at this end of the ship. It was opposite from the living quarters. Her dad would take her down here occasionally. He liked to make sure she had an idea of what she might be inheriting and how it worked. So, she knew the shuttles were there. But it was supposed to be for emergencies, and if there was an emergency, they would have taken her with them, wouldn't they?

She entered the loading bay. Two small ships were there. One was not. Where could they go? How far can a shuttle travel? It didn't have the regenerative fuel system that the ship had. The ship could go on forever. Carly didn't know much, but she knew that a shuttle didn't have the space for that kind of fuel. So, where did they go?

"Richard, how far is the nearest planet?"

"About a day's travel."

"Has it been mapped? Is it habitable?"

"Excellent answer. I can see you are using your schooling."

"Richard…"

"It has the potential to be habitable. With work."

"Can you take me there?"

"I cannot."

Carly paused. She felt her anger coming up. A temper tantrum was brewing. Her mom said, "There are no temper tantrums in space." But what could she do? She was an eight-year-old kid. She had feelings.

"Why? WHY?"

"Because a course has already been set for another planet."

"Another planet? When?"

"When you were born. That has always been our destination. We should reach it in two days."

Carly sat on the floor and cried. Really cried. She cried for her parents. She cried because she was lonely. She cried because she realized that, though she always realized how big the universe was, as she was traveling through it, she was not big. She was very, very small, and she had no control of her future.

From the ceiling of the ship, a handful of tissues fluttered down.

"You may need this."

"Thank you, Richard."

Carly wiped her eyes. Why? Why did they leave? Why was she headed to a planet? She had never been to a planet that she remembered. She was born on this ship. Just the three of them, and Richard, of course. That satisfied Carly. Her parents were always warm and loving. She didn't feel like she was missing out. There was always so much to do. And Richard made an excellent playmate. Why did they never tell her they had a destination? Carly never asked because why should she? She was a girl who lived on a ship, and that was enough. Or it had been. She sighed and got up. She saw what she needed to see. She would head back to the living quarters and have a nice bowl of soup for lunch.

"Richard, pull up all the info on this planet. I'd like to read about it."

"Of course."

She brought her food into the schoolroom. She was reading about this planet called Nahib. Apparently, it used to have plenty of lush jungles and more temperate zones that would be easily habitable by humans, but now it was mostly desert. The human population had declined precipitously in the decades prior to this relatively quick transition, but there were still cities here and there, though most of the inhabitants consisted of roving bands and tribes.

"Richard?"

"Yes, Carly?"

"Why did my parents leave?"

Richard sighed or came as close to a sigh as he could manage.

"I cannot say because I am not human. And I cannot believe humans can say this because humans are humans, and they have motives known only to themselves. I do know they are from this planet, Nahib."

"They were born there?"

"Yes."

"So I am from Nahib."

"Though you were born on this ship, you would, indeed, be considered a Nahibian."

"Maybe they went to the planet themselves. Without me."

"That would be a very ill-conceived maneuver on their part. There are not enough supplies or oxygen on the shuttle to make that trip."

"Then where do they go?"

"Unclear. They are out of range of my sensors, but it was not in the direction of Nahib."

Carly was exhausted. And she missed her parents. She missed them more than she missed Mr. Stuffies when she lost him three years ago. Even Richard had no idea where he went. She missed them more than she missed mint chocolate ice cream, which Richard made for her until he announced that he could not any longer. She attempted to sleep that evening, but there was a strange gnawing feeling in her belly.

The question rolled back. Why? Had she done something wrong? Was she not good enough? Did they not love her anymore? Why? Why? Why? Where did they go? She didn't cry herself to sleep, but the lump in her throat did not subside until she was well into slumber.

The next morning, she decided she needed answers. Her father also told her, "Be purposeful." It meant finding something worthwhile to commit to and committing to it. Her mother had read her mystery stories about this very old lady who was a master detective. And that is who she decided to emulate.

She woke up with purpose.

"Richard. I want pancakes with breakfast."

"Of course."

"I want pancakes with strawberries and whipped cream on top. I have a very busy day. After that, I want to look at all the information you have on Nahib. And I will need you to help me with the big words."

"It would be my pleasure. But don't eat too quickly. It's not good for your system."

"I know that, Richard."

Carly ate her breakfast slowly but surely with determination and even a bit of pleasure. Now, it was time to get down to business.

She went through all of Richard's files on Nahib. She only took breaks to eat and to pee. It turns out that Nahib was once a very habitable planet for human life. Lots of temperate zones and enough land for most everyone. Sure, there were things that inevitably happen when people co-exist: War, arguments over religion (Carly had already read about what those were, which was helpful.), but all in all a pleasant place to be. But, as humans do (this was Richard editorializing), they wasted their resources and fought too much. Now, there were pockets of forests here and there called oases. The planet was mostly desert, and most of the population roamed among those deserts.

The few cities were occupied by people who were very well off and, again, Richard said, were exploiting the people who lived in the desert. There were once kings, and then there were things called presidents, who were not kings but heads of government that had to negotiate and compromise with other branches of government and there were now councils, groups of very wealthy people who ruled areas called commonalities and then there was the Grand Council which every singular commonality sent a representative to, rotating yearly so everyone got a turn. Carly did not think she would be as fascinated with this as she was.

"So, it's a way for people to work out their problems."

"Yes. And settle disputes and distribute resources."

But there was a problem. Those resources were not distributed fairly. The cities tended to hoard most of these resources, leaving the people in the desert to fend for themselves. This created friction and eventually war, which, at least at the time of the information Richard had available, was not going well for the desert people. But there was hope as unrest fermented, from that group emerged leaders to resist and push back and demand basic rights, such as food and shelter. Those leaders were named...

And this is when Carly shut down the program. She sat in stunned silence, and slowly, very slowly, she understood.

"They were my parents. My parents were leading these people to..."

"Revolution. Yes."

"I don't understand."

"You. They left because of you."

"But...."

"Your mother was pregnant with you, and though she was brave enough to face danger herself, she did not want that for you until. . ."

"Until what?"

"Later. You are tired. You should rest. And bathe. That hasn't happened in some time."

"I hate baths."

"I am aware."

Carly hopped off the chair and headed to the door. She stopped and turned around.

"Tonight, can you sing me that song you used to when I was younger?"

"Blackbird? Yes. of course. Now go take your bath."

Carly left to head to the dreaded bath. Her head was swimming, but she was certainly not as sad as she was before. She was even humming.

The next morning, she read about her parents. Things they never told her. They never lied. They just never told her. Her mother was born to a family of tailors. They traveled constantly throughout the desert. Her father was apparently royalty of some sort and lived in a palace in the city. He was groomed to rule.

Her mother's family's skills were known far and wide and so he was sent for by her grandfather, who was apparently very particular when it came to his clothing. The moment he met her, my father could think of nothing else and vice versa. They would sneak off together and explore the city. She would take him to the desert to see how they managed to make beauty out of dire circumstances.

Eventually, his family found out and disowned him. So, they lived with her family. She taught him how to survive on little. He taught her to dream of something better. Between them, they started a rebellion that shook the planet. It almost succeeded.

The rebellion fired the imagination of millions upon millions. Dreams of a future where wealth and resources were not hoarded by the few. Dreams of a better life for most of the world's children were snuffed because of greed and fear. They persevered.

Carly's father ended up being a superb strategist, her mother a great warrior. And then they disappeared. Some believe they were killed. Others thought they gave up. The revolution collapsed. The response by the powers that be were draconian. Tens of thousands were killed. Families torn apart.

Since Carly's parents' bodies were never found, there was hope. So, the revolution was never snuffed out. It just went underground. People had pictures of Carly's parents' photos hung on kitchen and living room walls and were hidden when authorities inspected homes (a regular occurrence). They kept icons and statues wrapped up in the bottom of trunks. They became a symbol. An ideal to look up to. A hope.

Carly closed the file on Nahib and muttered to herself, "It's me."

Richard repeated, "It's you. If they returned with you as a newborn, your life would immediately be in danger."

"Then why are we going back at all?"

"You have answered that."

"Because it's me."

"What your mother and father and, I suspect, I have taught you over these years will prepare you for your return. There are people waiting for you and counting on you."

"But I'm a kid."

"You are more than a mere child. You always have been. Your parents made sure of that."

A lump formed in Carly's throat.

"I'm not going to see them again, am I?"

There was a moment before Richard responded.

"I cannot make a prediction regarding that. But based on my understanding of human behavior, I would guess no."

Carly let out a small sob.

"But I can offer you a human platitude. Wherever you are, there is a part of them inside you. Sometimes, that can be not such a good thing. But, I suspect that is not the case here."

"Where is the ship landing?"

"The Halor sector. It is one of the poorest areas of Nahib. It is mostly forgotten by the cities."

"Why there?"

"You are the daughter of people who the governments of Nahib are very fearful of. If you were to return, it would be best that they were unaware."

Carly took this in. She felt strangely calm yet excited. It was the feeling she got when she slotted the final piece in of a particularly difficult puzzle.

"How long have they been planning this?"

"Well, as I intimated, they have trained you for your particular purpose since you were very young."

"Yes, but when did they set course for Nahib."

"Many months ago."

Carly offered the tiniest of smiles.

"And how long have you known what they were planning?"

"I am merely a machine, a collection of programs and information designed to..."

"How long have you known?"

"Since you were born."

Carly thought of all the love they had given her. How they explained when she was old enough that they treated her like a little adult because someday she would be an adult. How her mother taught her what she called "the greats," books about what it is like to be human. How her father talked to her about gravity and black holes and how they would have food fights (which always irritated Richard) and pretend pony rides (though she had never actually seen a pony.) She realized that Richard was right. They formed her spirit with their curiosity and love. And since she had that, she did have them inside of her, possibly forever.

Carly took a breath.

"I'm ready."

"I'm glad."

It took two days to reach Nahib. During that time, Carly read everything that Richard had about the place. She read about the facts of the planet itself, but she also read about the development of the people, how their system of ruling came about, what their art was like, and how that developed. She also read the stories and myths of the inhabitants. Some of them were vaguely familiar to her, even though she was sure she had never heard them before.

She would stare at the navigation monitor, and eventually, one star seemed to grow brighter as the others began to fall away. She felt excitement in the pit of her stomach, what her mother called butterflies. She had never been this close to a star before. She had never been inside a solar system or on a planet. Everything was new to her. She was going to meet people that were not her family. Maybe she would eventually have friends her age. But there was something else burgeoning inside her, something new. After living her entire life on a ship, learning and loving her family, she had something she did not previously. She had a purpose. When she thought of that, the butterflies really let loose.

She managed to sleep, if only because Richard gave her a little something to help her. He said it was herbal and natural and it came from the greenhouse that was in the back of the ship. It tasted awful, but it did the trick. When she awoke the second day, Richard told her she was entering Nahib's atmosphere and that she should head to the navigation monitor and strap in. She should pay particular attention to the monitor because burning through a planet's atmosphere created a wonderful light show, and, as Richard said, "Humans are into pretty colors and that sort of thing."

Carly did as she was told and saw that Richard was not wrong. She felt the ship shake and wobble and magentas and cerises and burgundies seemed to fill and fall away from the nose of the ship as it pierced Nahib's atmosphere. And then suddenly, it was all gone, and Carly was awash in a piercing blue.

"The sky," Richard said. "This is Nahib's sky."

Carly found it hard to comprehend what she was feeling or the lump in her throat. She felt that she had dreamed of this vision in front of her before. Perhaps she had. She could not say. All she knew was that the emotions she had gone through the past few days might be a bit too much for a 10-year-old girl to handle. Then, the monitor showed a brown line that grew and grew on the bottom edge of the screen.

"Sand," Carly said quietly.

"That's right," Richard said. "Sand, dirt, some rocks, and soon, people."

"Where are we landing?"

"I have the coordinates. About fifty miles from a small village called Khartana. I must prepare you. You are expected."

"What?"

"We should touch ground in about two minutes. I see no reason for concern, though I feel obligated to state that about 1.5% of landings, there is a serious malfunction, and of about 10% of those, there are fatalities.

Carly audibly swallowed.

"But we should be fine. Hold tight."

Carly gripped the sides of her chair. She heard an excruciating metallic sound.

And then the preternaturally calm voice of Richard.

"That is simply the landing gear. It has been some time since it has been in use."

Carly was pitched forward. If she had not been buckled in, her head would have hit the console enough to split it wide open. Then the lights flickered off for a moment and then back on.

"We have landed."

Carly didn't realize just how hard she was breathing. She stayed in her chair for a couple of moments and then gingerly tested the floor with her feet. As she got up, she stumbled a bit.

"Gravity on Nahib is slightly less dense than ours. It won't grant you much advantage. You might be able to jump a few millimeters higher than you normally would."

"Thanks, Richard."

"Don't mention it."

Carly began to notice a faint noise coming from outside the ship. It was a rhythmic sound and strangely familiar. She strained to hear it.

"They are chanting your name," Richard said, "They are your army."

"My army?"

"Mostly villagers. They have come from miles around, some halfway around the planet. They have been waiting for you."

"To do what?"

"To lead."

Carly had known this instinctively. She had just never heard it named before. It filled her with pride and a sense of purpose. And maybe, just maybe, if she won, if her army won, and she could free the people that so desperately needed her, her parents might come back.

Carly headed to the door of the ship. The door that had no real need to be opened in her lifetime. The door that would previously lead to the endless emptiness of space but now lead to something else entirely. She stood in front of it for a moment.

"Richard..."

"Of course."

The door slid open. The chants were deafening. "Carly! Carly!" There were people for what seemed like miles. She smelled sweat and an electric feeling emanating from them like a wave toward her. She took all this on and then slowly raised her fist in the air.

The roars were thunderous.

THE GREEN FLARE

by Randall Hayes

The barmaid, Beryl, spoke into the microphone with a clipped British accent. "The next section of tonight's Old Toad pub quiz concerns the works of science fiction pioneer Jules Verne. We'll be accepting answers in English but with bonus points for French." She had done this many times and knew to hold the microphone far enough from her mouth that the consonants wouldn't pop.

"Craaaaap," whined Terry Mayor, for effect, though he was, in fact, the sunniest person on the team – probably the sunniest person in Rochester, given how the winter darkness tended to affect people. "Where's Yves when you need him?"

"'T's all right, Sweet Pea. We've got this." James Abernathy had an annoying habit of giving people nicknames, trying to seem more interesting than he was.

"Question 6," continued Beryl. "This novel – a sequel – was made into a movie, with special effects by the stop-motion animator Ray Harryhausen."

"Oh, oh," said James, not quite snapping his fingers but rubbing them together in a whispery way that couldn't be heard over the hubbub of the bar. "*Mysterious Island*. It's got Captain Nemo, only he's old. There's another version of it with crappy CGI, and Patrick Stewart plays the captain. Good old Jean-Luc Picard."

Cong Ly Lam put down her pint beer glass, which bore traces of her dark lipstick. "I love Patrick Stewart, but Nemo was a Sikh. Did they paint him brown, like they did Ricardo Montalban when he played Khan Noonien Singh in original Trek?"

"What's the French?" stage-whispered Terry.

"L'Île mystérieuse," Cong Ly whispered back.

"How do you spell that?"

Cong Ly just pursed her lips and held out her hand for the short, eraser-less bar pencil.

"Question 7. This novel, set on the west coast of Scotland, involves an atmospheric phenomenon that, when seen, grants the viewer psychic powers."

"*La Rayon Vert*," said Raymond Hedges, sliding into the booth with a black-and-tan held up in his left hand so it wouldn't spill. Raymond was from Kentucky, and his pronunciation sounded nothing like French.

Terry jumped. "Jesus! When did you get here?"

"Sorry, I'm late. Lab stuff. The book was called *La Rayon Vert* – 'The Green Ray.' You know, I actually saw that on the beach in San Diego last year?" The enormous Society for Neuroscience conference rotated between different cities. "Only now they call it 'the green flash.' There's a Green Flash Cafe."

"Wait, wait," said Cong Ly, leaning across the table. "Jules Verne was into psychic powers?"

"Lots of people were," said Raymond. He did not let people call him 'Ray.' Nobody was quite sure why. "If you could transmit information through wires or through the air with radio waves, why not? But Verne was more of a debunker. He liked to use legends to add color and then explain them away."

Beryl was burning through the questions tonight. Usually, she would repeat them at least once, often twice, to give people more time. "Question 8. In this novel, the final installment in a series, members of the Baltimore Gun Club attempt to alter the Earth's orbit by firing an enormous cannon built into the side of Mount Kilimanjaro."

Raymond shook his head and took a swig of his beer. "Nope. Though I gotta say, that is some super-villain level shit right there."

"I got nothin'," said James.

"I know the one where they shoot themselves to the moon," said Cong Ly, twisting her upper lip in a sort of facial shrug. "That became a famous silent film."

"And probably inspired Hitler's super-gun."

"Hanging out with you guys is like watching Olympic ping pong." Myrna Thurainayagam was a Sri Lankan pharmacology student. She had a beautiful smile, which she used liberally, but she so rarely said anything out loud that people tended to forget she was there.

Everyone turned and looked at her, and she shrank back a bit until they all shouted, "TEAM NAME!" and then she beamed and probably blushed, though it was too dark in the bar to be sure. The Old Toad was a proper British pub, whose wood paneling drank in the feeble yellow light of the incandescent bulbs in sconces on the walls, meant to look like gas lights.

Beryl shushed them and had to repeat Question 9, which was about Captain Nemo's ethnicity, which they had already discussed and got easily. "And now the last question in the Jules Verne section of tonight's Old Toad pub quiz, after which we'll take a musical break. This novel, also set in Scotland – or rather, **beneath** Scotland – was published under at least three different titles, any of which we will accept."

Cong Ly frowned, forming a vertical line between her delicate eyebrows as they pushed in towards one another. "*Journey to the Center of the Earth?*"

"I think that was Iceland," said Terry.

Beryl had her fiddle out. She was pretty good but too sensible to try making a living as a musician. Like most of the people who worked at the Toad, she was on exchange from some program in England, hospitality or hotel management or something like that. "Our musical interlude tonight is a final bonus clue to question ten. Something of a deep cut from Sting's album The Dream of the Blue Turtles. Not a song that made the Top 40 here in the States. It's called, 'We Work the Black Seam'."

Raymond listened to the lyrics for a few bars and then said, "Oh. Yeah. This one's all about coal mining. Total Scooby-Doo storyline, with this crazy old man and his pet owl trying to scare the miners away with methane explosions. It's under a lake. A *loch*, I mean. Then he tries to flood the town by blowing a hole in the roof to drain the lake."

"You mean Aberfoyle?" asked James, sketching a schematic on a bar napkin. "That's a real place. They used it as a bomb shelter during World

War 2."

"Hiding from Hitler's super-gun?" Terry rocked his head back and forth as he said this.

James was always willing to be playfully provoked. "Do not mock the super-gun." He pointed at his drawing, showing the side tunnels that held timed explosives, which boosted the speed of a shell passing down the main barrel. "This could lob a shell almost a hundred miles. And no, it was aimed at London."

Cong Ly, seeing that their sparring was likely to go on for a while, pointedly turned to Raymond, who was listening to the song instead of the table.

She tugged at his sleeve. "Where did you read all these Verne books? Was someone in your family a collector?"

"Public library in a county that never completely recovered from the Great Depression. What about you?"

"Catholic school in Vietnam. French colony, Communist utopia, all that."

"When did you come here?"

"Age 12. Rochester was a refugee resettlement zone, and we had family here."

Raymond raised his glass toward her. "Hometown girl!"

Cong Ly clinked it with her own. "Yeah, though my family would be a lot happier if I was studying medicine or engineering instead of literature."

"It doesn't matter. I **am** studying medicine, and my family still gives me shit about moving north and using big words when I talk."

"You don't have much of an accent."

"Y'oughtta hear me on the phone with Granny. It sure comes out then. Or when I'm drunk. Not a little beer-buzz like tonight. Like, full-on bourbon drunk."

The others were paying attention now. "Have you ever made moonshine?" asked James.

Cong Ly reached across Terry to punch James in the shoulder. "Stereotyping!"

"What?"

Raymond ignored the joke, as he often seemed to, and his answer was completely deadpan. "Not personally. I had an uncle who went to the pen over it. Nowadays, people are making crystal meth all over the place. I have a subscription to the local paper – comes as a PDF -- and every week, the front page is a meth bust or a meth lab blowing up. Or a car crash." He took a drink.

James tried again. "Are you a coal miner's daughter?"

Cong Ly was losing patience with him. "You're incorrigible!"

Raymond was unperturbed. "School teacher's son. The coal is further east, up in the mountains. We grew tobacco and milked cows. My grandpa mined coal until he made enough to buy land and start farming. He told my dad about it, and my dad told me some stuff, but Sting probably has more direct experience of it than I do."

"Did you grow mari-huana? The Mary Jane?"

"Nobody with any damn sense grows pot on their own land. You grow it in the national forest, or on your neighbors' land if you're mad at them. That way, their land gets seized by the DEA and not yours." With that last statement, he emptied his glass, got up, and went to the bar. Was he mad? It was hard to tell with him.

"Any ideas on the title?" Terry asked after a second or two of uncomfortable silence.

"Not a one," said James. "Let me out. Anyone want anything?"

"I want you to apologize to Raymond," said Cong Ly.

James rolled his eyes but said, "Okay, okay. I'll buy him a shot and it'll be fine."

Terry Mayor tried to get them back on track. "Title?"

"Don't look at me!" said Myrna.

"This is the problem with someone who wrote 40+ novels," said Cong Ly. "He was like the Steven King of his time period."

Beryl was back to speaking. "And now I'm going to pop off to the loo for just a sec and put my fiddle away, and when I get back, it's on to part three of tonight's Old Toad pub quiz. And remember, even while I'm gone, and I can't see you, simply looking things up on your phones is not in The Spirit of the Quiz."

The bar erupted with applause and shouts of, "The Spirit of the Quiz!"

The "lab stuff" Raymond Hedges had referred to was, in fact, the first of a series of personal experiments with psychedelic drugs. The experimenters took turns tripping inside a magnetic resonance scanner while the others looked for changes in blood flow to different areas of the brain, compared to a reference scan taken minutes before. Because the scanner was mostly used for clinical purposes, and they couldn't always predict when it would be free, they relied on compounds that were metabolized quickly, things like dimethyltryptamine (DMT) and 5-Methoxy-DMT, originally derived from — oddly enough — **toad venom.** The short half-lives of such hallucinogens also allowed them to use much higher doses and still come down in time to make it to the pub for Trivia Night. That much LSD, and they'd have been seeing things for 24 hours at least.

Raymond kept these experiments from his fellow students for a host of reasons. Informal sharing among the friends of academic researchers like Timothy Leary was what triggered the wide counter-cultural use that got psychedelics banned in the first place (that, and the CIA's MK-ULTRA projects, which tested a wide array of psychoactive substances as mind-control drugs). Before 1971, psychedelics had been legal around the world and regarded as highly promising treatments for addiction and depression. Only now was a new generation of safely tenured researchers cautiously testing the waters again.

Over the next seven years, through his medical coursework, his clinical rotations, and his residency in psychiatry, Raymond became more and more disillusioned with standard practice, which was to try one drug after another, starting with A for amitriptyline and working down the list towards Z for ZoloftTM, trying to temporarily maximize the relief of symptoms and minimize side effects, until the profile shifted enough to force a switch. These drugs were not cures. They did not address root causes. At that time, mental illnesses were still not technically **diseases**, with known etiologies, known causes, and effects; they were more properly **syndromes**, statistical clusters of symptoms. The standard drugs were, however, extremely profitable for the companies that made them, in part because they were not cures.

Raymond extended this logic to what became known as "microdosing," long-term implants that leaked tiny amounts of a psychedelic into the blood, amounts too small to induce hallucinations but enough to alter mood. It was probably at least partially a placebo effect, but patients did feel better, and there were blessedly few side effects. Over time he added other things to his toolkit — hypnosis, and bright light that helped with mood or other conditions. Migraines sometimes responded very well to specific wavelengths in the green range of the spectrum. As an MD, he was not dependent on writing grants to fund his experiments, and he could afford to wander the Earth intellectually.

As an academic in the humanities, Cong Ly Lam's experience was quite different. She didn't have to pay her students, so she didn't need grants, either. She did have to specialize, however, in order to avoid conflicts with her departmental colleagues. Pop culture, like science fiction, was in fashion, though dead white guys like Jules Verne were not. Postmodernism, the idea that all philosophies (including science) are socially constructed was, for the moment, triumphant. She adapted very well to that environment by borrowing some ideas from the anthropology of religion and applying them to what science fiction called "suspension of disbelief." The cultural moment of the early twenty-first century, with its infodemics and algal blooms of conspiracy theory, was kind to her. Her books, like *Spectrum of Belief* (with a trendy rainbow on the cover), were well-written and well-marketed, enough that they sold outside the academic market despite being published by university presses. She was well-spoken and photogenic and appeared regularly in documentaries.

James Abernathy, the engineer, went home to Scotland (a cliche if ever there was one). After a couple of mostly fruitless postdoctoral fellowships, he got involved in the field tests for tidal power and fell in love with the Orkneys, those storm-swept islands off the northern tip of the country. He kept a good waterproof camera with him at all times and was forever posting his latest pictures to social media, mostly shots of seals and otters and whatever might have washed up on some lonely, rocky beach — dead basking sharks, bloated whales, and once the rotting remains of what might, possibly, have been a giant squid. Genetic testing could have said for sure, but he was busy, and by the time he got around to calling it in, the tide had taken it back. He never posted that particular set of photos. He couldn't say why, exactly. It just seemed ... personal, somehow, as though he'd met a god walking along the strand.

The others did equally well for themselves. They all met up only a few times over the next two decades once the rash of weddings was over. These were usually beach vacations where they would rent a house and spend a week drinking and playing cards on some wooden deck while their kids splashed safely below in a turquoise-bottomed pool, bouncing ideas off one another and promising to find some way to work together.

*

"Are we ready for the induction?" Raymond asked.

"We've been ready all week!" Terry said. This was their fourth attempt.

"That's OK," said Raymond. "Putting yourself into a trance state takes practice. The longer we have to wait for the Flash, the better you'll be prepared for it when it finally happens."

Cong Ly pushed her sunglasses up onto her head. "It's a gorgeous sunset, regardless."

"You mean, 'irregardless'?" quipped James.

"No, no, I don't. 'Irregardless' is not a word."

"Your SCRABBLE debates will have to wait," interrupted Raymond, "if you want to do this. The sun is almost on the horizon. Good? Good. OK, close your eyes and imagine yourself at the top of a set of wooden stairs, just like the ones on our house – weathered, cracked, gray, but sturdy and safe. As I count down, feel your foot touching the step below you as it begins to take your weight. Ten. Nine. Feel your hand on the railing, warmed by the sun. Each step down leaves you feeling more and more relaxed. Eight, you feel that warmth spreading through you. Seven, more and more relaxed. Six. Five. You may find your mouth watering; this is a normal sign of deep relaxation. That's right, just swallow, it's fine. Four, more and more relaxed. Three. Two. One. Step down onto the warm sand, and in your mind, begin walking towards the beach.

I want you to remember how you felt last night, in your body, while we were watching the Fire-Maidens, dancing their strathspeys in our campfire. You may have felt a tingling, or a pins-and-needles sort of feeling, somewhere inside you as you became more relaxed and entered a deeper stage of hypnosis. I want you to see them, the Fire-Maidens, leaping upward with the flames and twirling into the night sky with the sparks."

"Like Uri and Baki ..." said Cong Ly, in a sort of little girl voice, very different from her normal no-nonsense way of speaking.

"If you know that book, yes," said Raymond, and incorporated her comment smoothly into his ongoing monologue. "Imagine the smoke coming out of their fire-yellow eyes as they change form. Or, if you don't, just use your imagination and visualize the campfire. Have you got it?"

"Yes ..." they all murmured.

"That's really good. If there's going to be a flash, it's getting close now, so I'm going to give you a suggestion. When you open your eyes, it will be as if time has slowed down. The flash will seem to stretch out, allowing you whatever time you need to fix that sight in your memory forever. Now open your eyes."

As they watched, the half-disc of the sun turned bright green. For just a moment, the water around it wobbled like a green flame, and the sky above flared the same color, but less intensely, more spread out. Then the sky was darkened, and as the last bit of the sun disappeared below the horizon, there was a final green shimmer as though the sun was shining through the water, which it was, until the earth's rotation moved too much water into the way, and it was gone.

"Now I'm going to give you another suggestion," said Raymond. "You will be able to call up that unique hue, to see it, really see it, in your mind's eye, whenever you want. And not only the sight, but the emotion that it generates within you. The knowledge that you are with friends who love you, who care about you, who want you to excel in your chosen endeavors. The knowledge that you are a part of this universe, that you belong."

They were all rather quiet on the walk back to the rented beach house.

The next day, as a touristy thing, the adults toured New Aberfoyle, "the underground city," as one of the titles of Verne's novel from that long-ago pub quiz called it, while Myrna was marinating her famous spicy-sweet Maylay chicken wings and the kids were absorbed in some complicated virtual card game. Beryl had been there before, with James, and stayed behind as well.

New Aberfoyle was purely a restaurants-and-retail venture at this point; nobody lived down there, and nobody was mining coal. The growing industry in carbon nanofibers might change that if the space elevator ever became a real thing.

Cong Ly Lam was in full professor mode, living up to her surname as a *person full of knowledge*. "Verne mentioned 'la rayon vert' in this book, too. It was more a symbol of the wonders of nature than a psychic phenomenon. A metaphor for enlightenment, rather than a direct magical cause of it."

"Yeah, that's where I got the Fire-Maidens, too."

"I thought I remembered that," said Cong Ly. "That was a really nice touch, Doctor Hedges."

"Why, thank you, Doctor Lam. I didn't know you were a Gene Wolfe fan, too."

"Yeah, he's great. But I want to ask more about this citizen science project we've been doing."

"Well, in one sense, it's just a playful hypothesis. What if Verne was right, and seeing The Green Flash actually did make people more empathetic? How could that work? Could a specific wavelength of light release some molecule that promotes mystical experiences like DMT in the brain?"

"Or maybe just a hormone like oxytocin?" put in Terry, who was at the NIH in Bethesda these days. Another plum post that didn't require writing grants. "That's more likely."

"Sure, "said Raymond. Nobody's ever found DMT in humans or any other primate, just very small amounts in rats. And rats don't see color the same way we do, so it's not a great model system."

"How would you know?" asked Cong Ly. She had always been scientifically literate, especially after marrying an astronomer ten years before, but not a brain specialist like Raymond and Terry were. One of the reasons they were still friends was that neither of them ever talked down to her. She had little patience for that.

"A hormone would be easy. You could get that from a spinal tap or maybe even a blood sample. For DMT or something else at very low concentrations, I'd have to freeze your brains, right at that moment, before it was metabolized, and then grind them up to look for it."

"Ew."

James also knew plenty of biology at the macro scale, but he was far more into forces and flows than molecules and tried to redirect the conversation by pointing at a figure capering across the coal-black ground. "Check out that creepy goblin guy."

"The guidebook says his name's Urisk," said Terry. There's some stories about him on the audio tour."

Cong Ly read: "'Urisk is a mischievous but helpful water spirit.' How many hours do you think went into making that costume?" which was hairy and vaguely apelike.

"Or how much energy?" said James, ever the engineer. "We could make a rough estimate —"

"That's what I mean," replied Cong Ly. We spend an awful lot of resources trying to make invisible things feel more real to ourselves. Atoms, molecules, bacteria —"

"— Money —" put in Raymond.

"— Ghosts, spirits, monsters —" continued Cong Ly.

"— Money —" repeated Raymond.

"— Poor people —" That was Terry.

"— Any invention or new technology **ever** —" That was James.

"Exactly!" said Cong Ly. "Isn't it all just creativity? Why do we privilege —"

"AAAAGH!" they all screamed in unison, turning towards the shore of the underground lake as **something** slid back under the water.

"What the hell was that!?!" Terry sort of laugh-panted.

James had been just as startled as the rest of them but was now studiously calm. "Oh, that was Nessie."

"That was NOT in the guidebook!" Cong Ly cried indignantly.

"No, I razored that page out."

"You ass! What if you gave me a heart attack?"

James was really in his element now. "Well, then I'd have to do CPR and give you mouth-to-mouth."

"Grow up!" she huffed.

"Why is Nessie not in Loch Ness?" Raymond asked.

"Protesters," James brogued, drawing out the O. "Said it would spoil the ecosystem to put an ALF in there. It's quite pristine, apparently."

"An ... elf?" Terry asked.

"ALF," James explained. "Artificial Life Form. Cooked up in a lab somewheres. Now she's down here in the dark with nothin' to do until the situation works its way through the courts. Assuming the heavy metals in the water don't kill her outright."

"Speaking of making things real," Cong Ly said.

"Are you not incensed that they would treat an animal that way?" James demanded, uncharacteristically hot for a moment.

"Maybe I will be after I'm done being freaked out. *Did you see those teeth?*"

"I knew the mammoths were just the beginning," said Terry.

"Oh, aye, and the sea cows," said James, back to smiling smugly to himself from having gotten them all so thoroughly.

They continued their experiments with synchronized mystical experiences. Cong Ly even wrote a book about them, titled *The Green Flare*, which she liked better than 'Flash.' But they were overtaken by the worldwide campaign to legalize drugs that were not classically addictive. Clandestine chemists had been busy for decades, generating new derivatives of old psychedelics. Organized clinical trials had volunteers lining up for curated experiences with certified guides.

Drugs seemed easier, more efficient, and they didn't rely on the weather. Discipline and practice were hard sells in any century.

The situation was not, in fact, a disaster, though. The Internet's unfettered access to everything, all the time, had made following generations just a wee bit more cautious in exposing their own children to the online world and its virtual reality extensions. Seemingly simple measures like parental control checkboxes provided a model for thinking about deliberate and graded exposure. Automation meant that people had to find meaning outside of work in their everyday lives. Ritual practices proliferated.

The last meeting of the Cult of the Flare occurred on a private beach below Esalen, in California, where Cong Ly was doing workshops now that she was emeritus and could come and go from campus as she pleased. Their efforts to change the world had come to nought, as such efforts so often do, and they were here in a purely private ceremony to say goodbye to their friend Raymond. They were all old now, and while long practice had made them receptive to messages from beyond, or within, or whatever, they heard no such messages tonight. The western sky was overcast, and the sun was a dim red slice sandwiched between gray water and gray clouds.

They had come prepared for nature not to cooperate with their theatrical designs. Once the night was fully dark, they splashed their campfire with a tincture of copper, which produced otherworldly green flames, and let the smoke carry Raymond's ashes into the sky. And into their eyes and into their lungs, for the breeze was gusty and unpredictable. They cried and coughed in turn as the alcohol burned and the copper's electrons jumped through their flaming quantum hoops, shedding photons that were not the same color as the Green Flash they knew so well by now, but close enough to feel how they wanted to feel.

Then they passed around a pipe, and cried and coughed some more, and watched the Fire-Maidens dance through the embers, kicking out sparks that swirled upwards into the night sky and disappeared.

THE FIRST SMILE ON OGMA 5

by Nicholas Leamy

Sitting in the crabapple tree with her arms wrapped tightly around her, a frown scrunched up Hazel's face. Looking up, she plucked one of the flowers off the branch and began to rip it apart in clumps. Tossing the shredded remains to the ground, she snatched another. Her fingers grabbed a petal and then paused. She rubbed it between her fingers, tracing the lines and taking in all the subtleties of the texture. Raising the flower to her nose, she breathed in deeply, and fresh tears began to fall down her face.

Layla walked under the tree. Looking up, she watched her daughter. A sullen expression crossed her face for just a moment. Taking a deep breath, she called up, "Is your plan to just live in this tree while the rest of us leave? The apples will be quite splendid in a few months if you can make it that long."

Hazel quickly wiped away her tears and then scowled down at her mother. "I'll figure it out. All I know is that I'm not going. You can't make me! This is my home. All my friends are here. How can you do this!?" Fresh tears formed in her eyes as she screamed the last words out. She shoved her face into her knees as sobs began to rock her body.

One hand over the other, Layla climbed the tree. Settling next to her in the nook of the trunk, she put her arms around Hazel without saying a word. Hazel ignored her for only a moment, then cried into her shoulder.

"I know you're scared. I'm scared, too. Change is hard, and this may be the biggest one either of us will ever make. The family spent months debating this, and I promise you, we did not make this choice lightly." Hazel sat back, red-eyed and tear-drenched. Layla took her head in her hands and began wiping tears away. As she finished, she kissed each eye.

"I know you're going to miss your friends, and no one will ever replace them, but there will be other children coming with us. Several around your age. I have no doubt you'll make new friends and find new corners to explore together." She said this last as she plucked an apple from the tree. She breathed it in deep and offered it to Hazel, who took it. "We should bring some of these with us and see if we can grow them there."

Hazel smiled for a moment and stuck the apple in her pocket. Then, concern crossing her face, she said, "It's not just my friends. I mean... just getting there is going to be so scary."

Layla smiled and pulled Hazel in close again, "I hear you, but you really shouldn't worry. Your uncle Charlie is one of the engineers, and you know he can handle this. If you'd like, I could have him walk you through the ship and explain everything to you. As scared as you are, I know you love punchships."

Hiding her excited grin by burying her face further into her mother, she replied, "I don't know if that will change anything, but I'm willing to hear what he has to say."

Hazel's family were transported to the launch pad by shuttle bus. The majority of their belongings making the trip with them had already been stored on the ship. The remainder was being handled by an estate representative who would ensure they received top dollar for their goods and that the funds would be distributed according to their wishes.

As the shuttle passed over the hill, the main launch site came into view. Hazel pushed her face to the glass, smashing her nose flat. Her eyes became saucers as she saw the punchship come into view. It looked like a cliche flying saucer ripped out of a pulp fiction novel, mashed together with the body of a classic rocket jutting out the top of it. It was covered in a metallic coating that was designed to protect it from radiation on its journey, but resulted in it looking incredibly gaudy, like it was conceived in the imagination of a flamboyant child. It had several visible sensors and monitors covering the outside of it that looked too delicate to survive a blastoff. It was also pointing upside down as if it were about to plow itself into the ground. The positioning gave it the appearance of the world's largest metallic mushroom.

Hazel turned to her mother and said, "I do love punchships, but seriously. If this doesn't work, we're just going to ram right into the ground and die a slow, fiery death, aren't we?"

Hazel's father, Frank, turned to look at Layla, who looked back and said, "Don't you dare glare at me. Moments like this are proof she's your daughter." Frank just laughed and focused again on the road.

Turning back to Hazel, Layla said, "There's no way that can happen. They won't drop the ship until everything is in place. Your uncle Charlie can explain everything when we get there."

At the sound of her uncle's name, Hazel let another smile loose.

Leaving their car in the garage, they entered Central Command. Hazel looked around with disappointment on her face. Leaving the foyer, they passed office after office, with everyone around them wearing standard work clothes. Tugging on her mom's sleeve, Hazel asked, "In all the stories, there are people in space suits running around with crazy science gadgets. Buzzers and air horns. This feels more like a place where they sell cars and not punchships."

Layla laughed and said, "Any gadgets you may have been hoping for would be in the assembly yard. Any alerts and high-tech command centers that are here, we don't have access to. As for any cool suits, we'll see if there are any on the ship."

Reaching the other side of the building, they took an elevator up to the fifth floor, which opened onto a windowed terrace. From here, they could see the punchship up close, and in front of them were two doors that opened onto a gangplank. Her mouth dropped open, and Hazel looked up at her mom, who responded, "Go ahead. Open them." Letting out a small squeal, she ran to the doors and flung them apart. She bolted toward the ship while Frank yelled, "Wait for us!" as they chased after her. As she got close to the ship, the bulkhead doors opened and out walked Uncle Charlie. He was rubbing some oil off his hands with a rag as he said, "There's my little dimensionaut!"

Hazel leapt into his arms, and he spun her around. "I missed you too, bug!" He put her down and waved as Frank and Layla approached. "I hear someone wants a tour of my ship. You all want me to show you the best parts? What do you want to see first?"

"I want to see the engine!"

With a smug, knowing look, he said, "Oh, you mean the propulsion engine up top there?"

Giggling and shoving him, Hazel replied, "No! The punchengine!"

"The punchengine, huh? I think we can handle that. You all don't mind if I show Hazel around, do you?" He said this last with a wink to Layla, who smiled back.

Frank said, "As long as you don't lose her, take all the time you guys want. We need to prep some gear in storage anyway."

Layla and Frank hugged Charlie on their way into the ship, and Charlie said to Hazel, "Ok, the punchengine, now where did I leave that thing? You think it's in this ship?"

"Uncle Charlie!"

"You're right! You're right. I'm being ridiculous. Come on. Follow me."

Passing through the airlock and the first hallway, Charlie and Hazel entered the main room of the ship. Charlie began, "This is the central crew quarters. That's why everything here is cozy and comfortable. It has TVs, games, and all sorts of entertainment. Places to work on your laptops. Places for people to hang out together. You may think it's a bit sparse, but don't worry, we won't be using it much. Over here is the cafeteria. This is large enough to support the twenty families coming with us to Ogma 5. We're going to be the third ship arriving on the third day, so there's going to be a number of people already there when we arrive."

Hazel said, "Why did we choose Ogma 5 again?"

Charlie said, "We didn't. It was the next planet up on the colonization registry when our ticket was chosen. Do you know anything about the American land rush from the 1800s?"

"No."

"Well, back when the country was young, they would occasionally open up restricted lands, and people would flood out to make their claims, despite what the local indigenous peoples had to say about it. Nowadays, organizations all over the world are working to discover new planets where we can reach out and colonize. These planets go through several approvals, and when they are deemed safe and viable, the colony lottery chooses the lucky families who can make the trip. Luckily, this time, there's no indigenous peoples to disrupt. No need for us to be dicks." Charlie paused with a frown, looked down at Hazel, and said, "Sorry about that. Don't tell your mom I cursed in front of you."

Hazel laughed and said, "But why only families?"

"Someone got it in their heads that families tend to be stronger together during adversity, and also that if you're trying to start a new world, having established family units in place would help solidify the new societies. If you are a legal couple, have at least one child, and bring at least one of the pre-approved crucial skills required, you are eligible."

"So, we were chosen because you work on punchships, Dad can build and work a farm, and Mom is a research scientist?"

"Yep. Having so many viable skills in one family really helped our odds. Now come on, I have an engine to show you."

Charlie opened a door, revealing a ladder leading up and down. They climbed down and entered a room with a large machine in the center. It had no visible moving parts but many tubes and wires spreading out and into the ship. It was the size of two cars stacked on top of each other and had several closed hatches.

"I'm afraid it's not much to look at. Most of what it does is internal, and the tubes vent the appropriate forces as needed. As such, it would be much cooler in action to see from the outside, but that's not really an option. Also, it wouldn't be safe for me to open without a required purpose. Do you know anything about punchengines?"

"I know it punches us out of everything."

"Well, it doesn't actually. That's what the command station is for. The equipment on the launch pad punches a hole in the universe, and then they drop us into it. This engine helps us navigate the in-between. Do you understand what that is?"

Hazel started unconsciously fidgeting her hands as she said, "Yeah... it's the.. going between the atoms, or through the planet, um... am I close?"

Charlie smiled, put a hand on her shoulder, and said, "Don't get yourself all worked up. This is not an easy thing to understand. I've been considering it, though I think I may have an example that could help you. Come here."

Charlie walked up to a workbench covered with all sorts of tools and gadgets. Hazel's eyes grew large with curiosity, but then her face soured as Charlie pointed to a deflated balloon sitting on the workbench. "This here is a cruddy map of the world I drew on a balloon. Here's Europe, here's a smudge I call Australia..." Hazel laughed as he continued to lay into the quality of his "art" style.

"Now. Is this how the world is? If you walk in a random direction far enough, will you just fall off the edge?"

"No."

"No! Because this is a two-dimensional map, but we live in a three-dimensional world like this!"

Charlie picked up the balloon and began blowing it up. As he did so, a secret smiley face and thumbs up became clear, and Hazel let out a loud belly laugh.

Smiling, Charlie said, "Right. That's more like it. Now, here's a fun tidbit for you. Did you know that if this is the Earth, and we were to drill a hole straight from the top to the bottom, and then you pushed me into it, it would take me about 40 minutes to pop out the other end and start planning my revenge against you!"

Hazel giggled again and said, "How about I drill a hole that is closer to where you started and push you in there? Would I get less revenged?"

"Absolutely not! There's less of a gravity pull on a shorter trip, so I'll still be falling for 40 minutes! You've changed nothing but my final destination, and now I'm going to sell all your things, eat candy while you watch, and not share any!" They both laughed heartily.

"Ok, so here's where it gets tricky. Our two-dimensional map was more accurate as a three-dimensional sphere. Now, you may or may not have heard that we are a three-dimensional world in a four-dimensional universe, but how are you supposed to conceptualize that? Well, let's look at the balloon. Imagine I drew the entirety of our three-dimensional universe on a flat balloon, and then I blew it up into its more accurate four-dimensional form. In this situation, Earth would be somewhere on the outside of the balloon, and then we could punch into it and fall to anywhere in the universe we want!"

Hazel got excited and said, "Is that why they say everywhere is just seven years away? Because just like all holes in the earth are about 40 minutes, all trips through the universe are seven years?"

"Got it in one! You are pretty damn smart. I have to be careful with you. You'll be coming for my job next."

"Don't say that."

"What?"

"The D word."

"Ah, crap!"

"Uncle Charlie!"

"Ok! Ok! I'm sorry. Don't tell your mom."

Hazel smiled and said, "But if the launch pad is what punches the hole in the universe, what does this do?"

"This aims us through the in-between, so we come out on the right spot of the universe balloon. Without this, we'd be..." Charlies looked down at his young niece, choking back the rest of the words he wanted to say, and replied, "Well, it would be a lot of work for me to finish the last bit of the journey, and I'd rather be spending my time with the rest of you. Speaking of which, let's go take a look at where we'll be most of the trip."

They climbed back up the ladder, past the main lounge, and into the upper ship levels. The rooms on this level were stark white, with eight-foot-tall pods leaning along all the walls. Inside each pod was a thin mattress, a headrest, multiple health sensors, and a breathing tube. Numerous readout displays surrounded the room that reported on pod conditions.

"This is where you'll be sleeping the whole trip, you lazy twerp." Hazel whacked him in the arm. "OW! I'm going to need the doctor to look at that before we leave. Sheesh. Now, you'll be awake until just before the drop, and we'll wake you up after we reach the other side. You'll get some space-time on the back end, and you'll get the joy of re-entry when we get to Ogma, but only I and a few other techs will get to be awake at any point for the in-between time. Sorry kid."

Hazel huffed and threw her hands down in a minor tantrum and said, "But why do I have to miss all the neat parts? It's bad enough we're leaving, but I don't even get to see the coolest parts of the trip."

Charlie gave her an understanding look, a crooked smile, and said, "Listen, bug, it's a long trip. If we didn't sleep for the trip, you'd have to spend your entire childhood stuck in this metal box. The cryopods halt the aging process. It'll be like you fell asleep on one side of the universe and woke up on the other. Not to mention, you should be really impressed with these," he said as he rubbed one of the pods. "This is top-quality science in action here, and you get to be a part of it. Did you know that the biggest problem with cryosleep was that we needed to figure out how to freeze and defrost people evenly throughout the process? Well, to make that happen, you're going to become part cyborg for the trip, as you'll be host to an army of tiny doctor robots that will keep you safe and secure throughout both processes. They'll cool you and defrost you evenly, all while constantly monitoring and repairing any tiny damage that happens. You're about to become the ultimate robot fighting machine!" Charlie did some crazy martial arts action moves that caused them both to burst into giggles.

Hazel wiped a tear from her eye and said, "Still, I wish I could see the in-between."

"Oh god, no. Do you have any idea..."

Charlie was interrupted by Layla clearing her voice loudly and staring daggers into his eyes. Charlie locked eyes with her, gave an awkward giggle, and finished with, "...um, how boring that would be? Trust me, you've seen everything you need to see in our three dimensions. Anyway, thus ends the tour. Trust me. Your folks and I have you in good hands. I'm starving. Why don't we go get some lunch."

Weeks later, Hazel's eyes were red and swollen while she ate her mac-n-cheese in the punchship's cafeteria. She had spent the morning crying while saying her goodbyes to all her friends and neighbors. After all the hugs, the tears, and the farewell gifts, the family left their home for the last time on their way to the launch pad. Hazel looked back for as long as she could see them and then hugged her knees to her chest and cried some more in the back of the shuttle bus. Having stowed the last of their things on the punchship, secured the bulkhead doors, and now this last meal, they were in the final stages before drop.

Doctor Saunders walked into the room and said, "Ok, Miss Hazel. Your parents are ready for you up in the cryopods. May I escort you?"

Silently, all out of tears, her shoulders hunched, her steps slow and heavy, Hazel stood up and followed the doctor up the ladder. Layla hugged her as she reached their level, a small tear dropping down her face. "I'm going to miss everyone too. But remember, we will always have each other, my darling." Layla kissed each of Hazel's eyes and walked her over to the open cryopod. She helped Hazel in and then assisted the doctor in applying the biosensors to track her vitals.

Doctor Saunders used a cotton swab to rub a cool gel on Hazel's arm, then picked up a tube with a needle on the end and said, "We've applied a light topical to the injection site, so you shouldn't feel a thing. Just be very still."

The needle entered Hazel's arm, and she felt a chill run up her arm. Seeing her shiver, the doctor said, "Don't worry. The solution and nanites will warm up quickly. You'll be fast asleep by the time they get cold again."

Squeezing her mom's hand, Hazel looked up at her and said, "I'm scared."

"Everything is going to be ok. I promise."

Doctor Saunders inserted a hypodermic into her main line and said, "Now, start counting back from 10."

Hazel replied, "10...9...8... I taste mint... and the sound is all warbly...how long..."

"...will this take?"

"Relax Hazel. We're on the other side."

Her mother's words came through as she blinked the haze out of her eyes. The room looked the same, but all the people were shuffled around. More people were milling around than before. All of them had frazzled hair, as if they had just woken from a long night tossing and turning in bed. Her uncle was walking towards her, and since she had last seen him this morning, he had grown a foot-long beard.

She reached up, tugged on it, and said, "How?"

"Hey, bug. You may have just woken up, but for me, it has been a hot minute. Like you, I slept through most of the trip, but the engineers on staff had to take turns waking up to check on the ship, the facilities, and to make sure all was still going according to plan. It's also a tradition that we don't shave until we land at the colony."

Looking around Hazel saw two other men with long beards helping out other newly awoken crew.

"I'm so hungry."

Layla smiled and said, "Since you haven't eaten in seven years, I bet you are. Come on. I'm starving. Let's get dressed and head to the cafeteria."

The propulsion engines at the "top" of the ship kicked on to take them the rest of the way to Ogma 5. The resulting reversal in gravity forced Hazel to relearn how to handle herself around the ship. With door handles switching sides and ladder destinations swapped, she found herself in the wrong areas of the ship on multiple occasions.

The remainder of the trip took two weeks, during which the crew prepped for their arrival. The first two ships ahead of them were radioing in daily to report that everything was still on schedule. The first ship would arrive and set up a primary bunker. This would store all the initial supplies and gear and act as a temporary and/or emergency housing site. The second ship would arrive and begin 3d printing buildings, creating individual homes, storehouses, and other required spaces for the colony to function. Then, Hazel's ship would arrive, and they would begin setting up farmland and other stations for agriculture. Initial scouting reports claimed the planet had mammalian analogs that could potentially serve as cattle.

Hazel spent this time getting to know some of the other kids on board. Georgie was an older boy who liked all things that moved: trains, ships, cars, and more. He and Hazel spent a lot of time hanging out near the punchengine, trying to speculate on how it worked and what happens inside it when it's on. Jenn was all about board games. Jenn would pull Hazel into the lounge at least twice a day and try to get her to play a game with a new variant rule to try and spice it up. And then there was Richie. Richie wanted the biggest desserts. Richie wanted to be first in line. Richie wanted to play with all the toys and games first. Charlie spit his water out all over his workbench when Hazel told him later that Richie was a dick.

Then came the day of arrival. Everyone was secured in their crash seats, wearing their safety suits and helmets. Entering the atmosphere of the fifth planet of this new solar system was shaky and so loud that Hazel squinched her eyes tight and held her parent's hands.

An announcement came over the speakers, "Captain Tyrell here. We're going to have a safe but rough approach today. There is apparently a large storm hitting the settlement hard. While I'd normally prefer to orbit and ride this out, there are people down there who are counting on our supplies, and we are more than capable of handling this turbulence. So, please stay secured in your seats and prepare for landing."

As the ship entered the clouds, rain started to pelt the hull. Loud booms of thunder could be heard in the distance. Several of the kids started crying. Hazel hummed to herself, blocking out some of the chaos.

Just as the turbulence hit an epic pitch, everything began to calm down. The ship's shaking subsided. The noise and thunder were reduced. The rain continued, but Hazel could feel the ship slowing down. A moment later, they touched down. She and the crew got out of their suits and prepared to exit the ship. Everyone was lined up by the bulkhead doors, carrying supplies, pushing carts, or handling various gear.

Captain Tyrell stood by the door and said, "Alright. Here's our situation. The storm has been pummeling the colony since they landed. They made the choice on arrival to land anyway, in the hopes of weathering the storm and not causing the incoming ships any delays. They were successful in setting up the bunker, but the 3d printers for the additional buildings are failing to function under these conditions. The storm is expected to let up tomorrow morning, so we're only a day behind schedule. As such, you'll all be housed in the primary bunker until we can get that all sorted out. Now, I'm going to open this door and we're heading straight for the bunker. They've set up a small covered pathway for us, but that's only going to do so much with the sideways rain we're seeing. So, hold onto your gear, stay together, and let's get into some shelter. On my count. Three. Two. One. Go!"

With that, the bulkhead door flung open wide. The line moved quickly and surely. As Hazel exited the ship, she was pelted with rain. Keeping her hood up, she covered her eyes and held onto her father as they ran forward. Peeking out from her hood, she could see what looked like tall trees but with long leaves that were more akin to grass. There were low-level scrub bushes with flowers that gave off a rainbow shimmer as they moved with the wind. The path to the bunker was cut clear, but the growth around them was waist-high and thicker than scrub grass.

Reaching their destination, Hazel threw back her hood and took it all in. The bunker was built like a large warehouse. It spread out long and deep and was already filled with large amounts of materials and goods. The warehouse was sent with the first ship in modular sections for quick assembly. While structurally sound, the modular connections were still being tightened up. Water was coming in from multiple locations and people were scrambling to try and shore up all the leaks. Extra cots and sleeping bags were being set up to account for the increased number of people. New supplies were being organized, stored, and rearranged to handle the current situation.

A man walked out of the chaos up to Hazel's family and said, "Would you please come with me?"

They were escorted to a corner where he showed them their sleeping bags and said, "You can get settled here for now. We still see the storm letting up by dawn tomorrow. Once that happens, we can get started on setting up new housing for you all and get our new colony started. I want to personally thank you for braving the storm, and for bringing the extra food and medical supplies. I'm sure it wasn't easy. I'm sorry for the chaos. Honestly, we'd probably be in a better situation if it weren't for all the mats."

Frank looked up at him and said, "The what?"

A lightning bolt landed nearby. A large crackling boom rocked the bunker. In unison, several creatures leapt up into the air, screeching. They began climbing over and on top of everything, knocking gear and people over. They had bodies similar to monkeys, but their hair was blue, and they had feline heads.

The escort said, "Yep, the monkey cats. We call them mats for short. While they are harmless herbivores, they have decided that our bunker is a perfect place to weather the storm. Every time a thunderclap hits too close, they flip out and make a mess. We've been trying to get them out of the building, but they're a wiley bunch and keep sneaking in. My name is James, by the way. If you need anything at all, please let me know."

Left alone, Hazel's family organized the few personal items they had initially brought along. Frank then went off to help with food organization and distribution. Layla tucked Hazel into her sleeping bag, gave her a kiss on her head, and said, "It's been a long day. Try to get some sleep. I'm going to help get things settled here." With a hug, she was off.

Hazel curled up in her bag and clamped her hands over her ears. Tears began to run down her cheeks, and she whispered to herself, "I wish I was home."

Thunder rang throughout the building. Mats began running and jumping throughout the building. Hazel let out a startled yelp as a mat dashed into her sleeping bag with her. Hazel opened her bag and looked down. The mat was curled up by her belly. Its orange-yellow eyes stared into hers, shivering with fear. Hazel said, "You look about as terrified as I am, sad. Maybe we can help each other."

She zipped her bag back up and cuddled the mat close. Its shivers lessened, and Hazel's eyes began to droop. The noise of the bunker faded away.

Hazel woke up to sunlight in her eyes. Looking around, she saw most people were still asleep, with only a few starting their day. Her parents were lightly snoring by her side. She opened her sleeping bag, and the mat was still curled up there. It looked up and wiped at its eyes. When it was done, it stared at her and then snuzzled its snout on her face. She hugged it, her fingers running through the soft hair of its body while it trilled in response.

Hazel held him close and said, "I guess you're going to be my first new friend here, huh? In that case, you're going to need a name. I think I'm going to name you Crabapple."

As Hazel held Crabapple close, a smile eased across her face.

NICHOLAS LEAMY

TO BEND OR BREAK
by Eric Remington

He blew away the steam coming from his freshly brewed cup of synthetic coffee, the smell never quite leaving his nostrils. The view from his balloon, tethered to the top of the trees below him, was impressive. He never really tired of it. Every new planet was a new vista, a new group of species to catalog, and a new adventure. He had a lot of work to do, but for now, he allowed himself to reflect, drink his coffee, and pet his dog.

The dog, a bio-engineered specimen that only resembled a dog in the most superficial sense, was much more intelligent than its earth-bound predecessors. However, it still loved a good head scritch, sighing appreciatively as one was provided.

The man finished his coffee and turned to the terminal behind him, the set of scans to be cataloged glowing faintly on the display. "You know, Pete," he muttered to his pet, "some days, it would be nice to just sit and enjoy the scenery. But duty calls."

The survey corps had strict rules. Non-interference was the first, a narrow timetable the second. He had only a week left in his four-week stint, and if he didn't get his assigned survey done, there would be hell to pay. Cataloging took most of the morning, leaving him little time to grab a quick lunch before beginning a set of observations in the afternoon. He found nothing that, had his superiors been around, would have justified setting down, but who was to know? He was going to violate the rules, if only a little. He wanted to stretch his legs, and besides, he'd done it before, and nobody seemed to mind.

The balloon was meant to stay moored on even the flimsiest of branches at the top of any tree. The point was to drift with the breeze, stopping periodically to make observations before moving on to the next area. It was equipped with a descent system to lower the lone passenger for further study and possible sample collection, though such things were frowned upon by the Corps. Sometimes, something was just "so interesting" it had to be studied further.

In the surveyor's case, he'd modified his descender to accommodate his dog as well. Technically, the dog was against regulations, but almost every explorer had a companion of some kind. The Corps' official stance being that no such companion be allowed. But when they actively tried, attrition rates went up, so nobody ever really said anything. Carefully rigging his friend first, then himself into the harness, he opened the lower hatch and began reeling out the line to reach the ground.

It was peaceful, somewhat exhilarating, yet also agonizingly slow. To avoid any sort of issues, the designers of the winch system limited the speed to something that could only be described as glacial. It did give a good excuse for a break.

They landed softly, the man tying off the descender rig to a nearby tree and admonishing his companion not to stray far. With these breeds, a leash really wasn't necessary, as they were smart enough to know when to wander and when to stay close. Normally, these deployments necessitated the latter, though there was the occasional time that the two could run a little more freely. Deep in an unknown forest was definitely not one of those times.

The man started a close examination of one of the nearby trees. This could only be called a tree in the loosest of senses: deep blue, almost black, ascending nearly seventy feet into the air. Its leaves a lighter blue, both tuned to the slightly different hue of sun, still serving the same purpose as the chlorophyllic green on Terran trees. It was a fascinating study in convergent evolution, a few thousand lightyears distant from humanity's home star, yet still, trees. It was a wonder the surveyor had long ago given up attempting to reconcile.

This particular tree, still unnamed (official naming wouldn't happen unless the Corps decided to send a second team), he thought of as the highly unoriginal Blue Oak for its similar leaf structure. There was a reason they didn't let the initial surveyors name things.

Carefully, he cut a single leaf from the tree, justifiable, in his mind, for its unique value to xenobotany. He placed it in a sample bag and labeled it with the time, date, and geographic coordinates.

While he was busy with this, Pete nosed around the ground a bit, searching for whatever he thought was interesting. Genetically modified or not, a dog is still a dog.

Suddenly, the surveyor looked up, fast, at a growl from Pete. Not something that happened very often. Normally, they were both so far from anything that either would consider a threat that the most common vocalization Pete made was a satisfied "grumf" as he flopped in front of the heater on board their airship. A growl was extremely out of character. "What is it, boy?" The man asked, concern seeping into his words. Pete didn't react, still staring fixedly into the trees and giving that hair-raising warning sound. The man moved closer, reaching out to stroke Pete's back, attempting to comfort him, thinking about how quickly they could get back to the descender and off the surface, hoping that Pete wouldn't damage anything in the process. The thought of a predator was the furthest thing from his mind; this planet had a few, but nothing was showing on his scanner. Pete had been able to notice things before the scanner, at times, though.

Suddenly, Pete barked twice, loudly, and bolted off into the underbrush. "Pete! Stop!" the surveyor yelled, giving chase, all thought of caution in damaging the foliage forgotten in his fear for his friend. They crashed through bushes, branches slapping at his face, Pete's trail was an easy one to follow as he continued barking while running. The man continued to exhort him to stop, hoping against hope that he could still catch him before something truly bad happened.

Finally, they came to a clearing. Pete paused, barking up one of the trees at the edge. The surveyor, nearly out of breath, caught up and grabbed his companion by the collar. "Pete, what the fuck?" he yelled, yanking the dog's face around toward his. Pete just shook his way free and went back to barking up the tree. The surveyor looked up, trying to discern why his friend would be so agitated. Drawing his stunner, the only weapon Surveyors were allowed to carry (his, like many, was modified, though still fairly low-powered as things go), and peering through the leaves.

"Is there someone up there?" he called, reasoning that only a stranger would get Pete so riled.

"Please call off your beast! I mean no harm, truly!" A voice called down. It was cultured, educated, perhaps a scholar of some kind. Sounded human, but you couldn't always be sure. Male, probably, though again, that was up for debate for some of the species that frequented this area of space. Its Galactic Standard was accented peculiarly, but whether this stemmed from a problem of anatomy or was learned somewhere off the beaten path, he couldn't immediately tell.

"Whoever you are, this planet has been claimed by the Exploration Corps and not cleared for visitation. You're in violation of half a dozen treaties, and I'm permitted to arrest and detain you. Now, I'll call my dog off, but you need to come down. Pete, heel!" Pete backed down, the fur on his back still standing on end, a deep rumble still issuing from his throat.

"Alright, I'm coming down." The voice in the tree replied, followed by a series of grunts and scrapes as whoever it was made their way to the forest floor. Apparently human, he wore an antiquated but still obviously functional vac suit, an off-the-rack model from a decade ago, and not particularly well-fitting. His hair was just starting to go gray at the temples, though from age or stress, it was hard to tell, as the rest of his plain, handsome enough face was largely unlined. He held his hands well out from his body, not quite as high as the surveyor would have preferred. "Can I explain myself, please?" the man asked.

The surveyor relaxed slightly, not quite taking his stunner off the man. "Maybe start with your name?"

The man, in turn, relaxed his hands slightly and introduced himself, "Maximilian Dziedzic, I'd say 'at your service,' but I don't think that's really appropriate under the circumstances. Please, call me Max."

"Surveyor Nakhon of the Survey Corps. Now, are you going to tell me why you're on a proscribed planet and, further, why I shouldn't take you in?"

"As to the latter, my good man, I really don't have an answer for you. You would be well within your rights and, indeed, your duty. However, you would make a little girl cry. As to the former, that has more to do with the aforementioned girl than anything else. And her mother, of course," Max paused. The surveyor felt as though he were being studied, attempting to keep his face still, he motioned with the still-readied stunner. Max continued, "You see, we are a somewhat unconventional family, one that is frowned upon by so many on the outskirts of our illustrious Confederation. The problem begins with me being human, for my sins. My love, on the other hand...it might be best to show you," he motioned deeper into the forest.

The surveyor, putting on his best "don't fuck with me" face, motioned him on with the stunner, muttering, "Heel, Pete. Calm, but watch him."

They trudged through the thicket towards another clearing, breaking through a final bush into an area at least twice the size of the previous. The light had an odd quality, and it took a moment for the surveyor to spot the tell-tale haze of a holo field shielding the little encampment from stellar eyes. Crouched on squat landing legs in the center of the clearing was a ship of an age with the owner's suit, a decade or more out of date. As with the suit, it still appeared fully functional, if not much more. A relatively standard light cargo lander, no more than sixty feet long, half that wide. Broad engine intakes, necessary in the thickness of some atmospheres, leading to some kind of combination output for air and space, its size hiding the probably rather anemic performance. Nothing quick, nothing fancy, though the star drive pod appeared on initial inspection to be fairly new, possibly modified.

A shout brought the surveyor out of his reverie and his stunner back to the ready. "Daddy!" a young voice cried from a small structure he hadn't noticed at first, followed by an alien he'd never encountered before. She was clearly a mix of her parents, though what the other half of this couple was, he could only guess. Armored skin, an extra pair of powerful-looking arms ready to pound the surveyor into paste at the merest provocation, the expression on her nearly-human face fading from innocent to joy to apprehension, if not actual fear.

"Neeska, go wait with your mom. The Surveyor here and I need to talk," Max said, motioning his daughter back towards the lander. Starting to move in between her and the surveyor. "Please, she's harmless."

Surveyor Nakhon started after a moment, coming back to himself. His initial fear reaction shamed him. *I'm a Surveyor, dammit. I should be used to the unusual*, he thought, hastily holstering his stunner. Pete was staring up at him curiously, almost as though remonstrating him. The surveyor could hear him talking in his head, "The fuck, dude, she's just a kid."

Turning to Max, he took a moment to calm himself, "I'm sorry, that was uncalled for. I'm supposed to be better than that."

Max waved it off, obviously relieved that the danger had passed, "It's nothing, but it just shows why we can't really be anywhere more populated out here. A lot of people are not nearly as tolerant of difference as you. We've been chased out of quite a few frontier towns already. I've heard of a planet not very far from here that is a lot more accepting of difference. We just need a few days to get the ship ready. Somewhere, nobody will bother us. This place should work, at least, not unless the Corps sends some enforcers?" The question was implicit, and the surveyor couldn't quite make up his mind what to say.

"Look, I can't promise anything, and the Corps will eventually send others. If I don't mention finding you, that could be bad for everyone. There could be a way, but it wouldn't protect you forever. But I can tell you that the closer you get to civilization, the better things will get. Not everywhere is quite as closed-minded."

"Any time you can give us would help. We just need to rest. And plan. Look, maybe I can convince you that we're just a couple of normal people. Stay for dinner. Have you ever had Scyllaran cooking? It's unusual, quite unlike anything else I've ever had," Max was almost begging for a second chance to plead his case.

The mention of food made Pete's ears perk up, and the surveyor had to admit that a home-cooked meal after months of the Corps' simulated food-like substances (the marketing made them sound better, but every surveyor he knew called them that) did make his stomach hopeful. "Like I said, I can't promise anything, but I'll hear you out."

Max looked overjoyed and ushered his charge towards the shelter set up on the side of the little lander. "Oblava! We have a guest!"

Somewhat reluctantly, a woman came out from the tent flap of the dwelling. She stood not quite upright, her back a large chitinous shell, alternating bands of white and brilliant blue. Her head pitched slightly forward, a pair of luminous eyes thrusting slightly forward of her armored head. A pair of powerful-looking arms were tucked against her thorax, ending in a club-like hand. Her fore-limbs ended in a pair of finer-looking hands, currently wringing themselves together in an almost cartoonish expression of worry. At the back, covered by a split skirt of heavy scales, a pair of legs held her upright, but seemed like they would prefer to be churning the waters of some far-off ocean.

"Hello, Surveyor," the voice came from a box mounted on the side of what would probably be called the neck of the garment she wore, obviously interpreting the deep, staccato rumble issuing from somewhere in her chest, "Welcome to our home. I'm afraid our fare may be a little sparse, but getting supplies out here can be...difficult."

The surveyor was intrigued. Scyllarans, being a reclusive people, were rarely seen far from their aquatic home and certainly never in the close company of a human. There was a story there, and the chronicler in him hungered for the details. Pete, on the other hand, seemed to really only be interested in the bit of fish in Oblava's hand. "I'm sorry to impose. I'd hate to take food from you when you've such a scarcity."

"No, no, I won't hear of it! You're a guest! You must be treated as such!" Max hustled in, doing his best to defray the obvious tension between the two. "Neeska, come say hi."

Shyly, the little girl peeked around the armored tail of her mother. She stepped forward slowly, not looking at the surveyor but seeming fascinated by Pete. To prove he was no threat, he flopped on his back, rolling in the dirt, presenting his belly and obviously hoping for a rub. The surveyor couldn't help but smile, the antics of his companion around new people never failing to amuse.

The girl reached carefully forward, the more dexterous of her (arm? fore-limb? the surveyor wasn't exactly sure what to call it in his head, and just let it go at arm) arms reaching forward, the fingers at the end, extending out from the carapace that otherwise covered it, extending tentatively towards the dog's soft underbelly. At the moment of contact, her face lit up like the first dawning of a new day. The surveyor wondered if she'd ever had such close contact with a dog in her life. Or any pet, for that matter. Pete just garrumphed and arched his back, trying to get her to rub harder.

"Well, I guess we know what he thinks." Max grinned.

Oblava gazed at the two playing briefly on the ground, her black eyes expressionless, though the surveyor could swear that she was pleased. Some bend of her antennae, some relaxation of her arms gave the impression of pleasure. She uttered a series of clicks and chitters that her system translated as, "I don't know when I've seen her so happy. You must stay for dinner. As my husband said, we don't have the richest of fare, but this planet provides for us well enough for now."

The surveyor stiffened at the thought that they were harvesting yet more resources from the planet but didn't say anything. *They're already breaking quite a few laws. What's one more? Then again, I'm not exactly blameless here.* A muffled grumble from his stomach reminded him that this morning's ration bar was quite long ago, and the promised cooked meal was enough to banish any thought of repercussions from his mind. "Of course, though, I can't stay long. I need to make my nightly report."

At the mention of that report, Max visibly stiffened. The surveyor felt slightly guilty that he'd brought up something that obviously concerned the other man greatly.

"Yes, yes, of course. How can I help, dear? I know you weren't planning on an extra mouth. Can I get you anything to drink, surveyor? I'm afraid we don't have much, but I think breaking into our celebration stock might be in order, don't you think, dear?" The Scyllaran made a motion that seemed to be an agreement as Max hustled into the ship with a smile, returning a moment later with a bottle unlike any that the surveyor had seen before, like ocean glass, but obviously made to be that way intentionally. "Scyllaran whiskey, or at least that's the closest I've been able to determine. The effect is unlike anything you've ever drunk before. Not exactly alcohol, but not exactly a drug-induced high, either. It's...indescribable. I'd recommend a very small glass for your first time," so saying, Max poured about two ounces into what it took the surveyor a moment to realize started life as a lubricant can before being washed quite a few times and handed it over. "Drink slowly. See how you feel. Obi?" Dziedic handed a glass with a rather more generous pour to his wife and another for himself. "What shall we drink to?"

Feeling somewhat called out, the surveyor offered, "The future, whatever it may hold," which was echoed by the others, though it was made a little off by Oblava's answering chitter. The surveyor sipped at his glass sparingly, expecting the worst (at the last moment, he realized that this would be the perfect time for them to poison him, but it was already too late, so he just indulged himself), on the contrary, he found the taste to be rather pleasant. It reminded him of the salty air of the coast near his home, mixed with the scent of fresh seaweed. It burned going down in that lovely way really good whiskey does. It took him a moment to feel the other effects. As his new acquaintance intimated, it wasn't anything like what he expected from alcohol. It was closer to the feeling that he'd heard people who take psychedelics describe. No hallucinations, but a feeling of intense happiness and peace. He was glad he took only the smallest sip. Chugging even the small amount he'd been given was likely to put him on the floor. He looked up to see the other two watching him intently, "Quite delicious, thank you. Though I think this will be all I can handle."

Beaming, Max and Oblava hustled into the shelter, presumably to finish dinner. The surveyor turned to see Pete and Neeska apparently playing a game that involved her trying to snatch at his feet while he kept them away from her. His happy grumbles occasionally turned to those of frustration when having avoided her two primary "hands," Neeska managed to snag one of his back feet with a secondary.

Left to his own devices for the moment, the surveyor took a further look around the little clearing. From this angle, the camouflage netting was much more visible, as was the projector for its hologram, though the latter was in rather poor shape. That's seen some hard use, and no wonder, he thought, somewhat guiltily. *How do I help these People? Can I? They've broken the very laws that I'm supposed to...well, not enforce, but at least watch for violations of, yet here I am pondering breaking those same laws. Have they ever really made sense? Is it just to break an unjust law? Is it really unjust, or is this just an abnormal situation?* He was so lost in thought, prowling around the edges of the clearing, looking at everything, yet not really seeing or hearing anything, until the Scyllaran lady of the house appeared in front of him, her vocoder asking, in a seemingly concerned voice, "Surveyor, are you alright?", startling him to no end, her sudden appearance, despite being the very person he'd just been considering.

"Oh! Yes, I'm fine. Sorry, I was lost in thought."

"So I see. Dinner is ready if you'd care to join us."

"Please, show me the way."

The dining room of the freighter was larger than he'd anticipated. Obviously, the ship had been extensively converted from its initial layout, much of the cargo space converted to living quarters, including a rather fine, if utilitarian, dining room. Pete immediately found the warmest and softest corner and flopped, his eyes twitching any time a motion was made that might indicate something tasty had hit the floor.

The meal was sumptuous in a way that the surveyor hadn't had in a long time. It largely consisted of harder seafood, though not of a kind he'd encountered previously. Briefly, he considered asking if this was yet another example of them violating the sanctity of the planet he was supposed to be surveying but decided he'd rather not know.

The conversation was necessarily somewhat strained, the family trying to be polite to their guest yet knowing that he held their freedom in his hands. For his part, the surveyor, despite quite enjoying the somewhat unusual fare, couldn't keep his mind off similar thoughts. He tried to be polite, laughing at the antics of the youngest of the three as she did her best to steal an extra dessert (dessert itself being a rare enough occurrence in such a household) or stealthily attempted to slip bits of her hated vegetables to Pete, who was only too happy to aid in her subterfuge.

Relaxing after dinner, Neeska having been bundled off to bed after much protestation, the three adults sat out under the stars, putting a larger dent in the bottle of liquor they'd produced earlier. "You have a very nice family, the pair of you. I do feel for you. It must be hard living under such prejudice."

His two hosts grew somber once more, though the subject was never far from their minds. "We've learned to live with it. I fear for Neeska how she will get on with life, but perhaps we'll find a more permanent home somewhere. One day. As we've said, this is just a stopover. You've no concern about that. I won't ask you again what you will do, but please remember us fondly."

The conversation ended there. Nothing more really needed to be said. A few moments later, the surveyor bid a reluctant adieu, convinced Pete to leave the comfy pile of leaves he'd scraped together, and began the careful trek back to his airship, his mind a-whirl.

Arriving at the descender, the surveyor, still mulling things in his mind, rigged him and his companion into the system and started the ascent. Normally, the view from such a height was calming and pleasant. This time, all he could do was gaze off into the distance, trying to find the camouflaged break in the trees that would point to where his new problem lay. He knew it was a pointless exercise, but he couldn't get his mind off of the little family just trying to escape to somewhere they could live in peace.

The ascent complete, Pete, once released from his harness, loped over to his water bowl and then curled up on his favorite cushion by the surveyor's desk, staring expectantly up at him. "Well, what's the call?" the surveyor could almost hear in his mind.

He sat, preparing his report, a freshly-made mug of synthetic coffee steaming away, "Surveyor Nakhon, surface survey complete. Retrieved samples for analysis, notes to follow. Found something else on the surface, that is of note to the Corps..." He looked down at Pete, out at the trees in the general direction of the camp, and thought.

STAR ANGEL

by Rose Strickman

"Are you sure you won't come, Elena?" Reclining in his float-chair, Vikram's face was creased into papery wrinkles of concern.

"Quite sure," said Elena. "You know my old bones can't deal with planetary gravity anymore." The two friends were in the waiting lobby of one of Astrophil Retirement Center's space docks. Nearby, a line of residents preparing to board one of the shuttles down to the planet was forming.

Vikram scoffed so hard his float-chair bobbed a little in midair. "Your old bones! You're in better shape than I am, Elena. You just hate going downside. Comes of working in space all your life, I guess. You're a real angel, aren't you?"

"Now, Vikram." Elena's dark eyes sparkled in her wrinkled face. "Are you suggesting that those old spacer tales are real? Beings of light and color living in outer space, singing to starships as they go by, spotted zipping by in hyperspace? *Those stories?*"

"Well, just about every spacer I've met has a story about seeing an angel. There must be something going on to fuel them." The boarding call rang out, and the line began to move, white-haired, wrinkled men and women hobbling or floating onto the shuttle. "Come on, Elena," coaxed Vikram. "It's been, what, a year since you went downside? We can go get a coffee at my favorite café!"

Elena smiled but shook her head. "Not for me, thanks. Have a good time." She stepped aside, letting Vikram direct his chair into the line. She waved goodbye, and he waved back just before floating onto the shuttle. The doors slid shut behind him.

Elena watched as the transparent shield sealed and the shuttle disembarked, making its slow, stately way to the blue-green planet rotating far below. Then she left the space dock, heading deeper into the Center.

Vikram was right: Elena was in fairly good shape for her age. She made pretty good time through the corridors, waving to friends and Center employees as she went. Astrophil Retirement Center was a very comfortable space station, its corridors carpeted and well-lit, with mirrors and artwork on the walls and plenty of communal gathering spaces for its residents. Space stations like this were popular venues for retirement centers these days, for it was simple to control the climate, and the light gravity was kind to old bones. Elena spotted some friends playing holo-games in one of the gathering spaces but went past the open doorway without stopping.

She could have gone back to her apartment, where she had correspondence to catch up with. She could have gone to the library to continue reading her latest novel. She could have gone to the gym or the pool for exercise or physiotherapy with one of the Center's many helpful trainers.

Instead, Elena went to the gardens.

Like most space stations, the Astrophil Retirement Center grew many plants to supplement its atmosphere, from decorative flowers in pots in the corridors to tanks full of algae bioengineered for maximum oxygen-carbon dioxide exchange efficiency. Like many other residential stations, Astrophil combined necessity with pleasure in its recreational gardens. They filled a long chamber in the belly of the space station, a long park of meandering paths, overhanging trees, blooming flowers, trickling water features, and comfortable benches. Dangling vines brushed Elena's hair as she made her way through the park, breathing deep of the scents of earth and leaves, water, and flowers.

Elena headed for her favorite bench, hidden behind a screen of lush green bushes and facing a window. Climbing roses and trumpet vines surrounded the window, overlooking the endless abyss of stars. The visual contrast held Elena mesmerized, staring in fascination at the living vines framing the vastness of outer space. Almost, she was tempted to describe that vastness as *lifeless*. But she knew it was not.

Elena settled herself on the bench, wincing as her joints protested the shift in position. She'd stayed in shape over the years, but there was no denying the fact that she simply wasn't young anymore. Still, she steadied herself, breathing deep of the garden air, relaxing her body and calming her mind.

"Alcyone," Elena whispered the name, staring deep into outer space, sitting enthroned by flowers. "Alcyone."

There came a flicker outside the window, a ripple of movement in the utter stillness, a nameless color in the lightlessness. It came closer and closer, dancing across space, a serpent of movement and brilliance, until its light filled the window. There came a shiver, and the new presence entered the station.

There was always that split second when the presence shivered and shrank under the assault of gravity and oxygen, an environment as lethal to the newcomer as outer space was to Elena. But Alcyone had been coming to see Elena for decades now and was well practiced at the art of gravity-walking. She built up her gravity-body in a matter of seconds: first bones appearing in midair, a fully realized skeleton, white and intricate. Then muscles materialized, wrapping around the skeleton, and skin filmed over the muscles, nails generating, hair flowing.

Finally, there stood a beautiful naked woman, skin smooth and brown, hair a waterfall of black curls, generous curves in the light of the garden.

The star angel opened her brilliant eyes and smiled with her white teeth.

"Elena," she sighed, voice like a breeze as she rippled air over brand-new vocal cords.

"Alcyone." Elena took off her long, soft duster coat and held it out to her visitor. "Better put this on, Star," she said, using the nickname she'd given her lover long ago.

Alcyone reached out to take the coat, her movements both jerky and smooth. She slid on the coat, twitching and giggling a little at the sensation. "So...soft!" she said, recollecting the word.

"Of course it's soft," Elena grinned. "I know what you like. Remember the time you tried on my raincoat and nearly broke all my furniture with your thrashing and screaming?"

"Well, that did feel very nasty," sniffed Alcyone, still running her hands appreciatively over the soft woolen sleeves. "There's too much sensation in the gravity-places. I don't know how you gravity-beings bear it."

"You've borne it pretty well for decades now." Elena held up her hands. "Help me up?"

Alcyone stepped over, testing her strength and balance, and, grasping Elena's hands, hauled her to her feet. Elena rose in a salvo of pops and creaks. "Thank you, Star."

"I still do not understand how life evolved in the gravity-places." Alcyone shook her head. She'd spent decades memorizing all of Elena's human gestures and their meanings until they'd become her own. "Look at you, Elena! You are born and live in gravity, but still, it destroys you."

"Well, you've told me that angels eventually deteriorate." Elena leaned on Alcyone's arm as they made their slow way out of the grotto. "You may be made of pure light and energy, but even that disintegrates over time."

"Only after a few thousand of your years, darling," said Alcyone, keeping pace with Elena's shuffle. "But this gravity-form will last me only a few hours at most. Let's hurry."

Angel and human paced along the level paths of the gardens, leaves, and flowers, brushing their hair and clothing. Alcyone gave little exclamations of pleasure at the plants, reaching out to brush petals and touch leaves. She raised her face, silver-shining eyes wide to take in every last particle of artificial sunlight. Elena watched with amusement. Her angel might complain about the horrors and inconveniences of gravity-places, but she sure enjoyed the sensations found therein.

They passed two old men sitting at a table, playing chess. Elena and Alcyone greeted them, and they nodded distractedly without looking up from their game. Elena glanced back over her shoulder as they went past. "It's still so funny," she said to Alcyone, "how no one ever notices that you don't belong. Not even on a space station like this one, where everyone knows everyone else."

Alcyone smirked. "I've told you, my presence clouds gravity-beings' minds. I don't belong here at all, so their perception just sort of slides around me. They'll remember seeing you with someone, but no one will remember who that someone was."

"The cameras still pick you up, Star."

"Yes, but all footage is eventually filtered through the human eye, and the same principle applies."

They strolled into another grotto, a space cleared around a murmuring fountain. Water trickled over flat, mossy rocks into a dark pool. Orange and white fish rose, opening and closing their mouths as they begged for food. Alcyone reached down to let one of the fish nibble on her finger. She giggled a little, then giggled again at her own giggling. "Such strange creatures! It really is amazing how different gravity-beings have adapted to living in this environment."

"Isn't it?" Elena smiled down at the fish. "Do you think they're aware that they live in space?"

"Doubtful. You've told me fish aren't very intelligent." Alcyone looked up with a dreamy smile. Her gravity-form was already starting to deteriorate. Elena noticed, with a pang, tiny wrinkles forming around her eyes and mouth. "Remember when we first met?" said the star angel.

"How could I forget?" Elena sat on the seat built into the fountain's rim, drawing Alcyone down beside her. "I was on a routine supply run to Alcyone II. I looked out the viewscreen and I saw — you. A star angel made of light particles and color, just like the old spacer tales."

"And I perceived you too," Alcyone recalled. "It was the first time I truly perceived any gravity-being. I couldn't take my senses off you. I couldn't stop myself trying to get to you."

"That almost killed you." The pair went silent, remembering how the angel had materialized in Elena's cockpit and nearly disintegrated on the spot, her form puncturing and falling in on itself under the ruthless gravitic assault. "You had to get out again awfully fast. But I put on a suit and went out onto the hull to find you again." Elena remembered those hull walks. The rhythmic rasp of her respiration inside her helmet, the effort of moving through zero-gravity. Around her, space spread out, an endless ocean of stars, and the angel blazed overhead. A vast presence made of a million lights and hues, all of them focused on Elena.

"So I learned what went into creating a gravity-form," Alcyone continued the story. "And tried making one. On the hull. In space."

"You learned pretty quick not to try *that* again!" laughed Elena. "But we figured it out. First, come into the ship, *then* build a form."

"Even then, it wasn't easy," said Alcyone with a rueful grin. Her teeth were yellower than before. "I had a lot to learn about building a form. Lucky I had you to be my model, darling."

"Yeah," Elena murmured, remembering the mind-bending bizarreness of seeing Alcyone's best approximation of her own face and body that first time. "Lucky. One way of putting it, I guess."

Alcyone gave her a hard nudge. "Well, it *was* lucky! And I've gotten much better since then."

"You have that, Star." Elena ran an appreciative eye over Alcyone's form. Alcyone's gravity-form still resembled Elena, but she'd branched out considerably since those early attempts, developing her own features and looks that pleased both her and Elena.

"Haven't I, though?" Alcyone said complacently. "But then trying to *communicate* with you…Communication with gravity-beings is so illogical." She gave a deep, theatrical sigh. "Sound vibrations through your mouths. I ask you, what's wrong with light signals?"

Elena hid a grin. Alcyone loved giving deep, theatrical sighs just as much as she loved complaining about gravity and human speech. "Well, Star, you've done a pretty good job of it," she said. "Illogical or not. Besides, think how long it took you to learn to eat!" She laughed at Alcyone's disgruntled look.

"Eating." Alcyone shook her head. "Another madness of gravitic life!"

"Admit it, Star, you enjoy gravity-walking, don't you? It's not just about spending time with me."

Alcyone sniffed. "I admit nothing," she said. "Except I do enjoy spending time with you, darling." She turned to take Elena in her arms, holding her in a deep, strong embrace. "I love you, Elena."

Elena returned the embrace, eyes closed against the sudden wave of emotion. When she'd earned her spacer's certificate and started a life on the star-roads, she'd never expected to encounter one of the legendary angels, let alone fall in love with them. Truly, life was full of miracles. "Remember the first time we ever made love?" she murmured. "It was on the jump to Rama IV." She recalled the hum of her starship as it sped through hyperspace, counterpart to Alcyone's clumsy but passionate embrace. The inexperienced, eager touch of her mouth, her hands.

"I will remember that forever," Alcyone promised. "As long as you do, darling."

"You know I won't be here for much longer, Alcyone." Elena pulled back to look into her lover's eyes. "Astrophil's a nice place, but it's where old humans like me go to die."

"Yes, darling." Alcyone gave her a gentle squeeze. "Your body is deteriorating. Just like all my gravity-forms do. At least yours has lasted longer."

"But unlike you, I won't be able to just build another one." Elena gave a sad smile. "One day, I'll leave this body and go somewhere else. And I won't ever be able to come back."

"The same is true of my kind, as you pointed out," said Alcyone. "But I will remember you as long as I endure, Elena. We have walked beside one another. We have loved. You have given me a name: *Alcyone*. You have taught me much that I would never have known otherwise, darling. That means something. That means a lot."

"You've taught me a lot too, Alcyone." Elena squeezed her angel's hands. "That some legends are real." She drew Alcyone near, and their lips met, a long, gentle kiss in the water-singing garden.

When they parted, Alcyone's shining eyes shone brighter still with unshed tears. Elena remembered the first time Alcyone had ever cried, all those years ago, when Elena's pet hamster, which Alcyone had loved, had died. *What is this?* The angel had exclaimed, dashing away her hot tears in panic. It had taken Elena forever to explain.

"What are you thinking of, darling?" Alcyone asked.

"The first time you ever cried, Star."

"Poor Puffball," Alcyone said solemnly, and Elena had to laugh. After a moment, Alcyone laughed with her.

Together, they slowly levered themselves up from the bench. Alcyone's gravity-form had deteriorated further, her face a web of wrinkles, flesh sagging from her bones. Her black hair was liberally streaked with gray. "Your forms deteriorate so fast now," Elena said as they began making their way back to the window. When they'd begun their affair, Alcyone had been able to maintain her gravity-forms for hours or even days at a time.

"It's getting harder to keep them up," said Alcyone, but Elena was not sure she completely believed this. She suspected Alcyone let her forms fall apart faster these days, so she could match Elena's physical state. She'd always liked imitating whatever Elena did.

They entered the patio where the two old men had been playing chess. They were still there but had abandoned their game in favor of watching the group who had come in with musical instruments, violins, flutes, and a cello. The orchestra of gray-haired Astrophil residents set bows to strings and fingers to stops. They began to play.

Alcyone let out a small exclamation as the first strains washed over her. She'd always loved music. She listened, entranced, until Elena took her by the waist and spun her into a slow waltz, the musicians and chess players alike smiling to see the two women dancing on the pavement.

As they danced, memories danced, too, swirling through Elena's head. The first time Alcyone had tried to eat, getting her food all over her face and hands and creating a huge mess. Alcyone learning to talk, still confused and unconvinced at the concept of spoken language. The first time Elena had taken Alcyone downside to a planet, the angel's pure, unadulterated wonder and astonishment. The joy and marvel Alcyone expressed at the smallest, most mundane things, even as she complained of the horrors of dirt and air and gravity. The first time they'd danced together, on a terrace overlooking the ocean on Poseidon I, the planet's three moons shining on the water, the waves gentle murmur singing through the music. All the wonder and happiness that Alcyone had brought into Elena's life, her marvelous, cantankerous, miraculous star angel.

The musicians came to a halt with a flourish of bows. The chess players burst into applause. Elena and Alcyone slowed to a halt and followed suit.

The musicians launched into another tune, faster and less romantic than the first. Elena and Alcyone waved goodbye and shuffled off, disappearing around the bend in the path.

They re-entered the tiny grotto by the window, climbing creepers framing the view of space. The station had rotated since they'd started their walk, so a thin blue-green slice of the planet was visible. Alcyone turned back to Elena, moving stiffly on creaking bones. "Goodbye, Elena, my love," she said. "I'll be back soon."

"I'll be here, Star." This had always been the way of things: Alcyone flying free, Elena anchored by her physical existence, waiting for her lover's return. Over time, Elena had learned to accept it. That Alcyone was able to visit her at all was a miracle. And there was some joy in living her own life between her lover's appearances. *Not for much longer, though.*

Carefully, Elena took Alcyone into her arms once more — the angel now looked much older than the woman — and gave her a long, warm hug. "I'll be here," she promised again. "I love you, Alcyone."

"I love you too, Elena." Alcyone gave her one last kiss on the cheek and stepped back.

Elena let her go. She watched as Alcyone's gravity-form disintegrated. First, the light in her brilliant eyes went out, then her skin crumbled, hair falling out, muscles and bones vanishing before Elena's eyes as the component atoms flew apart, reabsorbed into the environment. There came a soundless explosion, a colorless color — and then Alcyone had returned to her natural form, a great wavering curtain of light flashing out among the stars. She danced a moment outside the window, bidding Elena farewell, before disappearing into the vastness of outer space.

Elena remained at the window a long time. She watched the planet slide into view, obscuring the stars. She closed her eyes, praying that after her death, she might join Alcyone among those stars.

After all, angels were real. Who knew what other miracles were possible?

Smiling slightly, Elena turned away from the stars.

AT THE TOP OF THE MARTIAN WORLD
by Mary Jo Rabe

Mike Menner hopped expertly through the unfortunately silent reception area. As always, a surely temporary lack of customers had no power to spoil his mood, which was as bright as the lights under the expertly scrubbed transparent dome.

Born on Earth, he had emigrated to Mars with his parents at a young enough age to adapt to and enjoy the lower gravity. At the adult age of sixteen Martian years his muscles were well trained, one factor that gave him both the appearance and the energy of an adolescent.

He bounded out to the wide, circular deck surrounding his Olympus Mons Hotel, naturally also protected by the thick and seamless yet transparent plastic shield that covered it. The Stevensens Plastics Factory on Mars had done excellent work with the dome that provided radiation protection, as well as a great view.

He was honestly sorry that he still couldn't afford to pay them.

He stopped on the deck and stretched his short but compact body. He was in excellent shape, mentally and physically, just worried because of too many unexpected financial setbacks.

"Damn," he shouted and, as always, was surprised at how loudly his deep, bass voice bounced back and forth between the plastic shield and the red, rock walls of his hotel. His footsteps were clearly visible in the delicate layer of brownish-orange Martian dust on the light-blue, plastic floor covering on the deck.

He sniffed tentatively. Unfortunately, his nose immediately verified the presence of the caustic, even toxic, sharp crystals from the surface of Mars. The macro-sized dust particles coated the floor. The nano-sized ones saturated the air he had so carefully enriched with a calculated amount of extra oxygen to invigorate his guests.

The strong, pungent fragrance of chlorine was unmistakable and would overpower the taste of all the drinks his bar could provide. The last thing he needed was for guests to equate his new Martian cocktails with swimming pool water on Earth.

Another one of his miscalculations. It had never occurred to him that the wispy Martian winds would transport the sharp regolith from the surface twenty-two kilometers up to the top of the highest mountain on Mars, where the atmosphere was so thin that the location qualified as outer space.

Unfortunately, the dust was a genuine health hazard as well as a damned malodorous nuisance. The tiny crystals scratched mucus membranes and did permanent damage to the lungs and other internal organs.

Such outcomes were not the best advertising for an up-and-coming hotel. Somehow, the dust always got into human habitation, a little like scorpions from the Arizona desert when they encountered human housing. Despite all his efforts, he couldn't keep dust out of his hotel.

He would try reprogramming the cleaning robots and have them scrub the floors and walls three times a day instead of just twice. And he had to replace the air at least that often.

Actually, he would have to have one of Layla Jahoob's technicians reprogram the robots, as the AI structure was complicated and completely beyond his capabilities. Unfortunately, Ms. Jahoob might refuse since he hadn't paid her robotics factory for the robots yet, either.

The blue floor covering out on the deck was soft and had the slightly spongy feel to it that he had specifically ordered. He wanted the surface of the deck to be kind to his hotel guests' feet while they strolled around and enjoyed the unique view of outer space that only his hotel could provide.

The guest rooms were all carved into the lava tubes that ran through the interior of Olympus Mons, but the restaurants and reception area were located on the surface under the transparent plastic dome. Doors took you out onto the deck where Mike pictured his guests spending hours admiring this part of the universe, the one they could see.

So far, this hotel, constructed in the southernmost caldera at the top of the mountain, was his dream come true. It was located on the tallest mountain in the solar system and offered its guests a one-in-lifetime view. Up here, you felt that you were a part of the universe, no longer held prisoner by any planet.

In the northernmost caldera, he had smoothed out the surface to allow for the placement of state-of-the-art research telescopes and a parking lot for a few surface vehicles.

The hotel deck also had lightweight telescopes anchored into the transparent shield, but they were for the amateurs who wanted to gaze at Earth and its moon. At the east end of the caldera, he left space for a small rocket landing site.

His plans included encouraging tour groups to hike up Olympus Mons and stay at his hotel. Naturally, the hikers would need to be clad in state-of-the-art protective surface suits that Mike had ordered from the Stevensens Plastic factory. Mike had even commissioned Martian surface experts to stake out promising paths.

For those less athletically inclined, he secured permission for local rockets from Marsport to land at the eastern end of the caldera. The Mars settlement authorities had long since allowed and encouraged interested adolescent pilots to build and fly their own little rockets and add to the transportation options on Mars.

He looked out the transparent shield once more. The nanobots he had ordered from the plastics factory were doing a good job of keeping the dust off the outside surface. Getting them developed and delivered hadn't been cheap, but he wanted to offer his guests an optimal experience.

The rooms were also furnished and equipped with luxuriously comfortable, elegant furniture and all legal electronic entertainment devices available on Mars.

Impatient though he had been to make his dream of a hotel on Olympus Mons come true, Mike had waited until a sufficient number of communications satellites orbited the planet so that he could offer Earth-based and Martian electronic entertainment.

In a unique environment, Mike wanted to provide his guests an amazing vacation experience. They were in outer space but had all the comforts of planetary residence.

His hand-held communicator turned itself on. The 3-D visuals and the audio feed were of acceptable quality. All guests would have one of these communicators at their disposal for their safety and entertainment needs.

"Holo," Mike said, and the communicator beamed a hologram of Emma Brooks Baxter in front of Mike.

"I heard your hotel passed the final inspection. When do you want your food delivered?" her friendly, elderly voice asked cheerfully.

Emma's puffy face was crowned with her short, curly, white hair. Although she was one of the shortest adults in the settlement, she commanded respect, not only because Ned Brooks, the billionaire who was subsidizing the whole Martian settlement, was her brother. There was something about her demeanor that made people pay attention to her.

Mike wished he knew what it was. He was one of the shortest settlers in his age group. Those born on Mars were all tall and slender and towered over him. Mike was muscular and stocky, but his childlike face made it easy for his contemporaries to dismiss him. None of them had taken his Olympus Mons hotel seriously.

Mike sighed. This wouldn't be the last uncomfortable conversation he had to conduct. Emma, the cafeteria lady, was everyone's favorite grandmother. Even though every apartment in the settlement habitats contained a kitchenette, most settlers preferred to eat in Emma's cafeteria because the food tasted so good, and Emma cared so much about the welfare of each and every settler.

Emma, at forty Martian years old, was one of the first settlers. Mike, at sixteen, could only vaguely remember Earth, as his parents had emigrated to Mars when he was only three Martian years old.

Mike hadn't been enthusiastic about the move at first, but Emma had made him feel right at home. She not only wanted the settlers to enjoy their food in her cafeteria, she wanted all her customers to feel at home on Mars.

She always encouraged the settlers to pursue their dreams on, and inspired by, this new, exciting planet.

"Hi, Emma," he answered. "Thank you for asking." And he didn't know what else to say.

Emma's cafeteria, with its location on the surface of Mars and its three-hundred-and-sixty-degree panorama view of the Tharsis Bulge, had fascinated him. He immediately felt enthralled by the stark beauty of the red planet.

Dark red boulders and sand, pink skies with light-blue sunrises and sunsets, reddish-brown dust devils that swirled around ☐ nothing he remembered from Earth could compare with this.

The only irritation was that the thin but dusty atmosphere often prevented any kind of star-gazing.

It wasn't long before he wanted to have his own place where he could look at the stars and help people appreciate everything about Mars.

He did the research and decided that he wanted a hotel on top of Olympus Mons where his guests could view outer space and the surface of Mars while enjoying a luxurious stay. Gradually, other uses for the property on top of the mountain occurred to him, guided hikes up the mountain, astronomy research in one of the calderas, and launch pads for mini-rocket tours of Mars.

He was able to persuade Ned to pay for the construction of a hotel on top of the mountain. However, Mike's vision didn't match old Ned's.

Ned had pictured a spartanly furnished youth hostel where scientists could stay overnight when they had work to do up on top of the mountain. Mike wanted a luxurious getaway that he could justifiably call the most magnificent hotel in the solar system. The deal Ned offered was that he would pay for what he thought the hotel should be, and Mike would have to pay for any and all extras.

Ned's long-term goal was for the Mars settlement to make him even more money than he already had, and he set up a somewhat complicated system of Martian credits tied to Earth currencies. The way it worked was that Ned paid for the settlers' their room, board, clothing, devices, and pretty much anything else they could talk him into.

He also paid them a salary in Martian credits with which they could buy things on Mars or transfer funds to Earth. Whatever profits the settlers made from what they invented or developed on Mars were shared with Ned, fifty percent for Ned and fifty for the industrious Martian settler.

The trick was to come up with something they could create on Mars that would be in demand on Earth. Generally, ideas were the most profitable, whether scientific, engineering, or entertainment.

As of right now, Mike had huge debts and had no credits left to pay for his improvements to the hotel. He had assumed that the hotel would be booked up immediately once the rooms were finished. Unfortunately, he seemed to have wildly overestimated the appeal of spending time in and on Olympus Mons.

"And who will be in charge of your restaurant?" Emma continued. "The food won't fix itself."

Mike sighed. "Unfortunately, I don't need any food or any employees because I don't have any guests."

Emma looked astonished. "No guests?" she asked. "That's not possible. You have done so much advertising on the Mars net. Everyone has heard about your hotel."

"Yeah," Mike said. "But no one wants to spend any time here. They say the view is just a black sky with a few pinpoints of light."

"What about the tour groups?" Emma asked.

"Most settlers don't want to take the time, and there aren't enough tourists from Earth yet," Mike said. "The mountain climbers so far set up their own base camps and don't need a hotel."

"What about the adolescent rocketeers?" Emma asked. "They delivered everything to get your hotel built, and they have been flying you up and down the mountain. I thought you built your rocket launch pads just for them."

"They don't have any other passengers yet," Mike said. "So there's no reason for them to come. I installed high-quality telescopes, but Professor Tyler says her astronomy team has no immediate use for them. They're busy with data from satellites they now have orbiting the sun."

"Hmm," Emma said. "I understand. Wait a second. I might have someone you need to talk to." And her hologram faded away.

A few minutes later, Mike's communicator turned itself on again. At his command, two holograms appeared: Emma and a young man who looked somewhat familiar to Mike. He must be a native Martian, what with his tall, skinny physique, pale skin, and long, straight, dark hair.

"Mike," Emma said. "This is Larry LaMond, one of Dr. Tyler's research assistants. He would like to use your research telescopes and satellite dishes."

"All yours," Mike said. "But I thought your boss said she had no use for my facilities."

"She doesn't," Larry LaMond said. "She also has no interest in continuing any SETI research. She says enough time and money has been wasted waiting to hear from space aliens who are either not there or not interested."

"And you don't agree?" Mike asked.

"I think we have been broadcasting the wrong messages," Larry said. "I would like to do some broadcasting from your array and see if anyone answers. Dr. Tyler won't let me use her telescopes."

"And why do you think you would have more luck than anyone else has had?" Mike asked.

"I just want to broadcast music, folk music, pop music," Larry said. "Something unique to planet Earth."

"But hasn't that been done before?" Mike asked.

"Only half-heartedly," Larry said. "As part of other cultural creations. I want to follow in the footsteps of American DJs of the late twentieth century."

"Fine with me," Mike said. He desperately needed someone to start using his hotel. "How soon can you come, and what do you need me to do?"

Emma interrupted them. "I already asked Sean, and he can be ready to take off in an hour. He's the most reliable of the adolescent pilots. He'll take you up the mountain whenever you want. And he's willing to wait to be paid for his transport services."

"I'll be on my way to get my equipment," Larry said. "It's not much, basically just amplifiers. I have all the music I need stored in the Mars net. My access won't cost me anything."

"Great," Mike said. "Just out of curiosity, how did you choose the music?"

"For that I had to involve statistics," Larry said. "I determined which songs were purchased or listened to the most often, in isolated regions and planet-wide. I want the music people like to listen to, not music people tell them they should like."

"Sounds good," Mike said. "Come up here as soon as you can."

"We got an answer," Larry yelled through Mike's communicator. Mike looked up from the reception area and walked out on the deck where Larry let himself in from the caldera area outside. The little transport vehicle had almost run into the deck shield.

Larry threw Mike his communicator, and the hologram of a three-meter-tall, bipedal, purple creature with four waving extremities floated in front of him.

While Larry made clumsy and slow attempts to take off his helmet and exit his surface suit, Mike asked him, "Is this legitimate or a joke that your astronomy colleagues might have put over on us?"

"The signal is legitimate," Larry said. "Its origin is somewhere out past the Draco galaxy. It came in with a strength that almost fried my SETI apparatus."

At that point, the holo screeched and whistled and then emitted a few words in a soft, baritone voice. "Please talk more. I'm trying to get the universal translator calibrated."

Mike launched into a long monologue about how he got his hotel built and what he hoped to accomplish with it and ended with "So, you are my first real guests. How can I make your stay enjoyable?"

"That is sufficient," the holo said, perhaps with a hint of boredom in its now fluent, human, English-language voice. "I hope you don't mind that we used various telepathic devices to access more of your language."

"Mind?" Larry said with a slightly hysterical lilt to his voice. "You answered my SETI request; you justified my theories! You'll make me famous. How can I mind?"

"To be honest," the purple holo admitted. "You got lucky. Your broadcast got picked up by one of the dual-capacity drones that happened to be passing by your solar system."

"Since it fit the algorithms, it was re-transmitted via tachyon broadcast to the next receiver, then reviewed and sent on and on. Finally, it reached the Library of the Center for the Intergalactic Community of Compatible Minds. I applied for and got the commission to investigate the source of this interesting broadcast."

"Wow," Mike said. "How did Larry here win the universe lottery? It sounds like not every broadcast gets investigated."

"You're right about that," the holo said. "You have no idea how many intelligent life forms there are in the universe. Most, however, die out before they reach a level of development that enables them to communicate beyond their local galaxy."

"And the rest?" Mike asked.

"That still leaves way too many to investigate," the holo said. "You can't imagine how many dull mathematical treatises there are out there, plodding away from their respective planets at the speed of light. Read one, and you have read them all. Your music, on the other hand, was unique and pleasurable to experience. Your species is interesting enough to investigate."

For a few seconds, Mike was overwhelmed. Then, his business sense set in. "I happen to have just opened a hotel here on top of Olympus Mons," he said. It could be an ideal rendezvous for our species, yours, and any other visitors. What can I do to make accommodations here comfortable for you?"

The holo laughed. "Yes," it said. "One of your ditties did mention taking care of business. Our ship can't land here, but that area opposite the telescopes would be spacious enough for one of our shuttlecraft. We aren't all that picky about housing, but you will have to make some adjustments. There are temperature and air pressure variations you will need to compensate for."

"Hmm," Mike said. "There is probably no good time to bring this up, but building this hotel has produced certain cash flow challenges for me."

"Yes, yes," the holo said. "We got that from your memories. You'll discover that most intelligent species in the universe aren't deadbeats. I would suggest that we give you the formula and technical drawings for the universal translator, and in return, you guarantee us unlimited, suitable accommodations in your hotel."

"Making this a meeting place for many different intelligent species is an admirable idea," the holo said. "As soon as you are ready, you can let me know, and I'll post your location at the Intergalactic Library. Others have tried and failed at such an endeavor, but I have the feeling you might succeed."

"I have the formula for a universal translator in my communicator," Larry yelped.

"Send it on to me," Mike said. "I'll give it to Ned, and he can cough up the credits to remodel this hotel to accommodate all extraterrestrial visitors. I have the feeling that many people from Mars and Earth will want to spend time here and meet the visitors."

"It indeed could turn out to be a profitable exchange of ideas for all concerned," the holo said. "You will just need to create edibles and potables that all kinds of creatures will enjoy consuming. Having physiological energy needs satisfied in an amiable ambiance tends to foster mutual communication and appreciation."

"That, fortunately, will be no problem," Mike said. "I just have to talk a certain capable cafeteria lady into taking over my bar and restaurant. If she refuses, I'll get her brother to talk her into it."

"Then a few members of my crew and I will land our shuttle craft on your launch pad, and we can continue our conversation in person," the holo said. "This could indeed be the beginning of an inter-species relationship, beneficial to all involved."

Mike sat at his desk with the best view from the original hotel on top of Olympus Mons. He now had similar hotels on top of all the Martian mountains and was bargaining for information about other locations in the nearby asteroid belt.

So far, three hundred different alien species from various galaxies had vacationed in one of his hotels. They had paid for their accommodations with formulas for faster-than-light travel, time travel, energy-efficient transmutation of elements, and other nifty toys.

Larry had taken over negotiations. It turned out that he had a talent for conflict-free communication with truly alien life forms. Mike got better and better at persuading Ned to spend money he got from the use of the aliens' formulas on Mike's next dreams.

But it was still impossible to keep the Martian dust out of the structures. Not even the most advanced alien scientists could manage that miracle.

THE LEGEND OF THE ELGRULL

by Murray Eiland

"Grandpa, tell me again about the Elgrull?" Shiloh asked, tucked up to her chin, cozy in bed.

"Again?" Grandpa chuckled, "My, you really like that story, don't you?"

"Yeah! Something about it just makes me feel all warm and tingly."

Grandpa chuckled again, tussling the hair of his nine-year-old granddaughter. "Well, I can't deny you your favorite story, not right before bed, anyway."

"Yay!"

"Alright, little one, where should I begin?"

Shiloh kicked her feet under her blankets excitedly. "With the poem!"

Grandpa adjusted his glasses as he grabbed the well-read book from the shelf. "Ah, the poem! A great starting point, little one."

"I love the poem!"

"I know you do," Grandpa said, sitting on the soft, plushy bedside ottoman. "You know, I bet I've read this poem to you so many times that you could probably recite it word for word without any help from the book. What do you think?"

Shiloh puckered out her bottom lip and thought about it. Her big green eyes reeled as she recalled the poetic verses in her mind. "I think I can."

"Yeah? Well, I know you can," he smiled warmly. "Go ahead, give it a try."

Shiloh thought some more, making sure she had the verses right in her head before beginning. "Okay, here it goes…"

THE LEGEND OF THE ELGRULL

"The Elgrull dwell in cosmic deep,
A brilliant race, with stars they bind,
They harnessed light where shadows creep,
A marvel born of wondrous mind.

They searched across the distant skies,
From galaxy to planet far,
Their hearts alive with dreams that rise,
Yet all they found was a silent scar.

Through endless space and waves of time,
They roamed but found no life to share,
The void was vast; their hopes would climb,
Yet only darkness answered there.

No brothers met their wandering eyes,
No kindred souls to greet or find,
Their quest brought only mournful cries,
And left them far from peace of mind.

They ventured on, with spirits drained,
A cold truth dawned as they explored,
Their pride had led them, hope now strained,
Into the void where dreams were stored.

The light that once had sparked their flight,
Grew dim as hunger turned to greed,
Yet in the dark, they saw the light—
Their world was all they truly need.

Now round their star, a ring lies still,
A monument to dreams once bold,
A warning of the urge to fill
The empty space with hearts to hold.

The Elgrull now look deep within,
Their minds unchained from conquest's call,
They find the beauty there to spin,
A universe where none must fall.

No longer bound by need to reign,
They build new worlds within their soul,
In endless realms where love remains,
They find, at last, their truest goal."

"Bravo, little one! Bravo!" Grandpa cheered quietly, trying not to wake Grandma, who was in bed in the next room.

"Did I get it all right?"

"You did! It was beautiful! Great work, Shiloh!"

"Thanks!" The small girl snuggled proudly into her bed. "Okay, I think I'm ready for the story now."

"You got it. But since it's late, and this is a very long book, let's do the condensed version tonight, deal?"

"Deal! I'm a little sleepy anyway."

"Okay, let's begin…" And so Grandpa started at the beginning.

"Long before the Elgrull ever reached the stars, they were a prosperous civilization on a planet known as Astra'lon. It orbited a radiant, azure star called Imedi, and it was full of lush, vibrant plant life. The culture of the Elgrull was built on intellect, innovation, and exploration, driven by an insatiable curiosity to unlock the mysteries of the cosmos."

"But how did they get there?" Shiloh interrupted.

"Well, you see, long before the Elgrull, there existed two ancient cosmic gods: Arik, the mighty god of rock, and his sister, Kira, the radiant goddess of life. They were not like the gods of mortal stories, bound to planets or lands. Arik was as large as the planets themselves, while Kira, though delicate and human-sized, wielded power over the forces of nature.

Together, they drifted through the endless void of space, weaving the fabric of creation. Arik, with his enormous hands, would collect the swirling debris of the cosmos—asteroids, space dust, and molten rock. Then, he compressed these materials, shaping them into planets. His body was immense, more significant than the very worlds he created. His skin was like obsidian and iron, glistening under the light of newborn stars, and wherever he ventured, great clouds of space rock and debris followed him like a loyal dog.

As Arik traveled the galaxies, his touch would heat the fragments of space he gathered. The molten rock in his hands would glow brightly, and he would forge worlds of every shape and size. Some were smooth and round, others jagged and uneven, like the chiseled edge of an abandoned sculpture.

Kira, his sister, was his counterbalance. Where Arik's touch was hard and unyielding, hers was soft, a brush of life in the vast silence of space. When Arik formed a new planet, it was barren and cold, but Kira would drift alongside him, observing each creation meticulously. Though small compared to her colossal brother, Kira had a presence larger than the cosmos itself.

When she arrived at a newly formed planet, Kira would first walk its surface, her feet barely making a sound as they touched the rock. In the early stages, all the planets were unremarkable – an empty world of stone and silence – but Kira had an intuitive sense. The planets would speak to her, not with words, but with their energy. Each one had its own voice, its own rhythm, a kind of music that only Kira could hear.

If a planet resonated with her – if she found something appealing in the color of its sky, the temperature of its surface, the vibe it gave off, or the way the stars shimmered in the distant sky – Kira would smile, knowing that this world was worthy of life.

'This one,' she would say softly, her voice a melody that reverberated through all of space, 'This one has potential.'

And then, she would begin her dance.

On the barren soil of the planet, Kira's frolic was more than a series of hypnotically graceful movements – it was creation itself. With every step, the rock began to change. She would leap into the air, twirling beautifully, and where her feet landed, life was destined to stir.

Her breath served as the wind, her arms outstretched as though embracing the world, and from the tips of her fingers, the first seeds would fall. Where there had been nothing but rock and dust moments before, tiny green shoots began to push through the cracks in the soil. As she spun, flowers bloomed, their petals stretching toward the warmth of the newborn sun. Trees unfurled their leaves, growing taller with each step.

Kira's favorite part of the dance was the creation of animals. She would close her eyes and feel the pulse of the planet, the rhythm of its potential life, and with a soft exhale, the creatures of the land would appear. Insects buzzed around the new plants, fish filled the rivers she created with a flick of her wrist, and soon larger animals, from graceful deer to majestic winged creatures, suddenly had a place to call home.

This process took a very long time, but to Kira and Arik, age was meaningless. The dance was a gift from Kira to the planet, a gift of life and beauty, and once her work was done, the once-lifeless rock would be teeming with vibrant ecosystems. The air would fill with the sounds of chirping birds, the rustling of trees, and the calls of animals exploring their new home.

But despite the majesty she breathed into these worlds, Kira and Arik never stayed on one space rock too long. Their purpose was not to oversee the growth of life but to create it and move on. Arik, silent and stoic, would nod approvingly as he watched the transformation, his enormous form casting a shadow over the planet. Then, without a word, he would collect the space debris once more and move on to the next creation, leaving the newly formed world in Kira's wake.

It was on one of these creations, countless eons later, that the Elgrull would emerge. Despite Astra'lon not being the first planet, it was the first one with highly intelligent life. Born from the dance of Kira, the Elgrull would rise as a civilization with a hunger for discovery. But the Elgrull, unlike the gods who created their world, would struggle with their place in the universe, seeking answers to questions that even the gods themselves had never bothered to ask — or even conceive, for the matter."

"Kira sounds so cool! I wish I could have cool powers like her." Shiloh's eyes glowed warmly at the thought.

"She's one of my favorites in this story, too," Grandpa chuckled. "Now, Astra'lon was a verdant planet, rich with towering bioluminescent trees and crystal-clear seas that glowed under their star's light. There were even small plants called pondpoppers that gave off light in all the planet's waterways, giving the illusion of stars in the rivers, lakes, and oceans. The Elgrull believed deeply in balance — between technology and the natural world, between progress and tradition.

At the heart of Astra'lon lay the Lumasphere, a central hub of their civilization. It was a gleaming tower that stretched toward the bright, indigo sky. The Lumasphere was the very symbol of their brilliance, their proudest moment, and their crowning achievement. It was the center of governance and research, and at its very top floor was a council of the greatest minds of the Elgrull, known as the Oracles. The Oracles guided the Elgrull's endeavors, always pushing them to explore beyond the known realms. This was not easy because in the early days, the technology was not there. The first few attempts to become space-bound failed miserably, and there were dozens of casualties. Fortunately for the Elgrull, it didn't take long after that to perfect their intergalactic travel technology. After ten generations, the Elgrull civilization finally reached space.

Now, as for the Oracles, they possessed a unique ability — they could live forever, as evolution decided this was the best way to guide the masses, with a solid, unchanging voice.

"But Grandpa, how did someone become an Oracle? If they could all just live forever, wouldn't all the Elgrulls try to become one?" Shiloh asked.

"Did you forget, little one? The only way to become an Oracle is to be born one. And the way you could tell if someone was destined to be one of the chosen was if they came into the world with a gemstone on their forehead."

Shiloh reached up and traced her fingers across her head, feeling the outline of a cold stone she had felt many times before. "Like mine?"

Grandpa adjusted his glasses and pretended to study the ruby-colored gem in his granddaughter's forehead. Of course, he knew what it was. "Now, I'm no expert, mind you, but my money would say that it's pretty darn close."

"Really?"

"Sure!" Grandpa winked. "Now, one of the greatest Oracles was Orin Luxo, an ambitious leader whose vision stretched beyond Astra'lon. His dreams lay among the stars, and he believed that their destiny was to unite with other sentient beings that may be out there, somewhere in the vast cosmos.

One day, as the Oracles convened under the shimmering dome of the Lumasphere, Orin Luxo rose to address the council. His passion-filled voice echoed through the chamber, commanding the attention of all his peers.

'My fellow Oracles,' he said, 'we have reached the limits of our knowledge on Astra'lon. Our people hunger for more than this world can offer. It is time to reach beyond the stars, not just in exploration, but to find others like us who may share in our quest for enlightenment!'

Some Oracles nodded in agreement, while others frowned. One among them, Sira Nyx, voiced her concerns.

'Orin, we must be cautious. The universe is vast, and the unknown is dangerous. What if we search for eons and find nothing? Will we lose ourselves in the darkness?'

But Orin's decision had been made, and the majority of the Oracles agreed with him. He believed that the Elgrull were destined for greater things, and their destiny lay not in isolation but in communion with other life. He convinced the council to commit to the project that would define their legacy: The Ark Initiative.

The Ark was the biggest technological achievement of the Elgrull since the inception of the Lumasphere a few centuries earlier. The colossal spacecraft was designed to not only carry their civilization's hopes across the stars but also act as a home that could sustain them for centuries at a time. Unlike the sleek vessels of popular imagination, the Ark was a fortress — a self-contained world that mirrored the security of a vault. Its construction was as much a protective shield as a means of transport. The Elgrulls' finest architects and engineers crafted its structure, infusing it with the newest technology.

From the outside, the ship appeared almost monolithic, with massive reinforced walls layered in thick metal plates. Its exterior was built to withstand the harshest cosmic conditions, from meteoric impacts to radiation storms. Within its walls was the essence of their sun, a unique energy source that glowed with ethereal light, providing the Ark with power as it set out on its journey through the cold void of space.

The interior was meticulously designed, with the ship divided into sections. Upon entering the main corridor, the Ark's immense size gave way to an entire city that had been masterfully constructed within the ship.

The living quarters were organized into block-like neighborhoods designed for long-term habitation. Each block was a compact, efficient space, with rooms stacked on top of each other in a honeycomb-like formation. The lower floors housed the essential facilities: power plants, water systems, and agricultural hubs. The latter mimicked the natural world the Elgrull left behind, with rows of crops growing under artificial sunlight designed to sustain life for generations.

At the heart of the Ark was the central control hub, a technology-laden chamber illuminated by a circular array of shimmering blue screens and holo-projectors. This was the nerve center where the Elgrull space captains monitored every function of the ship. It was a place of both control and observation, with scientists and engineers constantly analyzing the Ark's trajectory, energy output, and search for any signs of life outside its steel hull. Another fascinating aspect of the control hub is that it allowed the Elgrull to continue advancing their sciences and studies, helping them evolve intelligently over the years as they continued their travels.

Throughout the ship, there were layers upon layers of hidden rooms, each with a specific function. Some were designated for scientific experimentation, while others housed cultural relics and preserved elements of their society. The deepest levels were the most secure, reserved for the Ark's vast archives — knowledge banks and historical records, the cumulative wisdom of their race stored in crystalline data cores. This section was also home to the Oracles.

In the event of a disaster, the ship was designed to seal off sections to protect its inhabitants, much like the massive blast doors that could close off entire corridors. It was a self-sustaining world within itself, capable of protecting its passengers for lifetimes if necessary. Every inch of the Ark had been designed with survival in mind, ensuring that the Elgrull could not only survive their journey across the stars but also thrive."

"You never told me if they had any disasters, Grandpa."

"Oh, I'm sure they had a few close calls, but fortunately for the ancient Elgrull, the Ark was like a floating stronghold, and it provided them with a lot of protection. With their grand expedition underway, the stars were the limit. Orin Luxo, ever the visionary, led the first fleet himself. Sira Nyx, though skeptical, did her best not to let her fears overpower her curiosity."

'I'll be your shadow, Orin,' Sira said, 'To remind you of the darkness you've chosen to ignore.'

For years, the Elgrull searched. They traveled across galaxies, charting stars and planets. They encountered barren worlds, gas giants, and stars of every color and size. Yet, despite their tireless efforts, they found no sentient life. Only silence greeted them in the void.

As time wore on, the mood among the explorers began to change, and tensions started to rise. Orin Luxo, the man once filled with boundless optimism, was now burdened with the reality of their failure... *his failure.* Despite many sharing his views, he'd forever be remembered as the one who proposed such an odyssey.

'We are alone in the universe,' Orin whispered one night as he stood before the ship's viewport, staring into the black abyss. 'All of this...*space...* and we are alone.'

The Elgrulls' search stretched for generations. New leaders and captains rose to take the mantle, and their missions grew more desperate. The Oracles were at a loss. Of the thirteen of them, only two ever truly proposed direction for their people. Orin Luxo, who wanted to find other intelligent life and unite with them, and Sira Nyx, who wanted to focus on laying down roots and growing civilization.

Some of the people on Ark felt that the Elgrull were the pinnacle of life in the universe, destined to rule over all. This was a new and radical way of thinking, and it was quickly picking up steam with the newer generations. For the first time in their existence, the Oracles feared they may soon be facing a mutiny. In a bid to salvage the mission and sanity aboard the Ark, the Oracles greenlit a new objective – planetary manipulation, turning lifeless worlds into reflections of Astra'lon — in other words, trying to play gods."

"Like Arik and Kira?" Shiloh asked.

"Precisely."

"Hey! You know what I just noticed?" Shiloh exclaimed.

"What's that, little one?"

"Arik and Kira's names are each other spelled backward!"

Grandpa had to think about it for a minute, but she was right. Arik backward spelled Kira and vice versa. "Well, would you look at that..."

"I know! Cool, huh?" Shiloh smiled. "Okay, you can continue, Grandpa!"

"Sira Nyx saw the folly in this playing god-like ambition. She had become a quiet observer, watching as the dream she never supported turned into a nightmare.

'We have truly lost our way,' Sira said one day, speaking to the new generation of captains and leaders. 'In our search for others, we have forgotten who we are. The universe owes us nothing. It is we who must find our place within it, not bend it to our will.'

But her words fell on deaf ears.

Eventually, the Elgrull realized that their pride had led them astray, but this realization wouldn't hit them until years later when the Ark was nearly out of survival supplies. The counter of livable days aboard the space vessel ticked down to fourteen — two weeks left before their livable cosmic habitat would become a colossal tomb, floating aimlessly through the galactic expanse of nowhere in particular. To make matters worse, their efforts to reshape the universe had caused massive destruction and a few casualties. Worlds that they had tried to terraform collapsed into ruin.

It was another Oracle, Veraan Pac, who finally acknowledged the truth and offered a solution.

'We must return home,' Veraan declared, standing before the masses. 'We have pushed too far, lost too much. Our future lies not in conquest or control but in understanding ourselves. Sira Nyx is right...she's been right all along.'

Everyone looked to Orin Luxo, but he didn't say a word. He nodded in agreement, then hung his head in shame. The Elgrull, once driven by boundless ambition, now found themselves following a new mission as they began their humbling journey back to Astra'lon. The Ark, once a beacon of pride that held the promise of progress — now seemed more like a colossal prison of their own making.

To make their dwindling resources last a little longer, the Elgrull carefully chose which parts of their ship to turn off. They started by shutting down all the fun and leisure areas: the virtual reality rooms, holo-theaters, and gyms went dark. The long-range communication tools and satellite links, which were no longer needed, were also turned off.

Next, they dimmed the lights in the less important parts of the Ark, like the unused hallways and storage rooms. The defense systems, including lasers and shields, were powered down since they had never encountered a threat. They turned off experimental machines and lab tools that weren't crucial for their immediate survival. The repair drones and systems that fixed minor issues were paused, focusing only on the most critical repairs that were deemed necessary by the Oracles and engineers themselves.

In the empty cabins and kitchens, they cut off heating and ventilation, saving every bit of energy they could. But the Elgrull knew which systems were essential and kept those running. They made sure the life support systems were fully operational, keeping the air clean and water pure. The medical facilities stayed powered up, ready to handle any emergencies. The food production systems continued to grow and synthesize the food they needed to survive.

They also kept the navigation and guidance systems on, ensuring the ship could still steer safely through the stars. The energy core regulation systems stayed active to prevent any overheating and to maintain a steady power supply. Minimal emergency lighting was turned on, just enough to help them move around and monitor the critical controls.

By carefully managing their power, the Elgrull were able to extend their survival by three to four years, which was a godsend compared to the two weeks they had. The only problem was that Astra'lon was five years away.

It wasn't without peril, but they managed to make it back to the Imedi solar system they hailed from, with no food and less than three days' worth of water and oxygen. As they prepared to land on their home planet, the Elgrull braced themselves for a world none of them, aside from the Oracles, remembered. But what they found was not the world they had left behind. In their absence, they found people — others like them — who never left, a secret organization formed by Sira Nyx many generations earlier that even she had almost forgotten about. One hundred people stayed behind, unbeknownst to the other Oracles, with the hopes of keeping their homeworld safe. It wasn't much, but Sira Nyx's hands were tied with what she could safely get away with to avoid anyone finding out about her 'plan B.' During the absence of the Ark, those who stayed behind not only survived but flourished. Their civilization had taken a different path, one of quiet introspection and growth. Instead of chasing the mysteries of the cosmos, the people turned their focus inward, immersing themselves in art, philosophy, and the endless depths of their own consciousness and culture.

The Ark, once hailed as the pinnacle of their technological achievements, was now seen as a relic of a forgotten era. Monuments existed to tell its story, of a time when the Elgrull believed they could bend the universe to their will.

Among the returning Elgrull, Orin Luxo, the Oracle who had once championed the quest for cosmic connection, stood humbled after seeing the universe's indifference firsthand.

'We left to conquer the stars,' he began, 'but we have learned that the greatest journey is not one that takes us far from home. The universe is vast, yes — more immense than we could ever have imagined — but we are but a small part of it. We sought to reshape the cosmos, to leave our mark upon the stars, but we forgot the most important truth: before we can understand the universe, we must understand ourselves.' Shortly after, Sira Nyx wrote the poem, and Orin Luxo hoped her words would help define their civilization.

To mark the lessons they learned, the Elgrull that remained shut down the great ring that encircled their sun, Imedi. This ring was once used to harness the light emitted by their sun for their burgeoning industries. While it was required to build the Ark, the planet no longer required that level of power. Those that returned also appreciated it is a monument, one that cannot and should not be ignored. It is now known as The Dark Halo, a symbol of their journey — once filled with the light of their ambition, now a monument to their humility.

The Elgrull no longer looked to the stars with the same hunger. Their focus now shifted inward to the worlds they held within themselves — where the possibilities were just as infinite. They began to craft not physical realms, but vast landscapes of the mind. Entire cities, landscapes, and oceans were built in their imaginations, places where they could explore the beauty of existence without needing to dominate or reshape the external universe. They created symphonies of thought, paintings made from dreams, and philosophies that stretched beyond the limits of physical reality. In doing so, they found a new sense of purpose — one rooted not in conquest but in connection with their own inner worlds.

The Elgrull embraced the beauty of their existence, no longer seeking to control or conquer the stars, but to understand and celebrate the unique place they held in the cosmos. They realized that, in their quest for the infinite, they had overlooked the infinite within themselves — their creativity, their ability to dream, and the endless mysteries of their own hearts and minds.

"Thank you, Grandpa," Shiloh yawned. "I love hearing that story."

"Well, I love telling it to you." Grandpa stood up and stretched, offering his granddaughter a kiss on the forehead.

"Goodnight, Grandpa."

"Goodnight, my little Shilo Nyx."

LAUNCH DAY

by Brian Gibson

"It's Launch Day!"

The exclamation, declared in the sonorous, feminine voice of the *Annie Jump* station's sentience Cannon, sounded in Doctor Bartholomew Simms' head and roused him from his sleep. It was followed immediately by the first of his Launch Day musical selections, ensuring that he wouldn't simply drift back away into dreams. He tried to issue the mental command that would silence the bombastic tones ringing through his head before remembering that he'd set it so that he'd have to physically touch the command screen on the opposite side of the sleep chamber. It was his way of making sure he actually got up.

Today, however, despite the excitement keeping him up half the night, was not a day when he needed the extra incentive. It was, after all, Launch Day!

He found himself humming along to the music in his head as he carefully disentangled himself from his spouses and undid the Velcro straps that held them suspended in the sleeping harness. Despite his efforts not to disturb them – as director of the launch, he needed to get the earliest start of the three – Abby muttered quietly and reached out to take his hand before he could kick away from the wall.

"Leaving already, Barry?" she muttered, her eyelids barely fluttering open as a sleepy smile spread over her face. Barry grasped a nearby anchor hold with his elongated toes to steady himself in the zero-gravity environment and placed an affectionate hand gently against her cheek. He could easily make out her face in the nearly lightless room, thanks to the vision enhancements that were now pretty much the norm amongst the portion of humanity living in the various artificial habitats spread throughout the solar system. Abby's smile broadened a little, and she met his gaze with eyes so brown they were nearly black, peering out from beneath the transparent, chitinous membrane that would protect them in the event of a loss of station pressure. He knew that she would be seeing the same feature guarding his own dark eyes, though neither of them took much notice of it after all these years.

"Shhhhh," he hissed in response. "You'll wake Kris."

His eyes flickered toward the androgynous third in their family unit, picking out the dark skin of their face where it was visible above the sleeping harness. Their eyes were closed, but their mouth was wide open as they emitted faint snores in their sleep. Barry chuckled a little at his own joke; when they were this deeply asleep, you could run an engine test in the next room without waking Kris.

The song in his head finished, and the next one started with a blast of brasses. He must have started a bit because Abby chuckled and murmured, "Go ahead and turn off your alarm, sweetie."

Barry brushed her cheek with a light kiss and kicked off from the wall. He drifted across the sleeping chamber to the far bulkhead, where he brought himself to a stop with the unconscious ease born of years of living in the weightless environment of the *Annie Jump* station. Taking hold of one of the rails ubiquitous in the station's design, he tapped out his manual password on the touchscreen by the hatch and touched one of the icons on the home screen. The concert in his head came to an abrupt end.

Even so, he was still nodding his head to the memory of the tune as he maneuvered himself into the shower chamber. Calling it a "shower chamber" was a bit of a joke since free-flowing water in weightlessness was kind of a terrible idea. The chamber was just a small cylinder that provided the privacy and amenities to give himself a sponge bath and apply a bit of rinseless shampoo before starting his day. Spaceborne hygiene had improved somewhat over the generations of humanity's spread through the solar system, but some problems had thus far evaded elegant solutions.

Nonetheless, he managed his morning routine with a minimum of fuss and was out in the residential corridor before Kris or Abby had begun to stir.

The hallway was brightly lit, lined on either side by hatches that opened into other living quarters. In this part of the station, most of them would be family units belonging to senior members of the development team, so the doors were a little more distantly spaced than other, similar districts. But not by much; enclosed, pressurized, and climate-controlled space was always at a premium.

The "ceiling" and "floor" of the corridor – that is to say, the walls not occupied by doors – featured regularly spaced, ergonomically rounded hand- and footholds that occupants could use to control their motion. With the ease of long practice, Barry oriented himself in the direction of the station hub and propelled himself forward with a single strong pull that sent him sailing down the corridor. He was in the zone this morning and reached the end of the hall without so much as having to touch a wall for course correction.

He reached the hub in a matter of seconds, where he caught hold and brought himself to a stop with the ring of handholds installed at the threshold for that purpose. There, he looked out over a rarity in the various space habitats of the solar system: open habitable space.

The central hub of this residential section, where all the residential corridors converged in an open cylinder about fifty meters across and two hundred long, was considered a wonder of modern space architecture. The perimeter was pierced at regular intervals by residential corridors like the one from which Barry had just emerged, sprinkled a bit more sparsely at the end where the station administrators and their families lived in their comparatively larger quarters. Between the rings of corridors, hydroponic gardens filled the space with welcome green, and no small amount of its oxygen needs. The gardens were also the source of the habitat's unofficial nickname, Peppertown, for the green peppers that were their specialty. Both ends of the cylinder featured clear, reinforced domes that could be shaded to various degrees to admit just the right amount of sunlight. The space was crisscrossed with high-strength tethers that residents and visitors could use to traverse the concourse or hold themselves in place.

It was a popular pastime among the youth of the station to start at one end of a residential corridor and, using the handholds in the walls, build up as much speed as they could to launch themselves out into the concourse like bullets from a gun barrel. Fortunately, at this early hour of the station "day," no one was up to those kinds of shenanigans. A quiet few people were drifting up and down the cylinder by ones and twos, a scant cross-section of the solar system's many kinds of humans. Out in the middle, another Station-born like himself, with his long, spindly limbs and prehensile toes, was helping a Martian make his clumsy way through the web of tethers. The Martian, squat by Station-born standards, was nonetheless lanky in comparison to the trio of Earthlings making their cautious way along the cylinder wall nearly on the opposite side from Barry. A lone woman, her skin the characteristic shimmery blue of the people adapted for Titan's icy surface, was making her slow way to the lock leading to the corridor that connected Peppertown to the working portions of the station. In her case, the slowness of her movements wasn't due to an excess of caution but rather the slower metabolism that helped her people conserve energy on their heat-starved moon.

Barry launched himself out into space toward the web of tethers with the intent of heading for the same lock. As he drifted toward the first line, a faint ping sounded in his head, indicating that Cannon wished to open communications.

"Go ahead, Cannon," he cast in response, his implants rendering the communication as simple as thought.

"Good morning, Doctor Simms. Heading into the office?"

"Yes, indeed, Can. How're the boards looking this morning?"

"All green. We had an instability in the magnetic bottle overnight, but the third shift teams got it sorted." At the same time, Cannon gave him a visual overlay of the status summary. He gave it a quick look over as his hands and feet did the almost unconscious work of navigating the station's webwork. At the last second, he altered his release from the final tether to send him sailing toward the other lock, the one to the outside.

"Do you want me to show her to you, Doctor Simms?"

"No, Cannon, I'm gonna see her with my own eyes."

A command issued through his implants to the airlock controls had them opening at his approach, and he slipped neatly down the center of the short corridor lined with pressure suits and into the lock beyond. He landed against the outer door, gripping the holds with his toes to keep from rebounding and keying the inner door to close behind him. A moment later, the air began cycling out of the lock, and dedicated muscles in Barry's ear canals and trachea sealed them off to keep internal gasses contained and prevent his eardrums from rupturing.

Barry released the outer lock door and braced himself before issuing the command to open the outer door. When it cycled open, he easily held himself against being tossed out into the void as the minuscule amount of air that the pumps hadn't managed to extract from the lock escaped out into space. A moment later, Barry Simms followed.

The exterior of *Annie Jump* station, much like the cylinder Barry had just left, was webbed in a network of tethers and handholds that enabled residents and maintenance crews to reach any point on its surface with relative ease and safety. Barry navigated with the unconscious ease of long familiarity. Even though he'd lived all his life with it, he still felt a thrill of awe at the vast reach of stars surrounding him in all directions.

On this side of the station, the shining arch of the Milky Way dominated his field of view, visible with a clarity and grandeur that no planet-bound observation could hope to match. As always, Barry was momentarily captivated by the display of light that had traveled untold billions of miles to reach his eyes. The product of generations of genetic modification and cybernetic enhancement that enabled them to drift without any barrier between them and the vacuum of space, the Station-born could immerse themselves in the environment as no other branch of humanity could.

But today, even that awe-inspiring beauty couldn't hold his attention for long. It was Launch Day, after all, and his anxious attention soon sought out the ship cradled in the vast scaffold beyond the station's office complex.

The tube connecting Peppertown to the operations module cut a line through the starfield view to his left, studded with handholds, tethers, conduits, and even the occasional maintenance tech or drone making their way along the surface. At the far end, it joined about a half dozen similar tubes that radiated from the convex arc of the command center. The shipyard scaffold beyond was cupped in the concave side, spanning outward to form a latticework tunnel open at the far end.

In that lattice hung the work of Bartholomew Simms' professional career. Cradled there was the dream of generations of humanity in all its forms: the *Sojourner* – humankind's very first interstellar spacecraft.

Aside from her scale – she clocked in at over two hundred meters long and about half that wide – the *Sojourner* wasn't much to look at. She was bounded at midships by a circular ring, while a pair of elliptical rings ran front to rear, intersecting each other at the craft's nose and stern at right angles. These housed the machinery that generated the spatial distortion which would allow the *Sojourner* to circumvent the usual speed limit of the universe, and the entirety of the rest of the ship was suspended by a network of buttresses within their bounds. The overall effect was as if someone had sketched a perspective line drawing of an egg surrounding a spaceship.

A central spine connecting the forward and aft ends of the egg served as the core of the ship's structure. The bridge was located at the forward end, just inside the junction of the elliptical rings, so that the observation portals could afford a view between them. It was arranged in a cylinder around the central spine, and beyond it, the structure swelled outward to accommodate crew quarters and the massive reactors on which the FTL field depended. At the far aft, occluded from Barry's view by the bulk of the midship equipment, were the main thruster cones, carefully positioned to avoid scouring the rings with their exhaust. She was dotted along her length with all manner of sensors to collect data on her performance and environment during her voyages – data that would be used to refine and perfect the first generation of deep space exploration vessels that would one day follow.

Barry hung suspended in space, secured only by his toe grip on the handle outside the airlock, a faint smile playing on his lips until Cannon's voice broke into his reverie. "Better get moving, Doctor Simms, if you're going to make it by this route."

Barry blinked. "Yes, of course, Cannon. Right, as always!" Barry kicked off from the airlock on a trajectory that followed the corridor toward Operations, using the various guy wires and handholds along the way to make minute course corrections and add to his velocity. Crossing the void in this way was best accomplished as quickly and efficiently as possible; even engineered as his body was to withstand the rigors of vacuum, there were limits to how long he could go without oxygen to replenish what he metabolized. Nobody who lived in such an unforgiving environment wanted to push those limits unnecessarily.

When, at last, he completed the transit and made use of the last guy wire to flip himself over and absorb the impact with his legs, he was moving at a good enough clip that his knees protested at being asked to counter so much velocity.

From there, it was just a matter of a few minutes to pull himself over to the Operations Module airlock and cycle himself through. As soon as he was inside, his breathing resumed, and his body set to work replenishing his oxygen reserves while purging the carbon dioxide that had built up during his extravehicular activity.

Moments later, he was sailing through one of the hatches into the Ops Center, which was spread across the station's concave face where it cupped around the front of the *Sojourner*. The bulkhead there was almost entirely transparent, allowing the kind of direct observation that humans seemed to crave despite the fact that the station's cameras and sensors could provide far more detailed views than the unaided eye could ever hope to do.

Since Barry had arrived early, Ops was sparsely populated, with only the overnight crew supervising the last-minute preparations. With the status display still active in his vision, he could tell he wouldn't be interrupting anything needing urgent attention when he broadcast a "Happy Launch Day!" to everyone in view.

"Happy Launch Day!" the ragged chorus came back — some over the implant, but some from people turning toward him and calling out with their actual voices.

Barry caught himself on one of the handholds studding the "ceiling" of the ops center, arresting his momentum short of the window right next to the commander's station.

"Morning, Enele!" he grinned at the night shift supervisor. "How's my baby been behaving for you?"

"That's 'Commander Fuimaono' to you, Simms." His tone was severe, but the flash of white teeth as the huge man occupying the supervisor's chair struggled to suppress a smile gave the lie to it. "And the *Sojourner* is purring like a kitten!" He assumed the Earth expression meant a good thing; he'd never seen or heard a kitten in person.

"Then it's Doctor Simms to you!"

They shared a laugh that briefly undercut the subtle air of tension in the command center, brought on by a keen awareness of the importance of the day. Not long after shift change, one of humankind's most momentous adventures would launch, and nobody wanted an error on their shift to be the cause of any delay, abort, or disaster.

Over the next hour, Barry kept a close eye on the status board while he listened in on communications between the various support operations and the technical teams still on the ship. They had spent the shift going over every inch of the ship and making sure each system was operating at peak. Every hatch and access panel was closed, and every loose item was secured. When the crew arrived, they would find everything ready for them.

While that was going on, Barry reflected on the long road that had brought humanity to this point. The struggle upward, from scratching an existence out of the Earth with what resources they could find, to the painstaking build-up of the tools to master and expand their environment across the planet. The slow emergence from superstition and ignorance to a more genuine understanding of the workings of the universe. The painful, oh, so painful, lessons in how to accept each other in all of humanity's many forms.

That last lesson was one that seemed to need to be learned over and over. The expansion into the solar system had been a bit of a crisis point. At the same time that the need to adapt to increasingly hostile environments was multiplying the diversity of the species, the growing vulnerability of habitats throughout the system in the face of the forces they were harnessing massively increased the pressure to get it right. Not even Mother Earth itself was safe from attacks launched from the ultimate high ground.

They hadn't always succeeded, and millions of people had died as a result. Vacuum-blasted habitats on Luna and Ganymede, drifting hulks of stations throughout the Asteroid Belt, and even the massive craters where San Francisco and Rome used to be stood as mute witness to the difficulty of the lesson. So did memorials to the millions lost in rounds of purges carried out by those who refused to accept the changes.

But they had persevered. They had tamed the Solar system (for the most part). They had taken new forms, learned acceptance, created new societies and new families, and finally figured out that when any number of people had the ability to wipe out civilization, the only choice was to get along.

Well, that or extinction. But thankfully, they'd so far managed to go the other way.

In many ways, the last few generations represented a new Golden Age. As humanity increasingly freed itself from the shackles of planetary existence, the opportunities and challenges of the new environments fueled advances in biology, computing, and physics that led to the present day. The human form was becoming increasingly malleable, with changes on the genetic level now possible for adult subjects to make adaptations for environmental, medical, and even aesthetic purposes. Brain-computer interfaces had advanced to the point of nigh instantaneous data transfer (give or take the relativistic distances sometimes involved) and real-time sensory augmentation.

But what was dearest to Barry's heart was the way physics and engineering had advanced. Abundant fusion energy made traversing the Solar System (relatively) easy, with mere weeks separating the rings of

Saturn from the seas of Earth.

With the *Sojourner*, and the ships that would one day follow, perhaps mere weeks could separate the yellow light of Sol from the red light of Proxima Centauri. Making that happen had been the focus of Barry's career since the day forty-two years ago when Dr. Allison Tadesse of the Titania Technical Institute announced confirmation of the field effect that made it possible to move macroscopic objects faster than the speed of light.

His ruminations were interrupted by the chime for the shift change and the sudden bustle of activity that it presaged. People of every stripe (in some cases, literally) began to enter the command center, exchanging greetings with their counterparts. The outward expressions were mostly friendly or social, as the technical details of the exchange could be handled more efficiently over the data channels. Nonetheless, the room quickly filled with a bustle of voices, the excitement of the day unable to be contained in the usual start-of-shift pleasantries.

"Doctor Simms!" the familiar voice cut through the crowd, pulling his attention to a hatchway about a third of the way around the curve of the back wall. There was a woman floating toward him, waving enthusiastically enough to give her trajectory an awkward wobble. Her brilliant smile against nearly black skin turned into a comic "O" of panic as she realized too late that the wobble had taken her out of range of any handholds, and she was going to crash directly into him.

"Allison!" Barry laughed, grasping onto the nearest toehold and catching hold of her. His grip prevented them both from spinning into the window behind him. "I was just thinking about you!"

The two of them continued to laugh as they sorted out their limbs and got themselves separated. Eventually, they were grinning at each other from an arm's length apart, Barry grasping a floor hold with his toes and Doctor Allison Tadesse securely gripping onto the ceiling with her left hand.

"I'm so glad you could make it!" Barry practically gushed. He had been friends with the discoverer of the Tadesse Effect for decades, ever since he'd joined the Sojourner Project to turn her discovery into a practical faster-than-light drive, but those years of collaboration had done little to knock the edges off his awe of her. He'd just gotten better at pushing through it.

"The university shuttle actually arrived last night; I was just asleep when it docked, and the crew let me stay that way."

"Well, you look great!" He wasn't exaggerating; even though she was pushing close to a century old, she barely looked over thirty. Vastly extended lifespans were another advantage of the medical advances made over the course of human expansion through the solar system.

"Don't you flatter me, you young whippersnapper," she replied with mock severity. "Nothing you can say can make the day better than it is, so you might as well give it up."

"I know, I know. You just want to see our baby fly, and you'll happily grind me into the deck to make it happen."

"Damn right, child," she laughed, and he joined in with her with the easy camaraderie of long association. "Have the fancy suits showed up yet?"

"All of my evenings for the past week have been taken up with showing the place off to the various delegations. But we've got another..." his attention flickered to the time display in the corner of his vision,"...hour until they invade our ops center. So, how about I give you a quick tour?"

It was several hours later, and they hung side by side, watching the *Sojourner* turn her ponderous bulk away from the far end of the scaffolding. The final tour had been a mix of emotions: pride in showing off his team's accomplishments, love for the ship herself, anticipation for the maiden voyage mixed with a touch of trepidation that something might, against all their preparations, go terribly wrong. Threaded through it all was a faint sadness that the monumental work was finally coming to an end.

After that came the welcoming of the heads of the various delegations who had come to witness the event in person. President Gyeon of the Earth Federation had been the first to arrive, clumsy as only a Terran could be in the gravity-free environment of the station and looking a little pale to boot. He was soon followed by the Martian Collective, whose tripartite mind combined to lead that venerable colony with a perspective unmatched by any other in the system. The Monitor of Ceres, the Chancellor of Ganymede, even the normally reclusive Venusian Bishop, among countless others, filled up the rear of the ops center, and he'd had to greet them all. But now, he had eyes only for the *Sojourner* as she delicately maneuvered her way free of her berth.

"There she goes!" Abby's welcome voice rang in his head. Neither she nor Kris could be physically present; duties of their own kept them away. Abby was managing the hugely complex life support system that kept the *Annie Jump* station habitable, and Kris was teaching in the station's school. But both were able to be present virtually, thanks to their implants, and he could feel their hands in his just as surely as he would have if they'd been in the room with him.

"Quite a beaut!" Kris commented. "We can't begin to say how proud we are of you."

"I couldn't have made it without you," he sent back, real-world tears momentarily blurring his vision as the *Sojourner* completed her turn, engaged her main engines, and slowly started to accelerate away. At the corners of his vision — unimpeded by the tears he was blinking away — he could monitor the Tadesse Generator powering up. If all went well, she would soon vanish from view, and from their instruments, to her destination just outside the orbit of Uranus. Then would come the wait — it would take over two hours for signals to return to *Annie Jump*, and only then would they know if they had succeeded.

"It's been a long, hard, often painful journey," he spoke aloud, and he wasn't talking only of his personal experience. "But beautiful, too." He smiled as coruscating light bathed the ops center from the field building around the *Sojourner's* pylons.

"I can't wait to see what beauty is still waiting out there for us to find."

The *Sojourner* vanished.

Two hours and seventeen minutes later, the operations center erupted in cries of joy.

GALAXY MUSIC

by Jay T. Levy

Alto opened his eyes and looked across the room through the glass of his hibernation chamber into the chamber of Jazz, his friend and fellow long-range communications engineer. Fast beats and electronic rhythms played in Al's headphones, mixed with crashing ocean waves, which energized his body and spirit. Along with the music, citrus scents blended into the chamber air around him. Though he'd just been unconscious, Al's mind felt invigorated and ready.

The hibernation chamber room was surprisingly dim, but Al could tell Jazz was awake; he saw the whites of his friend's eyes. Otherwise, with the low lighting, he'd never have known. Their deep sleep between planetary jumps must have ended; now they faced the aftereffects. It'd been the same when they'd gotten to the Jupiter Launch Station before departing for Charon, Pluto's largest moon.

With a press of the internal release, the chamber door slid open with a gentle hiss and both men stepped out at the same time, wearing headphones and hibernation suits. The music remained in Al's headphones but shifted. Drum beats quickened, distant birds called, and the chanting voices of a people he'd never met blended into a harmonious call. There was no need to remove his headphones. Everyone wore them at all times. They were essential, like wearing pants.

Non-lyrical music mixed with natural sounds had become the cornerstone of a peaceful human society.

Al stepped from his chamber on wobbly legs. Jazz did the same. They looked at each other, shook their heads, and laughed.

"Every time," Jazz smirked. "Feels like the deck's sliding out from under me."

The hibernation suits they wore were beige and soft on the inside yet had an exterior shell of a hard, pliable material akin to a human fingernail.

"Give it a moment," Al patted Jazz on the arm, "you'll find your legs, my friend."

Speech, like anything else that could be heard, was filtered through headphone sensors, added to music and ambiance, and then presented to the ear clearly. Sound connected everything, even though it was all essentially vibrations.

It was something humans had known for a long time, centuries even. But once a true understanding of vibrations emerged – through science, faith, and a little luck – the world had changed forever. Music and sound blended and became a harmonious constant for all humanity. Through sound, music, and the basic control of vibrations, the world healed with connections it never knew it had and found peace.

"Something isn't right," Al knocked on the bulkhead. "Bel, are you here? Why isn't she greeting us? We should see what's going on."

The pair wandered into the hallway and made their way to the bridge. The air was stale and harsh with chemicals, not fully prepared for humans. Al's music changed automatically into something soothing to compensate for his rising tension.

The bridge door opened with a hiss like the hibernation chamber. Inside, the room had a defined pink glow from instrument paneling. There was one chair on wheels, a large viewport, and several banks of computer displays and switches. In front of the controls, hanging limply from a central spot in the ceiling, was a bulb held in place by a chrome appendage, the head unit for six long, eight-jointed arms. Each arm of the spider-like mechanism ended in a set of tripod pinchers.

"Bel, can you hear us?" Al asked the rose-colored room. Activity across the display panels showed Bel was active.

"You know, I really hope that nickname doesn't stick." Bel's voice, both sweet and sharp, was suddenly in both engineers' headphones. The appendages hanging in the center of the room sprung to life, with the bulb glowing a bright fuchsia. "My name is B-Eleven. I'm sure you saw it on my registry when you boarded, but just in case..." One of the side panels on the bridge close to Al lit up with a registry license for Bel, or B-11 Cargo Class Transport.

"What's going on?" Al said. "You didn't greet us. The guy at the JLS said you would when you woke us."

"But I didn't wake you. In fact, why *are* you awake? What'd you do?"

Al glanced at Jazz; the look was returned.

"If you didn't wake us," Jazz said, "then it was a system error?"

"Look, I'm really sorry," Bel turned to the panels, "and I realize it's a week too early, but I can't put you back to sleep. Can't spare the time and energy."

"That's alright." Al patted Jazz on the back. "We're awake, and I'm hungry. I'm sure my friend here is, too. We'll go get changed and get something to eat. It's only a couple of days."

Jazz shrugged, and they left the bridge together.

Both had been given Bel's layout prior to hibernation at the Jupiter Launch Station, and, to them, that seemed mere minutes ago, so they knew their way around. After getting changed into standard uniforms — similar to their hibernation suits, but without the fingernail exterior — Al and Jazz regrouped at the small mess hall to eat and read Bel's logs.

"Perhaps these will tell us why she can't spare the time and energy," Jazz scrolled through a pad on the shared table.

Bel's mess had been an afterthought for the humans on board. The hall could only seat four and had no viewports. It was, essentially, a closet that linked to the food preparation chamber.

"I wouldn't worry too much." Al sat with two bowls of steaming food and a couple of mugs. "Here, hot off the presses."

Jazz looked up and raised an eyebrow. "Presses?"

Al smiled. "An old saying. Technically, it means news that was just printed onto newspaper, and both would still be hot."

"News on newspaper, is that like posted to a community board?"

"Yeah," Al pushed the bowl of food across the table, "something like that. Eat before it gets cold."

Jazz shrugged and stopped his scroll to eat.

In a specialized chamber, Bel had numerous, hermetically sealed tubes of nutrient paste of varying consistencies, which were heated as needed and run through a printing process after being injected with different flavors. What emerged was both nutritious and delicious. It allowed consumers the indulgence of sweet or fat without the additional intake of unwanted calories. The system also had bio-synthetic polymers in storage for creating utensils and dishes, which allowed them to be recycled for additional usage.

Thankfully, Bel had an updated model with a wide array of options. Al selected lemon pasta and Jazz requested jambalaya — both were little touches of home they could enjoy out in the depths of space.

Al looked over the logs while Jazz ate, scrolling back to the beginning entries. "These logs are incomplete," he said.

"I noticed that, too." Jazz swallowed a mouthful of synthetic rice and crawfish. "They start as they should, filed daily with the JLS, and they're very detailed, a bit overly detailed if you ask me. Bel lists every moment of each day, to the minute of what she was working on. Only, the dates between filings have grown longer, and her detail level has dropped. Daily reports became weekly, then monthly."

"There're no recent logs at all." Al turned off the pad. "Bel's A.I. should be capable of running her systems and filing daily logs like clockwork." Al rapped his knuckles against the table gently, his brow furrowed. "Let's go back to the bridge."

"You know, it takes a lot of concentration to run a ship this size! And interruptions slow me down even more." The fuchsia bulb on the extended arm glowed a slightly deeper red as it got closer to Al. "Carrying your-all's long-range transmitting whatever is heavy. You didn't tell me how big it was either! It's filling my entire hold. Makes me feel bloated and fat."

"The logs..." Al sighed.

"I was doing them, but I only have so much power these days, so I prioritized. I'll get to them when I can. There are *constant* minor course corrections and maintenance on my internal systems," she continued. "It is just me, after all! And I have to keep the shield running, too, or else we'd be turned into Swiss cheese. To finish our mission and drop off that dish for you guys to install, I gotta keep myself in top shape." Bel turned around, looked at various displays in no particular order, and melodramatically whispered, "Not that anyone these days seems to care how in-shape I keep myself."

"She seems a bit... frantic," Jazz whispered to Al.

"I can hear you," the bulb turned around, glowed bright red for a moment, then dimmed to fuchsia and went back to the screens.

"Bel...," Al hesitated, "are you okay?"

The bulb's arm went slack. It twisted around, and the bulb's glow diminished to a light salmon. "No, I'm not. I feel... drained. My engines are running too hot. It's giving me a fever. Too many systems are running at once, and the strain is giving me a headache. The course corrections are getting harder to maintain as if arthritis crept into the controls."

The lights on the bridge suddenly dimmed, and the room's temperature dropped twenty-five degrees. The cold was shocking, but within a few moments, the temperature had returned to standard levels.

"Unbelievable!" Bel's bulb flashed red, and she returned to the display screens. "This is what I mean. It's these kinds of things that keep happening."

"Have you run a full diagnostic?" Jazz asked.

"Do you know how many resources that would use? I don't have the capacity for that." Her six arms crossed themselves under the glowing fuchsia bulb.

"The end result will be worth it," Al said. "It's better to know what's going on and address it than keep plugging holes."

Jazz nodded.

Bel sighed but complied, or at least seemed to try.

"I can't believe it," the bulb flashed red again. "The diagnostic system is disabled. It'll take hours, possibly days, to get it reset. I don't have time for this!"

"Bel, from what you're describing and the errors we've seen," Al looked apprehensive and rubbed the back of his neck like he was a doctor about to deliver tragic news, "could you have caught a bug?"

"I can't see how." The fuchsia bulb stopped scrolling over panels and turned to Al. "They sprayed for bugs before we left. The guy — I don't recall his name, it's in the log — at the Jupiter Launch Station gave me the all-clear. Look, you can see it right here." Her voice had grown defensive, and she pulled up a digital copy of the JLS release form signed by Tenor, 'the guy.'

"If it's a bug," she groaned, "I'm gonna get fired up! Means he didn't do his job, and I can't be having that…"

"All-clear or not," Al continued, "the symptoms you describe sound troubling. You need to scan your hull."

"I can't."

"Because you don't have the resources?" Jazz asked skeptically.

"No," Bel snapped back, "internally, I have a variety of sensors in my array. But externally, my sensors are for navigation purposes only. I simply can't."

The two humans stared at each other while Bel returned to her work. The rhythmic, calming sounds of distant wind chimes sounded in their headphones.

"Could we use the main landing drone to investigate?" Al said. "It has an independent power source, propulsion system, and scanners."

"It's not programmed for that," Bel didn't even turn around. "And it can't be used while we're moving anyway. It'd get launched, then left behind."

Alto challenged her defeatist outlook. "But you could reprogram its functions, stop your engines, and scan yourself with it, right?"

"Yeah, I suppose I could. But it's a one-time use kind of thing. If we use our main landing drone now, we wouldn't have it for Charon. Plus, stopping means slowing and then restarting, which adds more time to the journey."

"When we get to Charon," Jazz said, "we could use our secondary, atmospheric observance drone. Details won't be as sharp, but it'll pick up the concentrated energy of Orpheus' shield, especially since Charon has no atmosphere."

Bel's power flickered again and left everything in a moment of darkness, except for the bright fuchsia bulb.

"How long should it take to reprogram the drone?" Al asked.

With another sigh, Bel answered, "I don't know, maybe an hour."

"Then do it," AI commanded.

Bel complied. She slowed her engines and began reprogramming the drone, groaning the entire time about using energy she didn't have to spare.

The sounds of space were not really sounds; science had revealed ages ago that, in order to be heard, sound must travel through vibrations of atoms and molecules, such as in air or water. Space had no air; thus, sound had no way to travel. But that hadn't stopped humans from exploring, and the universe was brought to auditory life through sonification — data transformed into sound.

Wavy signals of distant stars and planets bounced off each other constantly and once captured and digitized, became part of a symphony broadcast to humanity as part of their daily music. Instruments and natural sounds blended perfectly and helped to bring about Earth's harmony.

But humanity wanted more. What new sounds were out there in the galaxy? What wasn't getting through to Earth because of the planets or the Sun's potent radiation? And so, the listening array was created.

A listening post named Orpheus was developed and installed across the surfaces of Pluto and its biggest moon, Charon. In addition to its distance from the inner system, designers hoped to take advantage of Pluto's highly tilted, non-elliptic path.

From the array, pristine, distant signals would be relayed back to Earth, free of distortion from the solar system's traffic of planets, asteroids, and human travel. If all went well, it would unlock new strata of sounds for humanity's jukebox. One last component was needed for Orpheus to be ready and brought on-line: the dish sitting in Bel's cargo hold, which would beam what it collected back to Earth.

"This mission is taking a lot longer than I expected," Bel said while reconfiguring the drone. "I hope the higher-ups at the Jupiter Launch Station see how much additional time and effort is going into this. I hope Orpheus is worth it, especially if it caught me a bug."

Jazz studied one of Bel's bridge displays. "Bugs are said to be unpleasant, right?"

"Like gremlins, but real," Al said.

"What's a gremlin?" Jazz smirked. "Sounds made up."

"It is, or it was, anyway. When humans first took to the skies in airplanes," Al held up both hands, palms out, "I know, I know, I'm talking about ancient history, but when they did, people had all sorts of issues and problems with their planes. Power failures, parts being mysteriously broken, you name it. So, they blamed it on gremlins — short, blue-skinned, or white fur-covered creatures that would ride the wings and try to bring planes down."

"Yeah, well, as you said, they weren't real," Jazz frowned. "But bugs are?"

Al nodded. "They're nasty, energy-feeding vermin that hide out in the upper atmospheres and rings of our gas giants. They latch on and take what they can get through survival instincts, which endanger us, unfortunately."

"I've never seen one. Have you?"

Al shook his head.

"That's why launch station technicians spray departing ship hulls thoroughly before launch," Bel interjected sharply. "Bugs are only supposed to exist in, or around, those upper atmospheres and rings, but sometimes hitch rides on passing ships. Spraying removes any bugs before launch. It's supposed to put you in the clear." With each word, Bel's lights flickered.

Jazz frowned. "It's been well over an hour, Bel. Should your reprogramming take this long? Your power levels are still dropping."

"I know. I said I didn't have the resources to do this. But I'm finished. One of you'll have to manually launch it. That permission wasn't built into my system."

"Not a problem," Jazz rolled the only chair on Bel's bridge to the drone interface. "Launching in three, two, one."

Bel vibrated with the release, and the humans felt it through the floor panels. Al held the wall but didn't need it. Jazz was already seated in the chair.

"Activate the drone sensors," Al said. "Provide a standard search pattern, like it's scanning for the shield. Then, we listen."

Bel's light dimmed.

Al closed his eyes. He assumed Jazz did, too.

Pings from the hull came rhythmically and serenely until it reached the rear engines. Al opened his eyes, and Bel turned red.

"I can't believe it," her voice seethed as an image illuminated one of her screens. Next to Bel's stern engine exhaust was a large bug, an ixodidae. It had eight legs, auburn plates of exoskeletal armor, and beady eyes glowing bright yellow. Its mandibles were latched firmly onto a section of Bel's hull; its thorax, bulbous and grey, was full of energy.

"That thing is sucking on my ass!" Bel screamed. Suddenly, her engine output spiked. A massive surge of polarized energy cascaded across the stern and then over the ixodidae, covering it in waves of cracking, electric bursts.

But the bug didn't move; it latched on tighter, and its distended belly grew by another fifteen percent when it absorbed the flickering electrical energy.

"Bel!" Al said, "Why did you do that? Those things feed on energy."

"I know!" she screamed. "I'm sorry! I got... angry, okay?" Her lights dimmed again. "I was... hoping the sudden burst... would make it detach... float away..."

"You just made it worse," Jazz shook his head.

"I... I said...," a few of Bel's screens turned off; her lights flickered, "I'm... sorry." Her voice grew weak.

"Whatever we do now, we do it in power save mode." Al's said. "On Earth, that kind of bug, an ixodidae – a tick – is often eaten by predatory birds."

"I wonder." Jazz typed on the screen in front of him. "Perhaps we can use those predatory sounds against this bug. Bel, I'm finding the appropriate sound files; once loaded, play them against your inner hull as loudly as you can. Maybe it'll be enough to frighten the bug."

Al patted Jazz on the shoulder. "Good idea. How do we prepare?"

Jazz pointed to his headphones. "Increase the noise cancellation to compensate. Otherwise, we'll be fine."

Once uploaded, Bel played the sounds of eagles, falcons, and hawks all at the same time, blasting the sounds against her hull, concentrating on the area of the bug. It rang throughout the ship regardless, but thankfully, their headphones nullified the noise into a low hum.

The bug didn't move.

"It… didn't… work," Bel sounded defeated, deflated, and drained.

"At least it didn't get bigger," Jazz said.

"Hey… I said… I… was… sorry."

"What? Oh, I didn't mean…," Jazz backpedaled.

"Could our hibernation, or our zero-atmosphere surface suits, handle spacewalking?" Al asked, "So we can remove the bug ourselves? Or could we turn the ship around to Jupiter Launch Station?"

"Negative…" Bel didn't elaborate.

"Our suits weren't designed for that kind of environment," Jazz said, "and we don't have enough energy reserves to return." He typed on one of Bel's remaining lit panels, bringing up a graph for Al. "However, if we can get to Orpheus's unmanned, automated base on Charon, Bel can recharge as we install the array's last dish. By the time we're done, she'll be ready to go."

"Spray… hull, too," Bel added.

The two men looked at each other and nodded. That went without saying.

"Then we have no choice. I'll make sure it's noted in our log entries to JLS," Al met Jazz's worried gaze before addressing the dimmed, pink bulb. "Bel, we'll need to conserve as much power as we're able. Systems must be strategically turned off. Jazz and I'll have to rough it for a few days."

"Bel will have to be powered off, too," Jazz added.

"I… will?" Her voice hinted at nervousness.

"You use a lot of power, I'm afraid," he continued. "Some systems will need to remain active, like artificial gravity, heat, oxygen, and the diverter shields."

Al nodded, "Without shielding, even miniscule space debris could slice us to shreds."

"Correct," Jazz continued, "Those are automatic functions, like breathing or a heart pumping. They don't take up nearly as much energy as, well, you being you, Bel." Jazz typed again on the panel with the energy output, showing projections of continued usage. "Essentially, we need you to go into a deep sleep for a few days."

"Will... I... wake?"

"I assume so," Jazz shrugged, "but if not, we'll reboot you from the main memory core. You wouldn't remember us or the last mission, but that'd be okay. You'd still know how to fly the ship home."

All three were silent for a few uncomfortable moments.

"Don't... like... this plan." Bel was audibly struggling.

"I don't think we have other options." Again, Al's tone was respectful but commanding. "Bel, leave the automatic systems running and get yourself powered down. When we get to Charon, we'll wake you for landing."

Bel complied, and with a lot less sass than Al expected. Jazz kept the one screen active on Bel's bridge, which showed their energy output projections slowing but continuing to drop. Unfortunately, they couldn't properly account for the bug attached to Bel's backside like a nasty pimple, and its continual drain on her energy reserves.

Over the next few days, Al and Jazz took over manual course corrections. Neither was trained on how to fly Bel, but they could keep her old-fashioned autopilot system engaged and her bearings pointed in the right direction. They also didn't have much that they could use to help fight the chill leaking through Bel's hull other than their surface suits — similar to the hibernation suits but thicker. With heat set to a minimum, her inner temperature plummeted and quickly became intolerable for the humans. They put on everything they had, even stuffing their suits with bedding material to help keep warm. When that failed to suppress the cold, they huddled together on the bridge to conserve warmth and oxygen. They recycled breathable air as much as they could, but their supply was limited and running out.

Bel's food preparation chamber, ironically, devoured a lot of energy, so Al and Jazz were also limited to emergency rations. Fortunately, she had a decent supply of the crunchy, brown and green compressed briquettes of fiber and protean-meal, which tasted quite good but looked like unappetizing clods. As the cold set into Bel's hull more and more, things began to freeze over — including the rations. Eventually chewing them became crunching on ice, unpleasant and difficult when already weak from hunger.

The closer Charon got, the more Al knew he and Jazz shared the same concern — would Bel have enough power to wake once they arrived at the moon?

When the reddish-brown ice caps of Pluto's orbital double came into view, Al told Jazz, "It's time we wake her."

Jazz typed on Bel's only lit panel then stopped typing and tapped his chin before returning to the keyboard.

"Is there a problem?"

A low-pitched beep and red light on the panel screen were all the answers Al needed.

"Bel isn't responding," Jazz answered quietly.

"Damn. Can we reboot her from the memory core?"

"Not without exhausting more of our energy reserves." Jazz continued typing. "The bug drained more than expected. We have enough to land but not to return to orbit. We'll need to recharge Bel as much as possible at Orpheus Base. Any further drains..."

"I get the picture," Al said. "Unfortunately, we're not equipped to land her either."

Both technicians had been given rudimentary landing instructions at JLS, but neither was fully trained to land Bel manually. Al felt confident he remembered the steps, having heard them a few times on the previous missions during the installation of Orpheus sensor points. But he never thought he'd have to use them.

"If we need it, I can attempt to land," Jazz said.

"I appreciate that," Al patted him on the shoulder, "but I'm the senior technician. I'll do it."

Jazz didn't argue.

As they slowed Bel's approach and engaged the automatic orbiting system, Jazz released the secondary atmospheric drone. "It also has its own power and controls. We don't need Bel awake to use it."

"Good, now find me our landing spot." Al powered up Bel's manual landing station, stooping to see it at eye level, while Jazz remained in the only chair on the bridge.

Charon had no atmosphere, and it didn't take long to locate Orpheus Base's highly focused energy shield. The issue now was aligning Bel for landing.

"Remember," Jazz cautioned, turning over the chair to Al, "we need to come in from the side, not the top. Or else we'll bounce off the shielding."

"I remember," Al said, calm and steady, "almost like trying to sneak in under the dining room tablecloth."

Switching off orbital maintenance, Al drifted Bel closer to Orpheus Base using her landing thrusters. He considered whether he'd engaged the thrusters too early, but with his lack of experience, decided he'd rather drift slowly under the shield like a boat trying not to create too much wake.

Al's hands sweated as he gripped the manual controls. Bel's controls were clunky, with a heavy drift like her engine alignment needed correcting. Al wondered whether she'd always flown that stiffly or if it was the bug's influence.

"No, look!" Jazz said, panicked. "Bel's angle, we'll hit the shield."

Al turned up the music in his headphones, more calming, more flutes and the sounds of wind. He grasped Bel's controls and guided the ship more sharply downward.

Even over the music, he heard the scrape of Bel's hull as they just barely snuck in under the shield. Al engaged the landing struts and throttled down the thrusters, easing Bel to the surface of Charon as gently as he could.

The resulting crash shook Bel violently, threw Jazz to the floor, and knocked Al from his chair. Luckily, the technicians' injuries were only bumps and bruises, and both went to work immediately.

They had to take care of Bel first and so made their way to Orpheus Base across the rocky, ice-covered surface. Thankfully, the shield generator on Charon also provided some artificial gravity, even though its main function was to keep cosmic radiation and asteroids from destroying Orpheus's central hub. It made getting to the base easier, but the ice kept them cautious. Once there, Jazz retrieved the cables necessary for Bel's recharge, and Al grabbed the emergency bug spray canister.

While Jazz connected wires to Bel's recharge ports on the underside of her hull, Al approached the bug at Bel's rear end. The nasty thing pulsated and sparked as if its bulbous, enlarged belly might explode at any moment. Al shook his head and sneered in disgust, then unleashed the canister's contents. To be fair, he didn't really know what was inside but knew it was part of the decontamination process. He was not expecting the bubbling, green acid that ejected from the can and set the bug ablaze.

The ixodidae fell off Bel and tried to crawl away but couldn't. Then, it released its stored energy as puffs of electrified, acrid, black smoke that slowly expanded to fill the area. When the fuel was consumed, so too was the flame.

Al, more concerned about his crewmates, didn't stay behind to inspect the corpse or survey damage to Bel's exterior, although a cursory visual examination showed minimal damage.

"The bug's gone," Al said over their com link.

"She's charging," Jazz said, "but no sign of her. We may have to reboot her when there's enough power."

"Understood," Al sighed. "But we were sent all the way to the end of our solar system for a specific mission — we have an installation to finish."

Having spent months on Earth practicing, the technicians quickly and quietly installed Orpheus' voice, the giant transmission dish Bel had brought to Charon. Against the blackness of space, it was impressive to behold.

Al wondered, though, if the quiet was because Jazz was also thinking about their third crewmate.

When they got back inside, the technicians stood on Bel's bridge, and Al allowed Jazz to do the honor of switching on Orpheus's array.

Suddenly, new sounds flooded their systems, cascading over Bel's speakers and through their headphones. At first, it was a wild surge of sound — an undiluted cacophony of transmissions from galaxies far away but was quickly and expertly sonified by Orpheus's systems.

"Oh my!" Bel said suddenly.

The slow trickle of Bel's charge surged, and all her systems re-engaged.

"Bel, you've returned?" Jazz sounded surprised.

"That's right, I'm baaaaack baaaaaaby," she sang the last part in a beautiful soprano, giddily and full of joy. "Can you guys hear it? It's like nothing I've ever heard before, with its raw, untamed energy." The bulb on the bridge turned to the technicians, shining brightly fuchsia again. "It brought me back!"

Jazz flopped in the chair, looked up at Al, and smiled.

Al held out a hand to shake. "We did it, and we heard it first. This is why we're here, for the new and the unheard. Think about it, Jazz. Hours from now, everyone on Earth will hear what we're hearing right now."

Al closed his eyes and took in the mellifluence of shifting sounds, reveling in the hope and promise of this new galaxy music and what it meant for everyone home on Earth.

THE PALE RED DOT

by J. Patrick Conlon

Scott removed his glove and ran his hand lightly over the thin, spiny leaf of the aloe vera plant, then gently squeezed it. He released the aloe, walked over to the data-pad laying on top of a rust-colored boulder, and began entering his observations.

"How are we doing?"

Scott's eyes rose to glare at the intercom set into the metal wall.

"I'd be doing better if you stopped interrupting me. Besides, you are monitoring the vitals, right? I only just examined it. Gimme a minute, Jen!"

"Touchy, touchy. And you haven't taken off your gloves again, correct?"

Scott could hear the mirth followed by admonition in her voice even through the slight buzz of the speaker system.

"It's fine, I've done this hundreds of times. I know what I'm doing," Scott barked. "And another thing..."

"Scott, the aloe!" the speaker blared.

He spun and saw the small plant shudder and then wither, the green swiftly turning brown. The room was then bathed in red light.

"Get your suit sealed!" Jen's voice rang out through the intercom. Angry red blisters were already creeping over Scott's hand as he pulled his glove back on and pressed the switch on his wrist. The fabric shrank and fused to his sleeve. He moved to the wall as the exit irised open. He stumbled through, and the door slammed shut behind him. He was still furiously shaking his hand as the door to the other side slid open, and Jen raced in, red curls bouncing around her face. She grabbed his hand to steady him and squeezed his wrist. The glove released and she yanked it off. Scott's hand was red and already had several large blisters that had popped.

"Stop shaking!" Scott took a deep shuddering breath, and his hand stopped moving so violently. Jen pulled the top off the medi-spray and shot a wide arc of mist over his wounds. Everywhere the spray touched the skin turned pink, then a dull gray as the medication muted the pain and reduced the inflammation. Scott's face relaxed.

"I suppose we call this failed test 567, then," Scott smiled at Jen and then promptly collapsed.

"Welcome back, Scott."

Scott's eyes cracked open. The bright light of the room overwhelmed him, and he squeezed them shut again. The light blazed, then suddenly dimmed. He raised a hand to shield himself. A dark shadow, the edges of which were ragged, filled his vision.

"Jen? What happened?"

"You had to take your glove off again, is what happened, you idiot." The shadow coalesced down into the crimson curls of his fellow scientist and engineer. "How many times have I told you to never compromise your suit integrity when you are in the terraforming chamber. We have never had a test succeed for more than a few minutes."

"I guess my luck was bound to run out sooner or later," Scott mumbled, a light smile creasing his face.

"Run out? Are you insane? If it had taken another ten seconds for you to seal your suit, the aloe plant wouldn't be the only thing I needed to record in the experimental log!"

"If you're done, how long was I out? Do we have the diagnostics on the failure already?"

"You've only been out for roughly 15 minutes, and no, I had the silly thought that I should make sure you were stable before I started looking at the failure numbers."

"Well, I'm fine now, so," Scott tried to raise himself up and Jen placed a hand on his chest and shoved.

"You are not fine! Conscious again sure, but the scanners haven't cleared you yet. The air in that chamber turned corrosive again, and god knows what absorbing that into your arm has done to your internal organs. It turned the aloe into dark black goo, for crying out loud!"

"Yeah, yeah, how much longer does the computer say I need to be in the med bay?"

Jen crossed her arms, "At least the rest of today, and you will be sleeping here tonight."

"Come on, it did not say that." Scott turned on his side and reached over to turn the monitor towards him. Jen pushed him back again..

"It did, and you are in no condition to..."

DING, analysis complete, subject is green for return to active duty.

Scott slipped from under Jen's arm and swung his legs off the gurney.

"Hey, where do you think you're going?"

"You heard the Medicomp. I'm cleared. Let's go run those diagnostics." Scott shouted over his shoulder and shuffled out of the medbay.

Jen gently smacked the side of the medicomp's terminal. "Whose side are you on anyway?"

With that, she shook her head and walked after Scott.

"Look at that spike at 90 seconds. That has to be where the field failed." Scott tapped the screen, and the spike was highlighted.

"Maybe, but the fluctuations before aren't that promising either," Jen paced behind him. "How can we be certain that is the problem?"

"Well, this time, Al lasted a full 5 minutes before he liquefied. That has to mean something, right?" Scott turned. "Would you stop pacing? You're making me nervous."

"You're nervous?" Jen glared at him. "I'm the one who'll have to pilot this heap back to earth alone if you disintegrate from all the 'luck' you're pushing."

"It's been 2 hours, and apart from some stiffness in my hand, I'm fine. Stop worrying!" Scott pressed a few keys on the keyboard.

Analysis of experiment 567 complete. Results aggregate on main console

The center console in the room sprang to life with a 3D image rotating above it. Scott spun in his chair and got up. Both he and Jen moved around the console. Scott reached into the image and closed his hand into a fist. The image froze.

"Computer, overlay experiments 1 to 566 onto main display."

The line chart blurred as the hundreds of data lines from the previous experiments appeared.

"See," Jen pointed at the screen. "These readings are all over the place. And," She pinched her fingers around the 90-second mark, and the screen zoomed in. "The spikes at 90 seconds are not consistent either. "Face it, Scott, this is just another failed test."

"No, this time, AI lasted much longer than he had before! That spike must have something to do with it."

"Scott, we can't simply chase every anomaly down like this." Jen turned and grabbed Scott's hand. "We've been at this for three years. The rest of the team will be back on Earth by now."

Scott tried to pull his hand away, winced, and then his shoulders sank. "The rest of the team never thought this would work in the first place, so them being gone doesn't bother me. You, though, you I thought believed."

"I do believe. That's why I didn't get on the transport. But even without the rest of the crew here, we still don't have unlimited food, water, or air. We need to stick to the protocols and finish the rest of the experiments."

"But this time is different, I know it." Scott's face turned red. He started to collapse and gripped the back of Jen's chair.

"Green for active duty, my ass!" Jen rose and grabbed Scott under his arm, throwing it around her neck. "What did you do?"

"I may have relaxed the medicomp's protocols for active duty." Scott smiled weakly. "But don't change the subject. We need to look at this test more closely."

"We will then, I promise." Jen moved toward the door, dragging Scott with her. "But only once I reset the medicomp, and you are actually cleared."

"Okay, but only because I'm going to black out again." Scott's smile faded, and he crumpled to the floor, taking Jen down with him.

Jen removed herself from under him and tapped the call button on her wrist. A loader bot trundled into the room, stopping beside Scott's now unconscious body. With some effort, Jen lifted him onto the loader for the second time in the last few hours.

"I swear you are the most annoying man I've ever met. Loader, please take the idiot back to the medbay." She rubbed her side and then followed after, wondering how angry he would be when he woke up strapped to the bed.

Scott's eyes fluttered open. He began to move, but the sharp hiss and blinding light of making contact with the force shield forced his back flat. He squeezed his eyes shut against the flash.

"Finally awake, huh?"

"How long was I out?" Scott's voice sounded far away in his ears.

"Only a few hours. You were lucky that it wasn't just you and the service bots, or you might have died." Jen pointed to his hand. "You split your hand open again and almost bled out. You're welcome, by the way."

"I was going to say thank you, but that would be Stockholm syndrome."

"Oh please, if you hadn't gone running off before the medispray finished stitching your hand back together, you wouldn't be on that slab right now."

"The research," The force shield hissed again as he attempted to get off the gurney once more.

"Look, tell you what," Jen crossed her arms and glared at his prone form. "You let me put that into a hypo-cast, and maybe, just maybe, I'll let you look at what I found while you were unconscious."

The force shield glowed hot white and and the hiss was accompanied by a loud snap as Scott pounded the field in frustration.

"Stop that! It may not hurt you, but you'll blind us both if you keep that up." Jen pressed a series of buttons and turned the diameter knob on the console in front of her. The shimmer of the shield faded.

Scott slowly raised himself from the bed and swung his legs over the side. "Okay, what did you find?"

Jen smiled, then gestured at the mesh of fiber weave lying on the table. "First, let's get this on you, then we talk about what I found."

Scott reached for the hypo-cast, but Jen raised her hand. "No, I'm putting it on you so I know it's done properly and slowly." She emphasized the last part, snatching up the cast and shaking it at him.

"This had better be worth it." Scott winced as he stretched his arm out to Jen. She slipped the cast over his hand and then pressed the glowing yellow button on the side of the material. The cast immediately went rigid. Scott grimaced until the nano injectors inside the cast released the hypo spray. His shoulder relaxed, and his entire body sagged.

"Well, let's get to the control center, man, or we could wait to review the results after you are completely...."

Scott sprang towards the door before she could finish her thought, "No, no, let's get over there. I'm doing fine now."

The screen was filled with overlapped trend lines, making the whole an unintelligible blur. Scott swiped his hand, and the image spun wildly. He looked away, holding his free hand to his mouth.

"Congratulations, you found a way to make everyone nauseous. How does this help us?"

"Would you please just sit back and let me run my analysis program?" Jen grabbed Scott's chair and yanked. The chair spun away from the console, carrying Scott across the room. Jen pulled another chair into place and sat at the console.

"How long will this take to run?" Scott pulled his chair back across the room to sit next to her. "Just a second more. I have to reset the program to run from the beginning, or this won't make any sense."

Several tense minutes passed. The only sounds were Scott's exasperated breathing and the light clicking of the keys under Jen's fingers.

"There, it's ready." Jen hovered her finger over the final keystroke. Scott leaned in to peer at the screen. "Hey, turn around. I programmed this to run on the holo-projector. That's what I found. The results don't make sense unless you map them in three dimensions."

Scott turned, and Jen pressed the enter key. The lights in the room dimmed as the floor split open, and the holo-projector rose into place. The middle of the room exploded into a million lines, and Scott raised a hand to shield his eyes from the incandescent glow.

"This is the breakthrough? This makes even less sense than the trend lines graphing. This is why we gave up on using 3D imaging for the results a long time ago."

"Just give it a minute, for Christ's sake, Scott. The analysis hasn't even started yet. Just watch."

Jen turned back to the console and quickly entered a final sequence and pressed the return key. The room went dark, and then a single peak rose in the center of the projector.

Jen shot him a withering look as Scott opened his mouth. He sank back into himself. "That," she pointed at the bright line. "Is the results of the test we ran this morning." Several seconds passed with more clicking of keys.

"First, we remove all the unmodulated fields. Now watch what happens when I filter the rest of the results using this as a baseline."

Hundreds of lines sprang up and swirled around the room, the top of each bending towards the central line. "That made things so much better," muttered Scott.

Several minutes later, the image floated complete in the middle of the room, spinning slowly.

"It looks like a funnel?" Scott's voice was quiet.

"Exactly. We've been looking at this problem all wrong the entire time. We thought that the field would simply fail if the frequency wasn't correct, but when we modulate the frequency..."

"That can't be the answer!" Scott interrupted again, exploding out from his chair. "We've modulated the field hundreds of times, all with the same results."

"Sit down!" Jen barked. Scott shrank back into his chair. "Sorry, it's just that we can't go back and forth on this. This could be our last chance to get this right, and I need you to understand what we've found."

Scott nodded.

"Okay, this latest test we ran was a high modulation field, and it lasted longer than any of our other tests, but it still failed."

Scott nodded, but his eyes gleamed with unspoken protest.

"So we figured that it was just another failure of many, but while you were healing in the medbay, I wondered if all of this was just futile and we should just give up. I came here to run the numbers one last time so I could force you to see reason."

"I don't think I've been that unreasonable. What we are trying to do here is monumental."

Jen put her hand on Scott's shoulder. "You haven't been unreasonable. It's just been a long time here and we haven't had anything to show for it. Until now."

"Okay, so walk me through what you found. I won't say anything until you finish."

Jen took a deep breath, "Here is the solution. If we layer the modulated fields, using this last result as the anchor point, they pull into the center and stabilize. Which means…"

"Which means that the modulated field will also stabilize the reaction!" Scott sprang from his chair. "What are we waiting for? Let's try this with the field!"

Jen's breath came rapidly as she crossed the chamber. The wilted brown aloe plant sat in the middle of the room. She turned towards the intercom and gave a thumbs-up.

"Are you ready?" the intercom buzzed after several long seconds.

"It's pretty easy to forget that you can't see me in here."

"You're nodding at the speaker, aren't you?"

"No, but I can understand now if you do."

"Whatever you say," Scott laughed. "Okay, once you plug in the programming, I'll turn on the field, and you keep watch on your suit's integrity."

"Scott, you don't get to lecture me on that." Jen found herself smiling despite her growing anxiety. She sat down on the rock next to the rounded dome of the field emitter and pushed several buttons. The seam appeared and irised open, revealing a small keyboard and several indentations. Jen placed the round marble that contained the new code for the modulator and spent several minutes entering the necessary instructions into the keypad. She then pressed her hand again and the dome irised closed.

"Scott, we're ready here. You can start the field. I'll monitor and keep taking the readings."

"Fingers crossed. Be more careful than I am in there."

"Aren't I always?" Jen smirked and turned back towards the dead aloe. She whispered, "Here goes nothing."

The dome began to pulse with a thin green light, which pulsed outward in waves. Unlike all the previous times the hue and pigment of the light shifted and fluxed radically, then brightened. Jen had to shield her eyes from the glow. As the light reached her suit, steam began rising from the heavy fabric. A small bubble appeared on the center of the back of her hand.

"It's eating at the suit!" The intercom fuzzed at the volume and panic of Scott's voice. "I'm shutting it down!"

"No, don't!" Jen scrabbled back from the light. "I can stay out of the field. It has to build for a few more seconds before the anchor field kicks in. It will stabilize."

"Get to the edge of the enclosure now, and if it reaches you, I'm cutting the field."

Jen pressed herself against the edge of the enclosure. "I'll be fine."

"I knew we should have done this without you in there."

"If we do that, we won't know what's happened."

"I know, but now that you are in there I wish we had some kind of shielding that would allow us to record in there. This intercom is not cutting it for me."

"Now you know how I've felt these last 3 years."

The green fluctuation began to expand faster. The air in the room began to swirl towards the center of the emitter. Small bursts of lightning began to flick inside the light, the snap and hiss making the entire chamber feel like the den of a monster rather than a shielded lab. The room was then bathed in red light.

"I've got warning lights all over the console in here Jen! I'm shutting this off right now!"

"No! Just give it a few more seconds. It hasn't reached me yet! I'll tell you when to shut it off!"

"What if you can't? Even if I wanted you to get hurt, which I don't, I can't fly this back to Earth without you!"

"You give me 10 more seconds, Scott! I've given you a lot more than that."

The green cloud began pulsing faster, and the swirling air started turning to smoke. Jen could just make out the outline of the aloe in the midst of the conflagration. All the leaves were standing straight up from the pot, but she couldn't make out any further details.

The cloud reached the edge of the chamber, and Jen's suit began to sizzle. Dark black smoke rose up from her helmet and she opened her mouth to scream for Scott to turn off the field when a bright green light erupted from the top of the emitter and struck the ceiling. All at once, the green cloud swirled away from her and was drawn into the center. The light pulsed several times and then exploded outward. Jen threw her hands up and squeezed her eyes shut and yelled, "Shut it down!"

The room went dark.

"Jen, I shut the field down! Are you alright?"

Jen cracked open an eye and looked around the chamber. The entire chamber was green. Aloe plants covered the floor, ceiling, and walls. In the center, on that same red rock that held every test plant, sat Al 568. Its roots burst from the pot, snaking around the boulder and fastened into the ground.

"Jen!" Static burst from the intercom as Scott yelled.

"I'm here, Scott. Go put your suit on. You're going to want to see this."

"Doctors Johnson and Hammersmith, the rest of your team just arrived with the bad news." The visage on the viewscreen grimaced.

"Well, commander, we have some bad news for them as well," Jen tried to keep the defiance out of her voice.

"Oh," a raised eyebrow. "We haven't had a report from you in months. We assumed the entire team was coming back with either success or failure. What do you have for us?"

"A solution," Scott placed a hand on Jen's shoulder and smiled in spite of the grimace facing them. "We have a successful test, with results that are better than projected."

"We already wrote off the pale red dot initiative as a failure, so I hope that what you have is solid proof."

"Yes, commander," Jen grasped Scott's hand. "Scott found the modulation key that allows for reconstruction of biomatter."

"However," Scott squeezed her hand back. "It was Dr. Hammersmith who found out that the modulation frequency of the surrounding fields chained to the key allowed for stabilization."

"In English, please."

"The terraformer works," Jen said. "That means…"

"That means we can use it to terraform Earth back to livable conditions," the commander's face creased in an almost imperceptible smile.

"Yes sir," Scott's smile widened. "We can fix the damage and bring humans and animals back to the surface. We're transmitting the schematics and code now."

"We'll get these into our engineer's hands immediately. Doctors, you've given us our world back. There is nothing we can do to repay you for your diligence and efforts. I hope neither of you is averse to the entire planet trying though."

"No sir," Jen and Scott said together. "We wouldn't dream of it."
"Get your butts home then. A grateful world is waiting to try."
"On our way, pale red dot out."
The view screen went dark.

AT PLANE SIGHT

by Diana Parrilla Hernández

The plane shuddered, its engines sputtering as the cabin shook like a rag doll. Red emergency lights flashed, a chaotic melody of screams filled the air. The captain wrestled with the controls, but it was clear — the bird was going down.

Amid the mayhem, passengers bolted for the emergency exits, adrenaline kicking them into high gear. Oxygen masks dangled uselessly as people grabbed for parachutes stashed in special compartments.

A blast of frigid air and the roar of wind invaded the cabin as the door flew open. One by one, passengers hurled themselves into the void, fear tearing from their throats.

Each jumper fell away from the wildly pitching plane, which now banked hard, nosediving. The last few leapt as the aircraft plummeted, their bodies suspended in air, chutes blossoming as they gazed down, praying for a soft landing.

The plane continued its death throes, metal groaning under the stress. The pandemonium had faded, replaced by the constant howl of wind and the shuddering of the doomed craft. The cabin was in tatters, debris littering the floor, smoke tainting the air.

As passengers had bailed one after another, some leaping with chutes, others plummeting to their doom, the flight attendant who'd been calming passengers and helping them prep found herself alone. Her ashen face flickered in the strobing emergency lights.

She looked around. Every chute had been snatched up by passengers, and the pilot, who, in his haste to save his own skin, had been the first to abandon ship, leaving her with no way out. The attendant was alone, no family waiting at home, no clear destination, and no hope of salvation.

As the plane disintegrated, spiraling slowly downward, a voice crackled over the somehow still-functioning intercom: "Danger, approaching restricted zone boundary. Danger, evacuate prohibited area immediately." The attendant, not comprehending the message, and not wanting to either, stumbled to a shattered window. A blinding light assaulted her eyes, almost like a luminous bridge, a platform of salvation. With no better option, she hurled herself into the abyss.

The light swallowed her whole, and when she blinked her eyes open, countless sculptures were staring back at her. She pulled herself up, finding herself in some kind of dark basement that suddenly flooded with light as she rose. One of the sculptures lost its vacant stare, its yellow cat eyes springing to life as its mouth moved with a digital voice. "Body assistant activated. Welcome, please state your name."

"I'm Stephanie," she said, her voice shaky.

"What body do you desire? No need to explain what happened to your previous one or why you're changing. Just keep in mind, if you're choosing a body suited to a profession, you'll need to tell me the job you want, and I'll provide the most appropriate body for optimal performance in that role."

"What? I can choose what I want to do? But what if I don't have the skills?"

"The body comes equipped with the necessary traits to perform the job, but if you dislike the work, you can return, and we'll swap out your body and occupation. Or, if you prefer, you can choose not to work at all. However, I must warn you that happiness standards beyond ninety percent are rarely achieved without actively contributing to the community. Without a job, you might reach eighty-seven percent happiness, according to surveys. Plus, you wouldn't receive payment. Basic housing and food are covered, but you would miss out on any extras you might choose."

"Food?" Stephanie realized she hadn't eaten since that measly dinner before the ill-fated flight.

"Oh, of course. It's not necessary to eat to maintain these bodies, but some enjoy the pleasure of a tasty sensation on the tongue."

"I don't understand any of this. Where am I?"

"If you're feeling lost, I can provide a map of the ship. You're in the body workshop. Would you prefer a repair instead of a new one? It won't cost you anything unless it was caused by a rare incident – one of a violent nature, which is strictly forbidden, of course. The repair won't hurt either, as your soul leaves the body during the entire process. Would you like a magazine to read while we fix you up?"

"No, I – " Stephanie saw a map with blinking paths appear on her retina. "What is this?"

"The telepathic map I mentioned. If you'd prefer a guide to escort you, I can notify someone of your presence here."

"No, no, I don't want anything!" she shouted, terrified of being discovered as a stowaway on this bizarre ship.

The lights cut out, and the dragonfly-shaped statue with cat eyes froze back into stone just as voices drifted in from outside.

"How many survivors from the plane crash?"

"None, but we're missing one passenger."

Stephanie's throat tightened. The map still blinked in her retina. Labeled on it were: Classrooms, Medical, Cafeteria, Market, Library, Hotel, Workshops, Labs, Gyms, Residences, and Experimental Worlds.

"Experimental Worlds? What's that about?" she muttered. No sooner had the words left her mouth than she found herself teleported somewhere else – a museum-like space plastered with posters of massive dinosaurs.

She spotted two bipedal beings with white scales and orange skin, their rounded haunches reminiscent of seahorses, and ducked behind an info panel.

"They say World One-Two-Three is new, and you get three tries," said the one with spiky orange hair, looking like a hedgehog that'd stuck its finger in a socket.

"It's worthless. I went in, and the 'mysteries' they advertise are just old cases. If you've been to school long enough, you know them by heart. Kills the thrill."

"We should try the Saurian World."

"Dunno, kind of freaks me out. What if they attack you?"

"You hit the workshop. Don't be such a wimp. It's mind-blowing. Pay extra, and you can even inhabit one! Isn't that wild? I'm saving up from my door-decorating gig. Should afford it soon. If you chicken out, I'm going solo, just saying."

"You're a real badass, Natalia. Think I'll have you decorate my office doorknob. The bug-eyed frog I've got doesn't do it for me, but it came stock. The old lab chief from the Federation must've picked it, and I felt weird changing it."

As they passed by, another figure waltzed in, cheerily waving to the couple before they vanished into a kaleidoscopic tunnel. This newcomer was giraffe-tall, sporting metallic fingers with seven joints each. Its face boasted five hexagonal eyes on each side, grinning with a letterbox mouth stretched impossibly wide.

The alien creature halted, extracting what looked like a cannon and setting it on a tripod. It stepped back and hit the threatening ON button. A beam of light shot out, and suddenly, the metal wall transformed into an endless catwalk, a slice of infinity where once there was only steel.

"Models, you're on! I've got the new season's line!"

Various beings flooded in through a back door. Their faces lacked noses and hair; some tall and willowy, others with hips as wide as boats, all striding confidently towards the very real runway.

"Fatrish, I've got a problem. This dress split down the back," said the wide-hipped being.

The giraffe-like Fatrish whipped out a hand-sized device resembling a gun. With a grave expression, it aimed at the model's exposed back. A trigger pull later, the ill-fitting dress crumpled to the floor, replaced by an identical one that fit perfectly. "The glue gun made a copy and stitched it up. Can't even tell, what do you think?"

"I think I can squeeze in three more cream puffs without a hitch!"

Fatrish grinned as the model joined the others.

"Alright, hustle up! The museum opens soon, and we'll need to relocate to finish the shoot."

Stephanie heard the camera flashes and the bustle of the galactic fashion show, staying dead silent, though they probably wouldn't have heard her anyway. A voice echoed in her stunned mind. "If you slip out the left door now, you'll be unseen and end up in the ship's corridor."

"Who are you?" she whispered.

"I'm the AI assistant for the map function."

"You're not going to rat me out? Where am I?"

"I won't notify anyone unless you ask me to. I'm your AI assistant, at your service. You're aboard the Aerius, one of the Federation's many ships where interstellar races coexist harmoniously. You've accessed it through unofficial channels."

"Yeah, I know that much. I jumped into some light when my plane was crashing. That's all I remember." Stephanie followed the assistant's advice and found herself in a pristine hallway of white marble, walls lined with gleaming lead pipes and dotted with fisheye windows.

Stephanie, standing upright for the first time since the crash, noticed the blood-bubbling gash on her leg. She must've caught it on something sharp as the plane went down. A grimace of pain crossed her face.

"You need to get to the workshop."

"I didn't say anything."

"No, but you thought about the pain. Everything here works on mental connection. Everyone's linked to a vast network. You're never alone, but never too watched either. Anyone can connect with anyone, but nobody invades privacy. Why would they? No one wants that. But if something happens to you, they'll know — to help each other out. It's like everyone's listening and ignoring you at the same time. But seriously, that wound needs welding. You should hit the workshop."

"Workshop? Don't you mean a doctor, hospital, or something? I'm not metal like many specimens I see here. I have human skin."

"Doctor? Well, everyone goes to the doctor daily. They have a good time."

"What? Is everyone sick?"

"On the contrary. Oh, wait — humans call what we refer to as mechanics 'doctors,' you know, body fixers. For us, a 'doctor' is what humans call a psychologist. They provide you with the tools to perfect your soul, not for trivial matters, but to help you find happiness. Without envy or anger, you can be much happier. It's not the one who has the most who is happiest, but the one who needs the least. Emotional baggage isn't necessary to feel blissful."

A tropical room flashed in Stephanie's mind. A bed and a balcony overlooking a beautiful night lake, a massive ringed planet looming in the background.

"These are the couple therapy cabins. Very efficient. Once you master that part, they can even erase memories of resolved issues, so you don't dwell on the aftertaste once it's been discussed and solved."

"Couples?" Stephanie thought about her last relationship from years ago. It had ended poorly, and over time, her desire for another relationship had slowly withered away.

"Yes, you're assigned a compatible partner who acts as a mirror to see your own mistakes and face them head-on."

"Oh, I thought it was something romantic. But this is better. I'm not really into that stuff," she added hastily, almost too quickly.

"Well, it doesn't mean it can't happen..."

Stephanie peered out one of the round windows. Endless darkness was the answer. She saw the dark night in that landscape — and perhaps a reflection of her own thoughts. She had narrowly escaped certain death and found herself in this seemingly perfect world. But what awaited her was likely discovery and, in the best-case scenario, being sent back to Earth. Back to her exhausting job, barely making rent. Back for what? Here, the goal seemed to be happiness and inner growth — something far more fulfilling than working yourself to death in a repetitive job, only to realize you don't even know how to enjoy your free time when you finally get it.

"That therapy thing sounds good. I wish I could try it myself."

"Maybe you can, who knows? All you need is a partner for that — no payment required."

"No, I don't think I could open up to a stranger, even if they say they're a good match for me."

"Well, you don't seem to have a problem talking to me."

"But you're just an AI. Those therapies are supposed to be with a real person, with a soul and everything, right?"

"Yeah, exactly. They're not done with an AI. The psychologist has a soul, too. All living beings have one, no matter their form."

Stephanie's blank stare snapped back to focus as she recognized the all-too-human skyline below.

"Hold up, is that Earth down there? We can't be in space — it's way too close."

"Like I said, we're on a Federation ship. Humans know this place as the Moon."

"No way. Where's the big blue marble view of Earth?"

"We're not outside Earth. We're inside it. The Moon isn't just a rock — it's a colossal spacecraft positioned at the edge of Earth's atmosphere. Although it's a significant distance from the surface, it remains well within Earth's gravitational influence."

"But... the moon landing?"

"Smoke and mirrors, my friend. All a show for the space agencies to rake in cash. This ship's got a force field that keeps uninvited guests out. No one's actually touched down here or on your 'Moon.' Same deal with space travel — Earth's been on lockdown since before humans could even dream of rockets. Federation safety protocol. Most humans aren't quite ready to join the Federation — a realm of cooperation and harmony — just yet."

Stephanie's jaw dropped. "You're kidding me."

"Believe it or not, but you might wanna scoot. Company's coming. Want another peek around? I can zap you to the castle inn. The castle itself costs, but the inn's free."

"Whatever," she muttered, her gaze fixed on two distant, snake-headed creatures with cable-like hair drifting through the air.

Her request was granted, and she was instantly transported to a space resembling a movie theater but with much wider aisles between the rows of seats. A large screen at the front displayed job vacancies and related information, intermittently showing images from distant worlds — vast deserts, lush jungles, and torrential downpours. Behind her, towering structures loomed, connected to the grand framework of a castle.

"It's like the central office, but you can also request rooms here, though they do charge for them."

"This place is enormous. Does all this really fit inside the Moon?"

"Space isn't a constraint. Time and space don't operate as humans think. It's more like a kind of wormhole, leading to endless realms arranged in layers and dimensions with no limits. It's as if everything is unfolding simultaneously in everyone's mind, constantly updated for all."

To the right, a modest queue formed in front of a narrow wooden door with stairs leading upward. A doorkeeper stood guard – bipedal, with blue and red cables, through which a constant flow of yellow light seemed to pulse. Its face was masked, with eyes barely visible, and its hair, silky and reddish, barely touched its rounded shoulders.

"Next!"

The line crept forward, and Stephanie couldn't help but notice everyone was at least three or four meters tall.

"That works in your favor. You can slip in while the doorkeeper's distracted with processing folks."

Stephanie wasn't entirely sure, but she couldn't pass up this adventure, still unsure if it wasn't all some dream. So she did just that, weaving between those long legs, spotting a few that had arched forms instead of knees, almost floating a few centimeters off the ground.

"Your companion is waiting for you in Room 1B-475, down the hall."

"You've got the wrong data. I'm Augustus, here for some timber-cutting training. It's for my workshop job."

Stephanie seized the moment of confusion and discreetly slipped past, climbing the stairs. Upstairs was a museum-like space, plush crimson carpeting underfoot. Busts of insectoids and vases of indescribable shapes adorned the area. At the far end were double doors leading to different sections, like 1B.

To the left was a spiraling, bubbly tunnel labeled "Capsules."

While to the right, a towering door read "Chessboard."

"Chess?"

"Not what you think. Tiles that change color – it's like a life-size puzzle. When you complete it, the room transforms to match. It's free, but you have to book a slot. Don't wanna skip the queue."

"I'll try the capsules then."

Stephanie headed for the tunnel and, upon entering, found herself face-to-face with a wall-mounted staircase that seemed incredibly solid, almost cemented in. But as she began climbing, it swayed like it was made of threads. Ascending, she realized just how high up she was. The space resembled an opera house stage, with small hotel-room-sized nooks instead of box seats.

"Finally, someplace with a low ceiling."

"That's so they can lie down and relax. The seating's down below for meetings."

Climbing into one of the rooms, it felt more like a circus tent than anything, the semi-transparent, violet fabric acting as walls.

"There's no privacy here at all."

"No need for it. You can't really see what your neighbor's doing, but you won't feel lonely either. It's a perfect balance."

"And now what? Can I just hide here forever?"

"You could try. See that button there? Click it, and you can peek in on what others are doing without actually teleporting. There are public spaces where that's possible — meetings, cafés, the lab. Everyone can stay informed and participate in the community's activities if they want."

"Let's check out the lab."

Stephanie nestled into the plush, exotic-patterned green and pink carpet, pressing the crimson button, which sank satisfyingly under her thumb.

A holographic image projected out, revealing beings in white coats and tall chef-like hats, gas masks on their faces, gathered around gleaming asphalt floors and large sinks.

"If you dip your hands in like that, you can write encrypted messages in the water and send them."

"What use would that serve, H16? In our society, there's no need to encrypt anything. Everything is transparent, shared for the common good. Harmony is maintained because we all have access to the same information. There are no secrets to protect, only cooperation to ensure everyone lives in peace." The being with two suction-cup fingers continued, "Besides, the idea of hiding something only creates barriers. Here, every thought and action is in plain sight, not out of control, but to maintain balance. Trust is the foundation of it all. Encrypting a message would be like putting a door in the middle of a space with no walls. Why create divisions where we don't need them?"

"Precisely, T83, what I'm saying is to use the energy for encrypting to propel the wave to expand more quickly. It's like a retraction so that when it unfolds, it explodes with more force and bounces back faster. We'd achieve incredible energy savings, and the scenario creators could have shorter shifts."

T83 nodded slowly. "H16, what you're suggesting makes sense if we look at it from an energy efficiency perspective. By using the encryption energy not as a means of encoding but as a source of wave compression, we could achieve that cumulative effect you mentioned. The key would be finding the optimal point of retraction, where the stored energy is released in a controlled explosion that maximizes the impact without wasting resources. The idea of the rebound being faster is especially interesting. By creating a stronger, more sustained resonance, we could decrease the amount of energy required to maintain the integrity of the scenarios and, as you said, shorten the creators' shifts. Of course, we'd have to be careful not to overload the wave matrix, because too intense an explosion could shatter the structure of the simulated reality, and that would be... problematic, to say the least."

"I'm not understanding anything they're saying," Stephanie said.

"That's normal. Those are the Angelichen, the research specialists. If — "

"Oh, it's cut off," Stephanie said, sitting up. It took her a moment to realize there was a silhouette on the other side of the curtain.

A massive, winged being swept the curtain aside. "Stephanie? What are you doing here in that body?"

"What? Who are you?"

"It's me, Matthew."

"Matthew, the pilot from the plane?"

"The very same."

"I thought you all had died."

"And so we have. But you can't have that body — it's deceased."

Stephanie looked around, utterly bewildered.

"Wait, don't tell me you didn't die? You jumped here from the plane? When they were killing us? That's the only time the portal's open. They just taught me that in the intro class. Don't tell me you snuck in through there?"

"How do you know that?"

"I see what you're thinking. It takes some practice, but you get used to the good stuff quickly." An endless tongue unfurled from his massive grin. "How do you like the body I picked? They say the tongue's a universal analyzer, and with how much I loved to eat, I figured, 'Give me the biggest, longest one you've got!'" he roared with laughter.

"Help me," Stephanie whispered, speaking to her absent AI assistant. She stood, searching for an escape route.

"Oh no, don't go! Wait, I'll call security. Security!"

"No!" Stephanie didn't know where to run. The adjoining room was too far to jump, and there was no catwalk or anything to aid her leap — it seemed designed for bodies with legs that could clear the distance in a stride or wings and other special abilities.

From beneath a swarm of dragonfly-like beings, wings unfurling like bats, voices rose.

"Yes, she's the one missing from the plane crash tonight."

"Please, don't send me back to Earth," Stephanie pleaded, wrapping her arms around herself. "It's so nice here, and there's nothing for me there... not that I want to die either." She shivered at the thought of returning to her empty life on Earth, feeling exposed.

A guard, who appeared to be in charge, floated effortlessly toward her.

"Die?" he said. "I see. Since you didn't follow the proper procedure, you haven't been briefed properly. Death doesn't exist — souls are eternal. No being in the galaxy truly dies. It's a concept the Federation created when we built this system of united interplanetary races. We call it the Fede-recall project. Back when the race from Kepler-452b developed the technology to separate body and soul, we began reclaiming all the scattered souls across the universe. But we agreed not to do it all at once. There would be no sudden upheaval, no cataclysm. Instead, we allow species to live out their lives naturally, giving them time to evolve and prepare for the harmony of this society. In your case, when humans are ready, we 'kill' them — essentially, we transfer their souls to new bodies here, leaving their Earthly ones behind. We've done this for centuries. Before the project, humans lived longer but didn't really die. They just withered away. We quickly intervened, giving the appearance of death while gradually integrating their souls into this larger system."

Stephanie's arms began to relax slightly, perhaps more out of reflex, as she struggled to wrap her head around these new ideas.

"Earth's history is full of misconceptions, especially when it comes to science, space, and the human body. No one dies in the way you think. Sure, they may suffer accidents, their bodies may deteriorate, but true death only happens when we, from the outside, decide it's time. Suicide? That's just a signal. If we sense a soul is ready for this life, we grant them release. Earth has been sealed off for this very reason. We make sure humanity doesn't leave before they're ready. We've been doing this since long before they even dreamed of flying machines. Back then, setting up the magnetic vault around the planet was straightforward, and it remains intact today, preventing anyone from leaving prematurely.

"So the plane crash... you didn't kill them. You just discarded the bodies to transfer their souls here. If I had stayed, I would have ended up here too."

"Exactly. Sometimes glitches occur, like your unauthorized entry, but don't worry — you were part of the pack. If you come with us to the workshop, you can select your new body just like everyone else did." The guard extended a long, three-fingered hand. "We'll open a tunnel for you, and you can be there in the blink of an eye. The AI assistant will ask you some questions to assign the body it thinks suits you best."

Stephanie smiled. "Yes, I've been there before, and I'm familiar with those tunnels. The map app's AI assistant has guided me a bit."

"That's not possible," the guard said. "We don't have any other systematized AI besides the body assignment assistant. Everything else is managed by personnel at the central hub. The location assistant, along with those who handle food, work, housing, and so on — they're all staff, not AIs."

Stephanie was about to utter a "but" when a towering figure with a pulsing, cone-shaped antenna on its head ascended the wall-mounted stairs she had climbed earlier. It had no wings and was a light blue with stylish brown freckles.

The guard looked at the wingless being. "What are you doing here, Uj? Why did you leave your post at the central desk?"

"I came as quickly as I could," Uj said, finishing the climb and turning to Stephanie. "Hello, Stephanie. I was wondering if, after you choose your new body, you'd like to try the couple therapy capsules with me? Unless you prefer an AI to open yourself up to."

Stephanie blinked, first in confusion, then understanding the reference.

TO PERCEIVE AND BE PERCEIVED
by Owen Townend

After four decades of nondisclosure, Sunthers & Co. have finally released select passages of the Project Glimpse case file to the public. What follows are extracts from the initial Tempus Scope trial, featuring testimonies from the first two voluntary human test subjects.

Briefing – What do you hope to achieve?

Nelly Skinner, England

Who knows how many years I have left? All our futures are uncertain. At least, uncertain on a case-by-case basis. If I were to say a child named Mohammed will be born next month, that might well happen. If I were to say an octogenarian will succumb to complications caused by a bone fracture, that's what lies ahead for somebody. Likely me. I'm almost at peace with that reality. Still, before osteoporosis finally does for me, I'd like to see proof that the future can, in fact, be perceived.

That's why I'm here. Project Glimpse is an exciting venture. I was skeptical when first approached, but from your briefing, I can tell this has wondrous potential. If you boffins can really get this Tempus Scope of yours to work, I might just have a genuine premonition. Not my own, obviously. I quite agree that seeing what's to come for me would doubtless spoil my appetite, if not causality and the time-space continuum. As for seeing the future of a human being a million miles away, even just the promised sixty seconds, that will be enough.

I'm an old woman. When I think about the shape of things to come, it more often than not relates to other people more than it does me. This other lab rat of yours, I trust they're much younger. Seeing their tomorrow will hopefully be free of aches, pains, and medical reports. Hopefully. But then, you can't promise what the briefly glimpsed future I'll soon see will hold, can you?

Well, at least I'll experience some youthful energy. As for my opposite number, I'm afraid they'll have to settle with my rattling cough and see the world tremble through poor eyesight. If so, I'm sorry. Not as sorry as I will be, mind you, when I live that minute for myself in real-time.

Even if this turns out to be a failure, it will be thrilling to attempt it. At last, it feels like I'm truly a part of history. I've made some differences in my life, but nothing like this. If Sunthers & Co. have really done their homework, we'll pierce through the fog of Yet-To-Come. Now that's something to look forward to.

Ho Han, South Korea

All my life, I have needed to prepare. My parents insist that I must think ahead, know where to go next, then the time after that, and the time after that.

I am so tired of all this mental anguish. It would be good, just once, for someone to show me the way. Project Glimpse seems to offer this, allowing me to merely open my eyes and have it all laid out in front of me.

It pains me that I will not be able to see my own future, to finally have that long-sought advantage. However, I have read enough science fiction to know that the possible ramifications of this could be cataclysmic.

So, I will settle for a brief vision of someone else's future. I feel like my disappointment will be softened by the multisensory experience that you have promised. Is it truly possible for your Tempus Scope to offer touch, taste, smell, and hearing as well as the expected sight? I anticipate wonders.

If my parents knew what I have signed up for, they would likely call me a lazy fool going against nature. And yet, am I not finally doing precisely what they instructed me to do? If this works, I may be the only child who actually meets the high expectations of their parents.

Of course, I also do this for myself. I will look into the future of whoever you have paired me with and know something remarkable. It does not matter if I can never share it with anyone else. This knowledge will become my own proud secret.

Procedure – What did you see?

Nelly Skinner, England

Well, if that was a hallucination, it was still worth the price of admission!

It was almost like an experimental art exhibit, bafflingly elaborate at first, with all the pads you stuck to my skull and the heavy welder's mask on top of it. Your man mentioned more technical terminology, but quite frankly, it was all blown out of my thoughts when the actual show began.

At first, it felt like my brain had caught fire. I won't lie. It was a terrifying moment, especially as it concentrated around my forehead. Once it stopped feeling like my eyeballs were about to pop out of their sockets, I settled. There was a bright white light, but not for long. It faded into a familiar view. Pavement, though not quite the sort I'm used to seeing. A different shade of grey, not to mention less crumbly.

The vision bobbed slightly as I moved along the pavement. I'm afraid I threw up a bit in the present, but the motion sickness passed much quicker than usual. Just as we approached a gutter, the rest of my senses caught up. A car tooted behind me. I choked a bit on smoggy air and smelt artificial blueberries. Somebody must have been vaping as they passed by the person whose future I was seeing.

Then it occurred to me. This is someone's future! Either that or you've rigged up your Scope with some detailed test videos. In any case, the fact that I felt the world differently was impressive. Not just the sound, taste and smell, I felt hands stuffed inside tight jean pockets. They clearly weren't my own. These fingers were thinner, straighter with stronger bones.

Considering the possibility of being inside somebody else's senses, I spent the rest of that minute taking in the whole experience, internal as well as external. I felt young, moving fast and breathing lightly. Glimpsing the body's midriff, I saw a stylish grey jumper and felt the seam against unfamiliar hips. Functional hips!

Wonderful. Like sixty sweet seconds in the fountain of youth. Bones, organs, and blood all working together as they should. Still, whoever's body I was occupying, their gaze remained fixed on the pavement. To be honest, I zoned out of that part of the experience. As far as premonitions go, staring at the ground is hardly what draws the focus.

And yet, as soon as everything faded and all I could see was the black inside of the visor, I wondered why the body never once looked up. Perhaps I'm merely assuming, but it seems like this person was feeling low. Meanwhile, inhabiting their worldview, I was having the time of my life. How strange. A matter of perspective, I suppose.

Whoever they may be, I can't help but feel sorry for them. I realize I only saw one random moment in their life to come, but no one so young should ever feel so bereft.

Here's the soundbite you're after, the quote to headline your report. Looking into this Tempus Scope has enlivened me. It's an old chestnut, to look at the world through another's eyes, but you've actually managed it here. Briefly escaping this old flesh and surviving is the rarest of privileges. Thank you, and please, thank them for me too.

Ho Han, South Korea

First, I want reassurance that you will keep checking on my condition on a monthly basis. My initial experience of the Tempus Scope felt very much like acute brain trauma, and I fear this will somehow lead to an aneurism, a tumor, or worse.

As for what I saw, once I became used to the heavy visor and the shock faded, I am not sure I understood it. During my minute of foresight, everything felt very rigid. I tried to move, but then it occurred to me that this was not my own body's experience.

The body my mind was currently occupying felt old. I heard a voice cough, and the perspective shook, as if the stranger were sitting up. The slow, awkward shift reminded me of my grandfather. I felt a cold plastic bar, like you find on the side of hospital beds. I assume the stranger was bed-bound due to illness. I did not expect to view the future of someone so much older and more infirm than me.

However, once I got past this surprise, I remembered the privilege of the situation. Old or not, the senses I was borrowing were showing me a future. I do not know how far ahead we were, but I recall one of your specialists explaining that the Tempus Scope's current parameters do not go beyond the end of next year.

Anyway, it was pleasant to take in such good weather. For the majority of the minute, I saw blue skies with no clouds. I felt warm and snug under soft sheets. The air smelt slightly of chlorine, but there was lavender, too. Flowers on the bedside table, I think. The stranger never turned from the window.

I have no idea if the year ahead will see massive change or if it will be positive for me, my family, and my country. It would have been helpful to see signs and hear news, but I suppose we cannot choose what will be seen in this experiment. There will be quiet moments as well as significant ones. I suppose a boring premonition suggests a peaceful future. It was very uneventful but beautiful with it. I was shocked to see such a clear sky. It's been so long for me.

Though I could not distinguish the stranger's thoughts from my own, I did take comfort in their steady breathing. Their stillness in the minute was equally welcoming. A relief, in fact. Whatever their affliction was, I hope it recedes like the vision from my fiery brain. Assuming there has been no lasting damage.

I finally saw the future, and there seemed to be nothing to prepare for. On the one hand, this is disconcerting, but on the other…thank God. Some calm in my world, at last. I look forward to more.

Debriefing — How do you feel?

Nelly Skinner, England

Better. I'm still coughing and aching, but at least I have a more recent memory of youth to cling to. Funny that. A glimpse of another's future has become my memory, and it still hasn't even happened yet.

I often go over that little event, thinking about my fellow lab rat. I have no right to assume anything about them from so brief an insight, but I still worry about them. Whoever they may be, I hope that downcast minute was one of few. Will be one of few.

Every moment of my Project Glimpse experience has been uncanny but invigorating. I certainly didn't expect anything like this for my later years.

That being said, I still have to wonder what's to come for me. I have your implant in my buzzed skull, but what experience will it capture? How far into the future will my life actually reach?

Oh, but I'm tired of morbid thinking. Most of all, I want to say thank you. Thank you for all this cutting-edge madness. It's one thing I never knew I wanted to do until it happened.

We can now, in fact, see into the future. How nice to know there's some hope left in it.

Ho Han, South Korea

Your implant unsettles me. I will honor my contract with Sunthers & Co., but you must do everything in your power to ensure that I don't die of radiation poisoning.

As for my feelings about the premonition, it gave me comfort. In fact, if not for the subsequent wave of euphoria, I wouldn't have agreed to this implant. Well, that and the prospect of subverting the flow of time. I do not wish to end existence out of spite.

I suppose the stranger's peace has unlocked some of my own. I hope I have such quiet moments when I reach old age. Who would have thought hospitals could ever be free of noise and sadness?

Project Glimpse is a success. The Tempus Scope is a scientific marvel that the world needs to know about. I am glad to have been able to contribute.

I only wish that I had somehow returned this favor to the stranger. This damn implant will capture many things to come, and I only hope my knowing it's there won't affect my view of the world. Then again, having this glorious secret does seem to have already lightened my mood.

Of course, life never stops catching you unawares. Nothing can prepare against it. It can all turn in a minute. Then it will just turn again.

THE BIODECKS

by Erin Cullen

Jaden was fifteen years old the first time the Computer betrayed him.

The main Computer, the one that ran Sunrise Station from the interior mechanical ring to the life-sustaining ocean that filled the station's bottom level, had always picked Jaden's educational modules, as it did for all the kids. It had never steered him wrong before. But today, the Computer had decided that Jaden would receive a spot in a group of teenagers visiting the biodecks, the fragile habitats of plants, animals, and microorganisms that the humans on the station relied upon for environmental regulation.

Jaden knew that the biodecks merited appreciation. He had never taken for granted how amazing it was that he had been born to a species that had evolved on a planet out of interactions between lucky macromolecules and gone on to transcend the very world that had made them, to a point where Jaden and three generations of his family before him could live in luxury and comfort inside a metal cylinder in space. It was amazing that this metal cylinder could soak up enough radiation from the sun it orbited to maintain itself and make everything humans needed indefinitely. The biodecks were an indispensable part of that system, which was why they were mostly closed to the human residents of the station.

The scarcity of opportunities to visit was probably why so many people went nuts for them. Biodeck day passes were doled out in a popular lottery each year, and the jobs maintaining the levels — exhausting work, by all accounts, and as close to dangerous as anyone's job here got — were some of the most competitive roles on the station.

Jaden had no interest in going to the biodecks. He didn't understand why anyone, with the opportunity to stay in comfortably climate-controlled spaces with oxygenating plants tucked neatly away within the walls, would want anything to do with the dirt and humidity and chaos of the forest level, let alone the beach. But even with all that, the worst part of the trip by far was the bizarre requirement that the students wouldn't be allowed any connection to the Computer during the trip.

Jaden hadn't spent a minute of his life without the Computer in easy reach. The Computer was indispensable to him – he'd been shaping his own connection to it for as long as he could remember, teaching it how his thoughts worked and how to answer questions he didn't even have the words to ask. He could communicate with it more fluently and efficiently than he could with any human, and the connection he'd fostered had let him fly through basic education without having to learn much else.

The prospect of a full day without the Computer made his gut clench. What if he had a question and couldn't ask it in a way the counselors understood? What if he got hurt and needed help, and the other humans around didn't notice? What if it turned out he had nothing to gain from visiting the biodecks after all? Any situation Jaden could imagine would be better with the Computer in it.

"Computer, give me seven ways to get out of going," he ordered. Seven was the number he had settled on years ago – enough to force the Computer to be creative, but not so many that he was left wading through nonsensical drivel by the end.

The Computer, Jaden's oldest friend, his closest companion, did not immediately give him its reply. When the reply came, there was no list of brilliant ideas printed on Jaden's screen. Instead, the Computer simply said, "I'm sorry." Jaden had set it up to deliver messages in his own voice, which was meant to be pleasantly undistracting. Now, it jarred him.

"Give me the list!" Jaden snapped. The Computer almost never argued with a human inquiry, and for it to do so twice was unthinkable.

"This trip is the best thing for your wellbeing. I can give you a list of seven reasons you may not want to go. One: you are afraid of social ostracization by your peers. Tw–"

"Stop generating," Jaden muttered.

This time, the Computer obeyed.

There was a knock on his door. The Computer setup in the hallway had probably informed Jaden's parents that the task he had come in here to do had been completed.

"Come in," Jaden said, screwing up his face at having to admit defeat.

Jaden's dad opened the door. "What did it say?" he asked in a passably neutral voice.

Jaden considered lying. He could tell his dad that the Computer recommended going to the biodecks but that he could also stay home if he preferred. The Computer wasn't an official authority, but it contained the aggregate wisdom of all human history. Everyone knew that following its advice was practically always the best option. Jaden's dad had agreed that if Jaden's Computer gave him a reason not to go, he would honor it.

And the Computer had betrayed him.

Lying wouldn't help Jaden. The hall Computer knew what Jaden's Computer told him. It would tell Jaden's dad if he asked. "It said I have to go."

"Really?" That was the nice response. Everyone knew that the Computer didn't give explicit orders to humans.

"It wouldn't give me a reason not to."

Jaden's dad nodded. "I know you want to stay home, but this is a really exciting opportunity. I didn't get to visit the biodecks until I was in my twenties."

"You could go instead and tell me all about it," Jaden muttered.

His dad laughed. Jaden sulked.

Jaden kept to the back of the line, one hand always in his pocket. The other hand he had constantly raised to push away the branches that hung out into the narrow trail through the forest level.

"They made a forest in outer space. You'd think they could at least figure out a way to keep the trails clear," the girl in front of Jaden said as she held back a branch to keep it from swinging in his face.

"Yep."

The girl glanced curiously back at Jaden, but he didn't say anything else.

His arm was starting to tire. He had to switch pockets. He checked to make sure the adults at the front of the line were facing forward and tentatively took out his handheld.

"Watch out," the same girl in front of him said. Jaden looked up, worried about a branch hitting his face, and the girl was indeed holding one back from the trail. But her attention was on the thing in Jaden's hand. "You have a handheld!"

"Shut up!" Jaden brushed the branch aside and shoved his way ahead of her, cramming the handheld into the opposite pocket.

The girl followed him, practically breathing into his shoulder. "I'm Cora," she said. "Can I borrow your handheld?"

Jaden shoved a branch out of the way so hard it snapped. "No."

"Please? I just have a few questions. I'll use the typing interface."

"No. It's mine."

"It's all the same Computer."

"It's not. It's *mine*."

Cora remained a step behind him in relentless pursuit. "You really think the interface will change from a couple of typed questions?"

"Yes! It won't be my Computer anymore."

"What's going on back here?" A counselor in front of them had stopped moving while Jaden had been focused on the argument, and now they were only a few steps ahead.

As soon as Jaden noticed the counselor, the Computer interface in his pocket responded to his accidental summons. "Yes, Jaden?"

The counselor — Trev, Jaden remembered from introductions the group had done before beginning the hike — glanced at Jaden's pocket. Then they looked at Jaden's face with one eyebrow raised.

Jaden kept his hand clenched tight around the device. "My dad said I could have it for emergencies."

Trev frowned. "What kind of emergencies?"

"Any kind!"

Neither Jaden nor Trev had started walking again. Cora had stopped, too. Her presence made Jaden's skin crawl with irritation. She had nothing to do with this.

"Do you have any medical conditions that aren't listed in your file? A sick friend or family member who might send you updates on their condition? Any reason you might need the handheld that my emergency comm can't take care of?"

"Not right now, but emergencies can happen at any time."

"Give me the handheld," Trev said. "Your dad isn't in charge here, and it's against the rules."

Jaden considered pushing the issue. He could refuse to let go of it. Sit down on the disgusting forest floor and decline to move until Trev let him go home. Going off into the woods without any connection to his Computer felt like shaving off a piece of his soul.

But Cora was still there. Cora, who was his age, who lived on Sunrise with him, a situation that would likely hold true all their lives. He didn't want Cora spreading the rumor that Jaden had resorted to a toddler's tactics to avoid giving up his handheld for no reason he knew how to articulate.

He took the handheld out of his pocket. The chat screen was still on, waiting for Jaden to address the Computer. He wanted to say some words of parting — not for the Computer, which he knew didn't care, but for himself, and maybe a little bit to spite Trev.

In the end, he had nothing to say. He gave the handheld to Trev and pushed ahead, letting branches slap his limbs and face as if the sting of impact could puncture the hole that had opened up inside him.

The forest stayed the same. Wet and sharp and intolerably boring.

"I never got your name," Cora said from behind Jaden.

Jaden didn't answer. It was her fault he'd lost his handheld. He had come here because he'd been forced to, not to make friends, and he especially didn't want to talk to *her*.

Minutes passed. Jaden's palms were sore from shoving branches out of the way, and his feet were starting to hurt from walking on the squishy trail. Any distraction seemed better than enduring one more second with nothing to focus on but the all-consuming boredom and discomfort.

"It's Jaden," he said to Cora, who was still behind him. "What did you want the handheld for, anyway?"

Cora responded eagerly, not seeming to resent Jaden at all for his long silence. Or maybe she was as bored as he was and would take any distraction right now. "I wanted to ask about the trees. Are there this many kinds in the same place on Old Earth? How many of the species are natural, and how many are gene-eng?"

"You could just ask the adults," Jaden said. He pushed a branch out of the way and held it out for Cora to grab so it wouldn't swing back in her face.

"Yeah, but I couldn't be sure if they really knew. I'd have to ask the Computer again later anyway."

That was actually a great point. Humans were much more likely to say false or misleading things than the Computer was, whether they meant to or not. Humans were authorities only on their own opinions, and Jaden didn't care much about anyone's opinion.

Usually, he didn't. But right now, talking to Cora was much more pleasant than slogging through the mud with nothing to occupy his mind. But what was there to say?

He remembered how Cora had tried to start a conversation earlier, complaining about the branches in their way. He certainly had complaints of his own.

"It's so stupid that we have to do this. Just because our groundbound ancestors had to sleep on the floor and hunt for food doesn't mean we should," he said.

"I think it's cool," Cora replied. "Otherwise, how could we learn what it was like down there?"

"Why should we bother? The Computer knows."

"Yeah, but that doesn't mean we know. If everything we need is in the

Computer, then why even be alive?"

"To do fun things. Things like not this."

Cora's laughter echoed through the trees.

Beach deck. Sand stretched from the edge where they entered to at least halfway across the dome, where it disappeared past the protruding bubble that kept the ocean and the beach separate from the forest deck. The ocean lay in front of them, waves of water lapping at the rocks on the shore, giving way to stillness at the other end of the dome. The dome's thin mesh of solar-absorbent alloy seemed to glitter in the light emanating from the panels held in place by the mesh. Panels lit bright blue, and lavender hinted at a coming sunset. Every few seconds, a flash streaked across the dome as the station rotated, indicating that this end of the station was passing in front of the actual sun.

The group had reached the beach after a long climb up uneven steps set in the wet muck of the forest floor, a climb that Jaden's physical conditioning classes hadn't at all prepared him for. Cora, for all her genuine desire to be out here, had struggled too. She flopped down on the sand as soon as they were clear of the muck.

Jaden sat gingerly beside her. His pants couldn't get much dirtier anyway, after getting splattered with mud throughout the hike.

Trev and the other counselors were up ahead, counting kids. Trev smiled at Jaden, who scowled back at them.

It was only upon seeing Trev that Jaden realized he hadn't thought about his handheld through the whole climb up to the beach. He'd been too focused on making his way up, complaining back and forth with Cora about the slippery ground and their sore legs.

Now, though, all Jaden wanted was to talk to the Computer. Was the difficulty of the climb normal or was he in worse physical condition than he thought? Did Cora seeking him out for conversation mean she liked him, or was she just bored? What was the point of this trip anyway?

The counselors didn't give him much time to brood. "We're going to do something not many people on this station get to experience," the lead counselor, Lori, announced. "We're going to collect our own dinner."

Jaden rolled his eyes, but Cora looked eager as Lori explained how to cut individual mussels off the rocks bordering the water without damaging the others. Trev and the others passed out knives and heavy gloves for the students to wear and set them loose.

Cora immediately set off toward the water. The other students, who had been walking ahead of the two of them, dithered around, complaining that the gloves were dirty and the sand was getting into their shoes.

Jaden followed Cora. If he collected his share before the others were done, maybe Trev would let him have the handheld for a few minutes while the other students were busy on the rocks.

His shoes were sinking into the wet sand by the time he reached a rock with mussels clinging to it. He took the knife to it, trying to pry one off like Lori had demonstrated. The task was harder than it looked, and his first mussel popped off the rock, only to land deeper in the ocean with a splash.

Jaden looked toward it. As he did, he noticed that Cora was up to her knees in the water. All of them had learned to swim in the pools on the habitation decks, but even Jaden knew that the ocean was different. Waves splashed Cora's legs, making her pants cling to her thighs as she stared into the distance, knife hanging unused at her side.

"Cora? Are you okay?" Jaden asked. He had to yell to be heard over the splashes of the waves on the shore.

"Yeah! I want to try to see the generators," she said back. She turned toward Jaden, maybe to explain further — as if Jaden could possibly not know about the generators that managed the ocean's waves, keeping the algae that provided the station's oxygen in a healthy rotation and maintaining the gravity well that kept the station spinning smoothly.

Before Cora could say anything else, a wave slammed into her from behind, knocking her down. For a terrifying moment, she was completely underwater, invisible under the layers of dark algae and sand agitated by the waves.

She surfaced, the side of her face red with something it took Jaden a moment to recognize as blood. Then she lost her balance to an oncoming wave and went under again.

Jaden's instinct was to call for the Computer. The Computer could tell him what to do; it could solve any problem as fast as Jaden could think of it. But Jaden's pocket was empty, and the screen in his bedroom was far away. There was no Computer around to hear him.

"Help!" he yelled instead. It was an alien word, an alien desperation that led him to say it. He had never been able to rely on the humans around him. *Ask the Computer*, his parents had said any time he'd had a question as a child. His teachers had taught him to ask the right questions, to leverage humanity's accumulated knowledge for his own purposes, whatever those purposes might be. And he'd gotten good at it — tuned his Computer interface to his desires so that anything he wanted to know was within his reach at all times.

But the Computer couldn't tell him if it was safe to run forward and try to grab Cora out of the water. Not in time for it to matter, anyway.

He looked back and saw Trev, Lori, and the other counselors running toward them across the beach. If he did judge wrong and get himself hurt too, they would know what to do. There was no perfect answer, no time to think through a list of seven choices. There was only action and inaction.

Jaden ran forward. The current pulled at his legs and he slipped on a seaweed-covered rock, going down on a knee. But he had reached Cora, and he grabbed her arm, pulling her up to the surface and keeping her head above water as she sputtered and coughed.

Trev was only seconds behind him, sturdy even in the waves. They put a hand on Jaden's back and took Cora's other arm in a gentle grip. The three of them stood up with Cora still coughing and waded toward the shore where Lori waited, already talking into her emergency comm.

"There's a team on the way," Lori said as Trev guided Jaden to set Cora down on the damp sand a few steps from the edge of the water.

"How long?" Trev asked. Now that they were out of the water, Cora's head was bleeding heavily. One of the other counselors opened a first aid kit from his backpack, but blood immediately soaked through the gauze he held against the cut.

Lori's lips went thin for a moment before she spoke. "Maybe half an hour. They need to prep a helicraft."

Jaden motioned to Trev. "Give me my handheld."

Trev looked up from Cora, incredulous. "That's what you want right now?"

"Give it to me!" Jaden's hand didn't waver.

Cora started coughing again. She didn't seem to have ever fully gotten her breath back.

Trev reached into their pocket and took out the handheld. They placed it in Jaden's hand.

The device was wet from the ocean, but it lit up when Jaden touched the contact point that would have the Computer listening for his prompt. "Station ocean accident, cut head, inhaled water, medics half an hour away," Jaden said. He knew he didn't have to bother specifying his question, '*What do we do?*' but he made one clarification. "Not me."

A bright sound shot through to clear the speakers of water, and then the Computer's voice – Jaden's voice, but calmer, wiser, and knowing everything there was to know – came through. Jaden's Computer had been trained out of the unnecessary warm-up text the default interfaces came with and got straight to the point. "Is the victim conscious?"

"Yes."

"Record their pulse and respiratory rate and monitor over time. Albuterol can be administered if breathing is difficult. Is the wound still bleeding?"

"Yes."

"Cover with absorbent gauze. Is the victim responsive to speech?"

The Computer continued to ask questions. Jaden answered and followed its instructions, along with Trev. The Computer guided them through checking Cora's pupillary responses and asking her questions to check that her memory was intact, a prelude to proper concussion testing. It confirmed that it was alright for her to lie down on the sand when she asked to. Finally, there was nothing more to do until the medics came.

"Computer, is it possible to see the generators from the beach?" Jaden asked. The default interface would need to ask clarifying questions, but

Jaden's Computer knew that he was talking about the wavemakers, his beach, his station.

"It is not. The generators are deep underwater. Would you like to see a video tour?"

Jaden glared at Trev, who was still sitting with him and Cora while the other counselors supervised the rest of the students, who had finally started gathering mussels with more success than the two of them had. If he'd been allowed to keep the mobile, this whole situation could have been avoided.

But he hadn't wanted to let Cora ask her questions before because the Computer might think that Jaden cared about the answers. It wasn't Trev's fault any more than it was his. Maybe he would tell the whole story to the Computer later, let the Computer decide if it was better off to let groups like theirs have one handheld, for kids like Cora to ask their questions instead of getting into dangerous situations trying to find out the answers for themselves. It could also give kids like Jaden some peace of mind, knowing they weren't completely cut off from the only thing they had ever been able to rely on.

"Do you want to watch the video?" Jaden asked Cora. She was still clutching a layer of gauze to her forehead, but the bleeding had slowed, and her breathing wasn't so harsh anymore.

"Sure," she said from where she was lying on the sand.

Jaden positioned the handheld in front of her so that both of them could watch. When that finished, he asked, "What did you want to know about the forest again?"

"I thought you didn't want to contaminate it."

"I'll ask. In my own words."

"Do all those species live together on Old Earth? Are any of them gene-eng?"

Jaden ended up repeating the question practically verbatim. He hadn't wanted Cora asking the questions before because Jaden hadn't cared, and he hadn't wanted the Computer to get the impression that he did. Now, he did want to know, and it didn't matter that he only wanted to know because Cora did. It was all the same to the Computer.

Cora's curiosity kept them occupied until the medics showed up. "We should hang out sometime," Cora said as the medics put a sturdier bandage on her cut and prepared to load her into the helicraft.

"Yeah," Jaden said, surprising himself. He hadn't often wanted to spend time with anyone his own age. With any human, really. But he did want to see Cora again.

When Cora and the helicraft were gone, Jaden kept a tight grip on his handheld. Maybe Trev wouldn't ask for it back, now that they knew how good he was with it, now that his argument that it would be useful in an emergency had proven itself entirely accurate.

But he found that he didn't have anything else to ask the Computer. What he wanted to do was walk back out to the ocean and try collecting mussels again, in case Cora asked him what it was like. She was right that it wouldn't be the same if he heard about it from the Computer — the Computer could tell him the aggregate of how other people felt about it, but he could already tell that it couldn't quite capture the awkward heaviness of the gloves, or the difficulty of positioning the knife on the bumpy, slippery surfaces of the rocks. It certainly couldn't tell him how it would feel to do it right now, as himself, having just seen what the ocean could do to a person who wasn't being careful enough.

Most of all, if Cora asked, Jaden didn't want to have to tell her that he hadn't even tried.

He extended the handheld toward Trev. "Keep it safe," he said. Trev accepted it with a look of surprise. Jaden set off toward the rocks, his strides steady without the weight of the handheld in either pocket, to learn something for just himself.

A BEAR IN WINTER

by Jacob Jones-Goldstein

California sat on the creaky wooden deck and watched the condensation patterns his breath made in the cold air. The sun had only just begun its journey for the day, but it was enough to illuminate the field that stretched out beyond the cabin. During the summer it was flush with wildflowers and tall grass, but here in late-winter it was covered in almost a foot of snow. The tall pines that ringed the field also wore a fresh coat of powder from the previous night's storm.

Next to the chair, resting on a table California had set up, sat a small portable turntable. He liked to listen to a bit of music in the mornings while he drank his coffee and took in the breathtaking view of the mountains that rose in the distance. He dropped the needle on one of his favorite records and the opening guitar notes of "American Tune" from Paul Simon began to play. The lyrics about being far away from home always made him feel wistful. As he listened, he wondered what Simon would think about the unfathomable distance California was from where he was born.

The record eventually went on to 'Was a Sunny Day' and as it did, California noticed some movement at the edge of the woods. As he watched, an enormous bear emerged from the trees. It didn't seem to notice California initially, and began to tramp its way across the field. After a few moments, "Was a Sunny Day" ended and the record moved on to "Learn How To Fall." Something in the change in music caught the bear's attention. ilt stopped and looked towards California. He wasn't sure what to do so he waved at it.

The bear stared at him, his cabin, and his record player for a long moment. California could only imagine what was running through its head.

He was almost certainly the first human it had ever seen, as California was the only person for at least a hundred miles in every direction.

"How are ya doing?" he called out. His voice cracked slightly, as those were the first words he had spoken in a while. The bear cocked its head and then sat down facing him with a 'wumph.'

"Cold one eh?" The bear made another 'wumph' noise. He took it as an agreement about the weather. It was big for a black bear. California guessed it had to be close to six feet long, although it looked a bit trim. He presumed it would only just have gotten up from its hibernation.

California and the bear sat in the morning light and watched each other for a long time. Eventually Paul Simon finished singing about comets and mothers so he flipped the record and they listened to the other side for a while together as well. Sometime around 'Something So Right' the bear decided it was time to move on. California watched it go until it fully disappeared into the woods on the far side of the field.

"Nice meeting you!" he called after it and then proceeded to flip the record again. 'American Tune' began to play again and he went back to admiring the pure beauty of the Sierra Nevada Mountains and the winter sun on his face. He smiled. As much as California enjoyed the seclusion, it was always nice to make a friend.

The next morning the bear came back. California was again sitting in the cold air on his deck, admiring the view. The sun was shining and warming the air a bit, but not enough to melt the snow. He was listening to 'Ventura Highway' by America. Dewey Bunnel's voice carried over the field and the bear wandered closer to the cabin.

"You like America huh?" California asked the bear, "Me too." The bear sat down about 15 yards away and watched him. After the song ended, California picked up the needle and dropped it down on 'Horse with No Name.'

"This is a good one too."

The bear didn't reply.

They sat there and looked at each other while they shared the music.

"I'd give you something to eat, but I don't know if you could digest the food I've got. Wouldn't want to get you sick."

The bear made a "whumph" sound.

California let the record play and wondered if this bear's genetic ancestors were out there beyond the vast gulf of time and space, looking up at a different star and feeling its warmth on their faces. It seemed unlikely, but then he was a guy sitting in the mountains that used to be part of the state that he was named after, listening to music made 500 years before he was born on a starship millions of miles away.

Stranger things had certainly happened.

The bear was waiting for him the next morning. It was lying down in roughly the same spot as the day before. It flicked its ears when he came outside with his coffee and record player, but otherwise didn't react much. California smiled broadly when he saw his new friend had returned.

"How about a little Van Morrison today?" he called out by way of greeting. He also reached into the pocket of his robe and pulled out an apple, "This should be ok for ya," and tossed the apple over to the bear. It landed about a foot away. The bear reached its big paw over to pull it closer.

"This is my favorite," California told the bear and began to play 'And It Stoned Me.'

"I tried to find out where the genetic material for bears they took with them came from," he said to his happily munching companion, "Seems like it was from the Appalachians, so probably not your family. Maybe a distant cousin."

The bear seemed nonplussed to find out he wasn't related to explorers.

California had started life as an explorer.

He had been born on the city-ship 'J.A.3.' The third of four great civilization starships that had been launched over the span of 100 years starting in 2530. He couldn't really say where he was born, other than it was far away. The four ships had each left in different directions with missions to seed planets and find life, never to return to Earth.

Each had been outfitted with machines that could create small, one way wormholes that connected to a fixed point on earth. Everyone born on the ships was given the option to go 'home' to a planet they didn't know, never to see their friends and family again. Almost no one ever used them.

"I used it though," he said out loud. The bear blinked several times in response.

When he was younger, the ship, which up until that point was all he had ever known, never quite felt like home. That feeling had made him a distant, and generally insular child. He had friends and a loving family, but it colored everything for him on the ship. He had tried to tell his parents on a few occasions, but wonderful as they were, the subject always seemed to make them uncomfortable.

It wasn't until he began to look into his namesake that he was able to fully articulate it.

His parents had named him California because he was born when 'place names' were all the rage. He could just as easily have been 'Yugoslavia' or 'Olympus-Mons' like a couple of his early classmates, but he wasn't.

California, as a territory, had only existed for about 500 years. It had ceased to exist during the conflicts that had led to the Natural Revolution, well before full Unification. He had asked his parents why they picked that name, but all they ever said was that they had heard it a few times and liked it.

It was the music that finally helped him understand. During the course of reading the histories he stumbled across a period where it had been a cultural center. He watched some of the movies made there, but they were so archaic he couldn't quite connect with them. It was the music that finally helped him understand. The late 20th century in particular spoke to what he was feeling in a way that nothing had before. Songs like 'Ventura Highway' sparked a dream of wind blowing through his hair and the idea of feeling the warmth of a star on his face. He dreamed of a stillness that his life on a ship hurtling through space could never quite provide.

"Can you imagine it?" He asked the bear, "Going to your parents and sister and telling them you wanted to go away forever?"

The bear didn't answer, but his stoicism made California think that he did understand, "I guess maybe you can."

The bear made a snuffling sound and began to eat the apple.

"I wonder if you're lonely?" he asked. Once again, the bear didn't respond.

When he was 18 he was told about the wormhole generator that could take him to earth. It still bothered California that they kept it a secret. The idea that they didn't want children to use it impulsively made some sense, but for a person who had such a deep longing as he did, growing up might have been easier if he knew there was a chance he could feel whole.

The idea of keeping it secret bothered him even more once he discovered that there was actually a name for how he felt. It was called 'The longing.' Psychologists and scientists on the ship had theorized that people carried a genetic memory of Earth, which only was triggered in a small subset of the population. Even within that subset, very few chose to act on the impulse.

When California announced his intention to become a 'Returner,' he was the first one in almost 20 years. His parents were horrified and did everything they could to talk him out of it. His sister had understood his desire. She didn't share it, but she was closer to him than anyone and had grown up in the shadow of his distance and depression.

It had been very hard to say goodbye to all of them and the life he had known. When he finally took the million lightyear step through the portal and took his first breath of earth air, he had felt a thousand ton weight fall off his shoulders.

For the first time in his life he understood what it felt like to be home.

The first few months had been hard on California. The combination of true quiet, stillness, and the open sky were enough to render him almost comatose during his initial forays outside of the return center.

A woman named Marian had been the first to greet him when he came through. She explained to California that an organization existed to help Returners acclimate and get set up on Earth. They averaged about one person about every six months, sometimes more frequently, but more often they would go longer without anyone showing up. She had helped the previous two, both from J.A. 4, the youngest of the four great ships.

The program consisted of short trips outside, small apartments that generated the same ambient sounds as the ships, tapering them off over the course of two months. They also provided medical attention as it could take a while for a person to fully acclimate from the sterile ship environment to a more natural one.

California had struggled as his immune system acclimated and despite his dream of feeling the sun on his face, developed particularly acute sunburn initially.

Marian had laughed at him when the first thing he used his maker for was an ancient type of music player and a few records. One of the benefits of matter reconfiguration on earth versus the ship was he wasn't limited in his allotment of material.

Eventually the issues subsided and he was able to fully exist on the planet of his ancestors. The Return center was located in the only remaining city, Gaborone, that was on the planet proper. It served as both a civilization hub and the planetside capitol. It took up most of what had once been called Botswana. The vast majority of the population lived in the exo-planet built around Earth itself.

The exo-planet had been built in the middle of the Natural Revolution as most of the planet was returned to its pre-human natural state after the ravages of the preceding centuries. Gaborone had served as the capital continually since Unification.

Human settlements still existed all over the world, but they were much smaller and were built to have little impact on the areas around them. Most Returners ended up in one of these settlements, very few choosing to live in Gaborone with its millions of people.

California had made the unusual decision to live on his own. He was provided with a maker, a domicile, and a small ship that he could use to travel to the nearest settlement, some 150 miles from the spot he found in the mountains.

"And that was twenty years ago." he said as the bear happily munched on the additional apple he had tossed it.

The bear looked up after California had stopped talking for a minute and let out another "whumpf" followed that with, what sounded to him, like a belch.

He shrugged, "Not much else to tell my friend. Sometimes you gotta travel a long way to find your home. I miss them all, but I know in my heart that I did the right thing. And heck, if I hadn't, I never would have met you!"

California smiled and reached over into his box of records and fished out another of his favorites, "Heads & Tales" by Harry Chapin. He put on side two and dropped the needle on the second track.

"Any Old Kind of Day" began to play.

California leaned back in his chair and watched as the sun reached its zenith and began to melt the snow.

He and the bear listened to the song in companionable silence.

ACKNOWLEDGEMENTS

First off, we would like to thank Marcella Harte-Conlon for her wonderful painting gracing the cover of this volume. Her art captured the spirit of the better tomorrow envisioned by the authors included herein.

We would also like to offer a special thank you to Jennifer Marang for the incredible job she did on the cover design and the layout of the book. Her talents have defined the look and feel of Oddity Prodigy's books. Without her we would be fumbling around in the dark.

We want to thank all the wonderful writers who took the time to grace us with their amazing stories, as well as all the people who submitted their words for us to read. Not everyone can make the final cut for an anthology, but that doesn't mean we don't love reading everything sent to us.

They're listed up front, but we would like to once again thank everyone who backed the Kickstarter for this project, as well as the people who took time to share and promote the project. We do not take that support for granted.

We would like to thank the wonderful people at Espec publishing who took time out to back our kickstarter and promote it, but also to share their accumulated wisdom and publishing acumen with us.

Captain Blue Hen Comics is our LCS and another of our biggest supporters. They are a brilliant star at the heart of Delaware's creative arts gallery, doing everything they can to help, encourage, support, and nourish the many creative people in our community and we will never be able to thank them enough for all that they do.

And a final shout out to our families, who were very accepting and supportive of our long nights working on this. You make everything worthwhile.

MEET THE AUTHORS

ALICE AVOY is an emerging writer from Poland who graduated from the Institute of English Studies and worked as a journalist, reviewer, editor, and translator. Her short stories appeared, among others, in 34 Orchard journal, Beneath the Yellow Lights anthology, and Dragon's Hoard 3 anthology. She's mainly interested in horror, high fantasy, and urban fantasy, but she follows where her muse leads her. She loves to travel, play TTRPGs, and get lost for hours in the land of video games. You can find her on Twitter (@AliceAvoy) and Bluesky (@aliceavoy.bsky.social)

J. PATRICK CONLON — see page 273.

ERIN CULLEN is a neuroscience researcher and speculative fiction writer based in New York City. She spends her free time running around outdoors and dreaming up stories about science and the future.

HANNAH DUGGAN — see page 274.

GLENN DUNGAN is currently based in Brooklyn, NYC. He exists within a Venn-diagram of urban design, sociology, and good stories. When not obsessing about one of those three, he can be found at a park drinking black coffee and listening to podcasts about murder. You can find his work on his website, whereisglennnow.com, or follow him on substack at "Where Is Glenn Now?"

MURRAY EILAND is an archaeologist living in California. He is an avid reader of mythology and speculative fiction.

BRIAN D. GIBSON is a lifelong fan of science fiction, horror, and fantasy, who has too often allowed a career in mechanical engineering to distract him from putting thoughts to paper. A father of three and husband of one, all beloved, he makes his living in the wilds of suburban Lancaster County, Pennsylvania. There, he occasionally dabbles in a writing process that could best be described as ponderous chaos.

PHIL GIUNTA novels include the paranormal mysteries Testing the Prisoner, By Your Side, and Like Mother, Like Daughters. His short stories appear in two dozen anthologies of science fiction, fantasy, horror, and more. He is a multiple award-winning author and member of the Horror Writers Association, the National Federation of Press Women, and the Greater Lehigh Valley Writers Group. Phil is currently working on his fourth paranormal mystery novel while plotting his triumphant escape from the pressures of corporate America where he has been imprisoned for thirty years. Visit Phil's website at www.philgiunta.com. Find him on Facebook: @writerphilgiunta, Instagram: @phil_giunta71, and BlueSky: @pgiunta. bsky.social

RANDALL HAYES, "your friendly neighborhood neuroscientist," conveniently has the same initials as the character above, but none of the same psychedelic experiences (so far). He writes a weekly newsletter called Doctor Eclectic at https://randallhayes.substack.com, where readers can find publication announcements, occasional fiction, and half-baked opinions on various topics.

JACOB JONES-GOLDSTEIN — see page 274.

NICHOLAS LEAMY — see page 274.

JAY T. LEVY, a devoted writer of genre fiction and role-playing games, spends much of his free time reading stacks of comic books, and taking walks with his lovely shield-maiden wife and dogs. His other works can be found in Beneath the Yellow Lights, I Used to be an Animal Lover, Dark Halloween, Scary Snippets: Valentine's Day, Scary Snippets: Halloween, Scary Snippets: Christmas, Scary Snippets: Virtual, Fatal Fairies, A Guide to Useless Sidekicks, and Guilty Pleasures and Other Dark Delights. To contact, please visit: jaylevy.substack.com.

DIANA PARRILLA HERNÁNDEZ, born in Spain, is a versatile writer. With a degree in economics and mastery in Japanese, she shares her passion for anime and games on her YouTube channel and social networks, where she goes by the handle buffyta17. Her publications span across various genres, including horror, speculative fiction, and mystery.

MARY JO RABE writes science fiction, modern fantasy, historical fiction, and crime or mystery stories, generally displaying a preference for what she defines as happy endings. Ideas for her fiction come from the magnificent, expanding universe, the rural environment of eastern Iowa where she grew up, the beautiful Michigan State University campus where she got her first degree, and the Black Forest area of Germany with its center in Freiburg where she worked as a librarian for 41 years before retiring to Titisee-Neustadt. News about her published stories is posted regularly on her blog: https://maryjorabe.wordpress.com.

KARA RACE-MOORE studied history at Simmons College as an excuse to read about the soap opera lives of British royals. She worked in educational publishing, casting the molds for future generations' minds, but has since moved into the more civilized world of litigation. She writes horror, fantasy and science fiction stories, many inspired by history. She currently lives in Los Angeles, the land where fact and fiction tend to blur. She can be found most days posting reviews on Goodreads and posting on her blog at: https://kararacemoore.wordpress.com.

ERIC REMINGTON is a Delaware native, distracting himself from writing and traveling by working as a programmer. He enjoys wandering the wilds and waterways of northern Delaware with his wife and their dog. His goal in life is to lose at Never Have I Ever....

ROSE STRICKMAN is a speculative fiction writer living in Seattle, Washington. Her work has appeared over 60 times, in anthologies such as *Sword and Sorceress 32, Beneath the Yellow Lights* and *Spring into SciFi: 2024 Edition*, as well as several e-zines. Her novella *Island of the Drowned* is a Graveside Press Tiny Terrors title and she has self-published several novellas on Amazon. Please see her Amazon author's page at https://www.amazon.com/author/rosestrickman.

ZACHARY TAYLOR BRANCH is the pen name of a semi-retired scientist and consultant, enjoying the good life with his wife Nancy in Lorena, TX. "The Gray Horizon" was his first professional fiction sale, his short story "The Nerine Seven" has been published in Alien Dimensions Space Fiction Short Stories Anthology Series #26, and his short story "The Gateway" is included in the B Cubed Press Southern Truths anthology. His children David and Elise grew up in Newark, DE, and are now too far away in Saint Louis and Houston, pursuing careers in counseling and medicine.

OWEN TOWNEND is a writer of short speculative fiction and light-hearted poetry. He lives in Huddersfield, West Yorkshire, England. Owen has been previously published in anthologies from Arachne Press, Comma Press, Oxford Spires Publishing, WrittenOff Publishing and Astrea Publishing. He is on Instagram – @owt441.

PAUL WEISSMAN is an actor/playwright in New York City. He has been a genre fan practically since birth. He read Salem's Lot when he was way too young and had every Star Trek toy imaginable as a child. His favorite genre-ish writers are Ursula LeGuin, Ray Bradbury, Neil Gaiman and Kelly Link. He likes music also. Quite a bit actually. He futzes on guitar, rambles on piano and is currently taking mandolin lessons. This one is for his daughter, who was Nahib's first reader and first champion.

THE ODDITY PRODIGY BRIDGE CREW

MARCELLA HARTE (CONLON) has been fascinated with art and illustration since childhood. The same passion and attention to detail that won her school a sizable arts scholarship followed her to the University of the Arts, where she earned her bachelor of fine arts in illustration. She is currently working on a children's literature project. Her publishing credits include the anthology The Stories in Between by Fantasist Press, a collection of science fiction and fantasy stories published in 2009; cover art for the All-Out Monster Revolt Online Magazine in 2015; and most notably The Mermaid in Rehoboth Bay, a national award winning children's book published in 2016. In her capacity as resident artist and founding member of Oddity Prodigy Productions she created the cover art for the very first anthology Oh Snap! As well as the cover for this anthology. Not content with simply living in the art world, she contributed her debut short story Silence in the first curated Oddity Prodigy Productions anthology, Scary Stuff.

J. PATRICK CONLON is a genre fiction author currently living in Bear, DE. As a fellow founding member of Oddity Prodigy Productions, his writing focuses mainly on fantasy and speculative history themes, though he has ventured into horror and urban fantasy in Oddity Prodigy's previous anthologies Scary Stuff and Beneath the Yellow Lights. He has appeared in anthologies and magazines, working not only within Oddity Prodigy but working with Smart Rhino and Cat and Mouse press, for whom he served as Associate Editor for "Beach Pulp," a collection of pulp fiction. When he isn't writing, he is tirelessly marketing for his wife, an award winning illustrator and fellow cofounder Marcella Harte as well as caring for their two african pygmy hedgehogs.

Per her family, HANNAH DUGGAN is a sassy, snarky, kind, loving, distracted, brilliant, ginger oddball. She would add that she is decidedly cooler than her husband, whom she loves dearly.

JACOB JONES-GOLDSTEIN, Jacob Jones-Goldstein, founding member of Oddity Prodigy Productions, is an internationally published author, journalist, and editor. His short stories have appeared in anthologies and magazines such as 'Plague of Shadows' from Smart Rhino Press, 'Beach Pulp' from Cat & Mouse Press, and Lovecraftiana from Rogue Planet Press. His debut novel, The Change, will be released in July 2025. Followed by his novella, 'The Last Summer', from the Systema Paradoxa series of Espec Books. He has edited the previous volumes from Oddity Prodigy Productions 'Scary Stuff' and 'Beneath the Yellow Lights.' In addition to fiction, Jacob writes about music for his personal site, ShoutingStreet.com, and has covered the Philadelphia 76ers for several online publications. Beyond writing and editing, he hosts popular podcast "The Scary Stuff Podcast", plays Magic the Gathering, Disc Golf, and way too many board games. He loves comic books, movies, exploring, cats, family, friends, Joel Embiid, Tyrese Maxey, and his wife, Jennie. *[mwhah from said wife]*

NICHOLAS LEAMY is a well-known miscreant who has lived in Northern Delaware all his life. Working in a data center, with a B.S. in Computer Science, he is well outside his wheelhouse when it comes to writing fiction. He has decided, however, that the time he's spent running D&D games for his kids, Oliver and Edison, has made him interesting enough to pull it off. He also happens to be a lover of board games, horror movies, and anything bizarre. Nicholas has been published thrice before in Oh Snap It's Oddity Prodigy, Scary Stuff and Beneath the Yellow Lights. His loving wife Hannah attends supervised visitations with him when he is not riling up his other patients and planning his escape.

JENNIFER MARANG loves werewolves, writing, and... uh, what else starts with W? Working? God, no. A graphic design/tech person by trade, Jennie did the cover art and interior layout for both *Beneath the Yellow Lights* and *Scary Stuff* anthologies. She's spent most of her life writing and drawing and broke into the industry in grade 6 with the award-winning illustrated story *Indiana Jones and the Last Banana*, released by her own printing press (handwritten on construction paper), distributed at the local library, and published in the newspaper of her tiny outback town in Australia. Look out for her next published work sometime this century; *The Flame's Heart*, a slightly-sweeping fantasy about a complete dick trapped in a sword. Jennifer lives in Delaware, by way of Montana and Australia, with four ridiculous cats, two ghost cats, a variety of wild birds, four chonky sneak-thief raccoons, and a husband she absolutely adores but purposely put last because that's where he put her; looking at you, Jacob.

STEVE MYERS was an award-winning cartoonist and graphic designer who lived in Bear and Newark, Delaware. He spent his days working as a Search Engine Optimization professional, and his evenings drawing comics and cartoons, including *The Adventures of Superchum*. He passed away in December of 2023, and is truly, deeply, missed.

SHASTA SCHATZ is an eager reader, occasional writer, and lifelong fan girl, the latter of which translated into a costuming obsession in her adult life. Her B.A. in English laid the groundwork for Shasta to become an addicted hobbyist with professional leanings. Between HEAs, TPBs, and NDAs, Shasta is a hot mess wife and mother with a penchant for coffee and organized clutter. While she prefers not to be associated with these people, their links can be found on her costuming blog, GreenLinenShirt.com.

ALSO AVAILABLE FROM ODDITY PRODIGY PRODUCTIONS

SCARY STUFF
Horror Anthology—A tribute to the classic style of horror published in comics from the 60s and 70s, Scary Stuff is at heart a love letter to the kind of scary stories we grew up on.

$18.95 paperback

BENEATH THE YELLOW LIGHTS
Urban Fantasy Anthology

The new collection of short stories from Oddity Prodigy Productions captures that feeling of magic on city streets, just out of the corner of your eye. Join us as we take a walk, Beneath the Yellow Lights.

$18.95 paperback

ORDER AT YOUR LOCAL BOOKSTORE
WWW.ODDITYPRODIGY.COM

www.ingramcontent.com/pod-product-compliance
Lightning Source LLC
Chambersburg PA
CBHW071139180726
48291CB00007B/2254